PENNY PICKLEPANTS

AND THE TWENTY-PICKLE PIE

PENNY PICKLEPANTS

AND THE TWENTY-PICKLE PIE

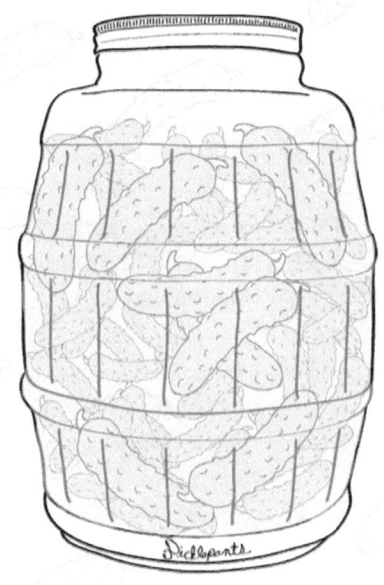

BY

A.M. JONES

JANES Works Publishing

an imprint of JANES Works Co.

For Mom, who instilled in me a love of thrift shopping,
For Noah, Elijah, and Spencer, who eat pickles almost as much as I do;
And for Jim, who always believes in me.

Library of Congress Cataloging-in-Publishing Data
Jones, A.M.
Penny Picklepants and The Twenty-Pickle Pie / by A.M. Jones
p. cm.
Summary: A young girl with a knack for style and fashion fights to save her family's
pickle plant to keep her dream of being the youngest professional pickle taster ever
alive.
ISBN 978-0-9849642-5-3
[1. Humorous – Fiction. 2. Coming of Age – Fiction. 3. Family Life – Fiction.
4. Girls & Women – Juvenile Fiction. 5. Family – Juvenile Fiction.] I. Title.

35 34 33 32 31   9/9 0/0 01 02
Rochester, New York
Printed in the U.S.A.
First American edition, July 2012

CONTENTS

CONTENTS

CONTENTS

PENNY PICKLEPANTS

AND THE TWENTY-PICKLE PIE

CHAPTER ONE

Dear Secret Pickle Society,

It all started with Willem Prins Groot de Jong. Willem was being forced to marry Margaretha Goossens de Smet, a girl he had never met, a girl he did not love. Though he protested, Willem's father, Petrus Prings Groot De Jong, would not hear of it. Growing tired of Willem's constant whining, he locked Willem in his room. Petrus needed his son to marry Margaretha to secure the family fortune.

The night before the wedding, Petrus locked Willem's door and bid him a good night. Unbeknownst to Petrus, Willem had it all set: money, clothes, and a secure passage to start a new life with his true love, Femke.

Eventually, after one horse ride, two trips in the back of wagons, three passages aboard three different ships, four rides in rickshaws, and five different disguises, the runaway lovers finally arrived to their new home. Though they did not live in the way to which Willem was accustomed, they had each other, and that was enough... that is, until the money ran out.

Luckily Willem discovered a new food in this strange new land known as achar. Willem became fond of one achar vendor in particular, and because of his fondness, the business quadrupled overnight. Word had spread that a royal Dutchman loved the vendor's achar, and people came from all over to try it. The vendor made Willem a partner, and soon the Patel Achar Company became the biggest achar provider in all of India.

One night, Willem heard that another Dutch royal had landed at the port and was looking for a long-lost son named Willem. Kicking himself, realizing he should have changed his name to something like Acharpants, Willem knew there was only one thing to do. Fearing his fate of being grounded for the next 20 years, Willem fled immediately with his family to a new land to start his own achar plant, but this time he would change his name. In the new land, he called the achar a pekel and changed his last name to Pekelpantaloons, figuring that if the Dutch royals ever made it to America, they would never discover him with that name.

Over time, the spelling of the name would change, eventually settling on Picklepants. Of course, achar is simply a pickle. So there you have it, the true story of the humble beginnings of the Picklepants Pickling Plant of Pottsville, Pennsylvania. After taking the preceding story into consideration and pondering its full ramifications, please, please, PLEASE (down-on-my-knees begging please!!) let me join your Secret Pickle Society.

Yours Truly,
Penny Picklepants ♡

"Penny, it's time to go," my mom yelled up from downstairs. "Penny, I'm waiting—time to go shopping," she said, a bit more impatient this time.

Great! The four words that I dreaded the most from my mother's lips—I know it sounds crazy as most 11-year-old girls would love to hear those words, but not me. It wasn't because I didn't love shopping. Trust me, Penny Picklepants loves shopping. It was just that I loved shopping at the mall—with my friends—with lots and lots of money. The problem was that when my mom said, "Time to go shopping," she did not mean, "Penny, I want you to take this purse filled with lots and lots of money, meet your friends at the mall, and shop 'til you drop." No, it meant going to the local thrift store with my mom—minus the friends—minus the lots and lots of money—minus the shopping 'til dropping.

You would think if your parents owned their own business, they would be loaded, but no, not my parents. At the beginning of every school year, my mom liked to point out that we didn't have any money—and trust me, we had had the same conversation about a gazillion times. It always goes something like this:

"Mom, Olive,"—my best friend—"and her mom made a deal that if she kept her room clean for two weeks, she could get a new pair of jeans. Could we do something like that?"

"No, you keep your room clean because I tell you to keep your room clean."

"Well, I need some new jeans, so can you take me to the mall anyway, so I can get some?"

"No! We don't have the money."

"You have money for a bunch of other stuff. Can't we just work my new jeans in with that other stuff?"

"No! Now go clean your room!"

The object of my desire may have changed from time to time, but the dynamics never did. Every year, we always ended up at the thrift store, scrounging through the 99-cent bins looking for tees and sweaters and jeans and shoes that neither looked nor smelled new. My mom thought she was teaching me a lesson. I just thought she was being mean.

"I'm coming," I yelled downstairs, letting out a huge sigh.

I had to go incognito to the thrift store in case I saw someone I knew. I put on my favorite baseball cap, oversized aviator sunglasses, and a blonde wig that I found in the Halloween box.

As I came down the stairs, the look on my mom's face was one of those "I don't think so" kind of looks—another constant conversation we had, albeit nonverbally. But I was older now, and I could make my own choices.

"Is that what you think you are going to wear?" my mom asked with a little bit of "I already told you 'I don't think so' with the look I just gave you" inflected in her voice.

"Mom!" I protested. "Don't you know how embarrassing it is that I have to go to the thrift store to do my school shopping? Just once, I would like to go to the mall and pick out my own clothes and not have you pick them out for me. I am almost a teenager, you know—I need to look like one."

"I know that, dear. That is why I don't let you pick out your own clothes," she quickly retorted, with that smirk of hers.

"But I am going to be in sixth grade," I bemoaned, "I need to look every bit the part. I need the perfect tees with the perfect jeans. I can't be wearing last season's hand-me-downs—I can't believe you are a girl and you don't even get it!"

By the look on my mom's face, I could tell she was not amused by my last comment.

"Penny, I know you think that with the factory we have a money tree that we can magically pick money from," she began.

Oh great! Here we go again. I couldn't stand it when she started to lecture me about life—I mean, I was 11-years-old, soon to be 12! I was practically on the cusp of maturity, so I already totally and completely got life, or at least how to have one.

"Real life is expensive and there are…" my mom continued,

trailing off before getting to her usual "when I was kid and we had no money" story. She had a concerned look on her face.

"There are what, Mom?" I asked. "Wait! Is something going on with the factory? Because you and Dad have been acting rather stressed lately—more than usual. And Dad is…"

"Penn, don't worry about the factory," my mom said. "Everything is going to be fine. Listen, I'll make a deal with you. If you agree to get a few things at the thrift store, I will take you to the mall."

"Are you serious, Mom?!" I squealed.

"One item!," she said holding up her index finger. "And it has to be around twenty dollars."

"Yes, yes, yes! Let's go—Mom, I love you, I love you, I love you!"

I had to add that I loved her, because I did, plus I knew it meant a lot to her. Yes, it was only $20, but for my mom, it was a monumental occurrence, so I had to show my appreciation. It was odd though, how she said, "everything is *going to be* fine," instead of, "everything *is* fine," with the factory—there's something more to this than she is letting on. Oh well, it can wait. It's shopping time!

Just as we were about to walk out the door from the kitchen to the first of many trips to the mall—okay, the thrift store, *then* the mall—my dad yelled for my mom from the kitchen. Sheesh! Just like my dad to ruin the beginning of a perfectly good (thrift-store aside) shopping trip.

"Pam? Can you come here for a minute? I need to talk with you."

Ugh! Of all the times Dad!

"Penny and I were just about to leave to do some school shopping, Peter. Can it wait?" my mom replied.

Please, oh please, oh please let it wait.

He walked into the kitchen with a huge smile on his face and he actually seemed happy, like Christmas-morning happy.

"Actually, I was just going to tell you," he said, giving my mom a kiss on her cheek—Ugh! Better than the lips I guess—"That I have just finished paying Pottsville Community Bank the very last payment for the factory. We are now the owners of the Picklepants Pickling Plant, clear and free!" my dad said.

"That's so great Peter!" my mom replied in between her squealing and hugging and giving my dad a kiss on the lips.

Double ugh!

"Wait! I thought we already owned the factory," I chimed in. "I mean Grandpa Picklepants owned the factory before you and Great-Grandpa Picklepants owned the factory before him, and Great-Great-Grandpa Picklepants..."

"Yes! We get the idea, Penny," my dad said. "All you need to know is that there was a second mortgage on it, a payment, but the bank says we paid it off. Besides, you're a kid. You're not supposed to worry about the factory. You should be worried about kid things, like shopping."

Wow! My dad so got me. Well, sort of—I mean, of course I worry about the factory—I am going to run it one day after all.

"Peter! That is such great news. To celebrate I will make a nice dinner tonight," my mom said, with perhaps a hint of relief in her voice.

Of course, right when my mom said that, the phone started to ring. Are you kidding me? It was like the forces of anti-shopping had combined themselves against me today!

From the look on my face, my dad must have been able to read my mind, because he laughed and then said, "You guys go—I'll get the phone."

Finally, we were off. Granted it was to the thrift store, to make me appreciate spending a few of the hard-earned dollars the factory brought in, and to make my mom feel good about not having to spend so many of those hard-earned dollars—never mind the price of my dignity, a subject my mom obviously either didn't care or know anything about—much less my ranking on the ladder of sixth grade society. All my mom ever seemed to care about was finding bargains and deals that had the most bang for the buck. I swear, if she spent half as much time trying to help the factory as she did hunting for bargains, we would have plenty of money for me to go to the mall, and only the mall.

As I climbed into the red-grocery-go-getter, aka my mom's minivan, I had a sinking feeling that, like all those times before, this shopping trip was not going to end up at the mall. She had promised trips to the mall before, and for one reason or another, we never ended up there. I called it my mom's wily shopping trickery. She called it good parenting.

"Now Mom, remember you promised you were going to take me to the mall, right? So that I can buy anything I want in the store of my choice, right?" I said, with all the maturity-sounding voice I could muster.

"Yes, Penny. Now stop worrying so much about the mall and let's get to the thrift store. I have a feeling you are going to find some great stuff there this year."

"Mom, you say that every year," I said, still with my mature-sounding voice.

"And you always do," she replied.

"Whatever. Let's just get this over with," I said with my signature Penny Picklepants eye roll.

My mom used to tell me that if you looked up "eye roll" in the dictionary, there wouldn't be any words, just a picture of me doing my patented eye roll. I used it to express a variety of things I could be thinking, but it got the point across loud and clear every time. When someone got the infamous Penny Picklepants eye roll, they knew it was better to just drop the subject and move on… at least, I'm pretty sure they did.

Luckily, on the way there, my mom went to her "mom-never-neverland" and started to think about whatever moms like to think about, like dinner and laundry, and boring stuff like that, which meant I got to listen to my favorite radio station. Mine and Olive's favorite song came on, which I had to crank and sing to at the top of my lungs—wow, I sounded pretty good! Maybe while I am touring the world, as a professional pickle taster— my dream ever since I was little was to be a professional pickle taster and it certainly helped that we owned a pickle factory—I would also tour the world as famous singer. I would stay in the best hotels. By day I would have pickle plant owners begging me, just BEGGING ME, to taste their pickles and for me to give them the "Penny Picklepants stamp of approval." And by nights, I would sing to my adoring fans the wonders of life and love. My inspiration for such deep, philosophical thoughts would be Jiminy Jams—more on him later. Ah yes, the wonderful life and future of Penny Picklepants was clearly coming into view.

"Penny," a seemingly disembodied voice jolted me from my

daydreaming. "Penny!" my mom repeated.

"What?" I said, realizing we had arrived at the thrift store.

Daydreaming is so much better than real life. I was secretly hoping, in the midst of my daydreaming—ahh, daydreaming—that my mom would accidentally forget about the thrift store and drive directly to the mall.

No such luck.

"We are here," my mom said.

Well, here goes nothing. I looked out the window, looking for anybody I knew. It was doubtful I would see anyone on this side of town, much less JayJ—I really doubted she, of all people, would be in a thrift store—but it's better to be safe than sorry.

Who's JayJ, you may be wondering. To tell you the truth, I'm still trying to figure that one out. For now, let it suffice that JayJ Rothefeller was none other than the diva archnemesis of all archnemesises. For a more detailed description, just keep reading.

Cautiously, I crept out of the car, and did the double, then triple check. I looked up and down the street for anyone remotely resembling somebody familiar. The coast was clear. It was now or never I told myself, so I beelined it as quickly as my little feet could take me into the store, leaving my mom in the dust. Of course, since I was so preoccupied with looking up and down the street, even while on the move, I didn't think to check the entrance to the thrift store. In all my efforts to be incognito and not cause a scene, I ran right into someone leaving the store. I then fell right on my bum, causing half of my disguise to go flying in different directions.

"Oh, I'm so sorry," I said. "Did I hurt..." but before I could finish my sentence, I realized who it was I had just run into.

Good-golly miss-molly! Looking down at me was none other than JayJ Rothefeller.

Life? What did I ever do to you?

"Penny Picklepants! Fancy bumping into you here… literally," she said, with that smug little smile of hers spread all over her face.

"Are you okay Miss Picklepants?" asked Mrs. Rothefeller.

"I'm fine, thanks," I said, dusting myself off and nursing my bruised ego.

"Are you dropping some stuff off too, dear?" asked Mrs. Rothefeller. "It just feels so good to give to those in need, it just puts a smile on my face," she said, with a big cheesy grin.

Puke! Somebody please bring me a doggy bag pronto, about to lose my lunch over here.

By this time my mom had finally caught up.

"Oh, JayJ, are you okay? I saw the whole thing as I was walking over," she had the nerve to say. Yeah, don't worry about your own daughter sitting on her rear end, completely humiliated! "And you are so ever kind and thoughtful to donate some of your things," she continued. "Isn't she so kind and thoughtful Penny?"

My mom was so out of touch. "Uhh, sure," I said.

"But no, JayJ, to answer your question," my mom then said.

Oh please Mom, oh please, oh please, do not embarrass me so much that I have to move to a new country, learn a new language.

"We are just here to find Penny some school clothes," my mom blurted out.

And of course she told her.

Seriously? Was this woman just bound and determined to ruin

my life? Does she not know that this blonde-haired girl already holds the fate of all of the school's social groups in the palm of her hand? That is it! My life is over, whatever life was left! I am officially leaving tomorrow for Canada. I mean that is a totally different country (right?) and I am sure I can pick up Canadian in no time. I mean, it is a foreign language, right?

"Oh really?" JayJ piped up, with a big smirk on her face. "Well, I am meeting all the girls at the mall for my school shopping. I guess we can't all save the world like you, Penny, right?" she said. "Let's go mother," she said, walking away, before stopping and turning back. "Oh, and by the way, Penn, just love the hat and the glasses —and that wig. It's like you are in witness protection or something. Maybe you could start a new trend—witness protection fashion."

"No, unlike some people, I just like to give to the poor anonymously," I said, as I got up and stormed into the store, leaving my mom to say the goodbyes—and I'm sure apologize for her daughter once more.

After that embarrassing, more like disastrous, meeting with JayJ, my mom was more determined than ever to get some thrift shopping in before I dragged her to the mall. I just needed to make sure I maintained my "oh so happy to try on anything even though it was cool 20 years ago—scratch that—not ever" attitude. It was the only way to get my mom to follow through on her promise to take me to the mall. As long as I acted appreciative of the hand-me-downs, I think she thought I was learning a lesson or something.

I looked through the racks, one article at a time, listening to the constant start and stop of feet along the worn out linoleum tile that at one time must have been stark white, but now had the dull sheen of yellowish brown. I could hear babies crying. I thought, "Right back 'atcha kid, but at least your mom's trying to make you happy."

All I wanted to do was to hide inside the circular racks of clothing like I did when I was a kid. Why do these things always happen to me? Nothing embarrassing ever happens to the cool kids.

I was thumbing through the clothing racks, when something struck me. Rather, something hit me, literally. A little boy, cooped up in his mother's overflowing cart threw a bouncy ball at the back of my head. He was laughing at the fact that he had hit his target, his mother oblivious to the whole thing, lost in her own thrift-shopping world.

I was about to tell my mom that I was ready to go home, empty handed, when I saw something. Could it be? No way! I don't believe my eyes. Do my eyes see clothing that I dare say looks actually cool?

Not wanting to draw any unwanted attention, I nonchalantly eyed the cool looking clothes from a distance with the bargain hawk eyes I inherited from my mother, albeit put to better use.

I started to move—slowly, purposefully—gently casting my gaze in different directions to distract other would-be buyers of cool clothes.

Out of the corner of my eye, I saw a girl whip her head around and spot me and then the clothes—my clothes! She began walking towards the clothes—MY clothes! Her head turned to me, and back to the clothes. I sped up my pace, looking at her, looking at my clothes. She matched my pace, looking at me, looking at my clothes. Then our glances met and quickly descended into death glares. It was a full on thrift store showdown. Me and her—her and me—neck and neck. Who would get their first? I broke into a sprint—she broke into a sprint. The race was on, but I was going to win this race—I had to!

I have never been a fast runner, in fact, I am the slowest runner in our class. But when we ran at school, it was only for a time and a grade. This time, it was for all the glory of fashionable clothes. I found my turbo button, hit a few racks in between—that was gonna leave a mark—and just when I was on the verge of reaching out and grabbing the clothes—MY clothes!—I tripped! Of course, of all people, and of all the things to do, I tripped.

"Nooooo!" I yelled out loud.

Seriously? Again? Why me?! Isn't it someone else's turn by now, life?

I fell hard on the floor. My ankle hurt. But I reminded myself, cute clothes were on the line here. I had to make them mine at all costs, even if it meant a sprained ankle and few minor cuts and bruises along the way.

I pushed myself to get up and regain my bearings—I spotted the enemy. And doth my eye deceive me? There the girl stood, pinned between the little boy in the cart that so lovingly threw his bouncy ball at the back of my head and a rack of used sporting equipment and dirty stuffed animals.

The clothes—MY clothes—were mine, all mine.

"Thank you" I whispered to the boy, as I limped to the finish line, and to my rack of fun, hip, and cool clothes.

Score! They're all my size. I looked back at the boy smiling, the girl glaring. Thrift shopping? More like survival-of-the-fittest shopping. All's fair in love and shopping I suppose.

"Mom?" I yelled, "Come quick! I found a bunch of stuff that I love, seriously LOVE! And they're all my size."

"That's great," she said, giving me the twice over. "That run in with JayJ really did a number on you didn't it?"

There was no point in explaining my disheveled appearance. I was the victor, and that alone was enough.

"Okay, you go and try them on and make sure they fit," she said.

Eww! Thrift store changing rooms? Gross!

"But they're all my size. I already know they fit. Can we go to the mall now?," I asked.

"Penny, I am not buying you a thing unless I know it fits. If you want these clothes, you will march into that changing room and show me that they fit."

Ugh! There's always a catch.

"Yes! Yes! Yes!" was all I kept saying to myself even though I found myself standing in a dingy, way-too-small for comfort fitting room simultaneously thinking, "Eww! Eww! Eww!"

I couldn't believe that I found all these amazing clothes for super cheap. And my mom loved that I actually found clothes that I liked—she would have no choice but to take me to the mall now. Plus, they all had major labels on them, which would totally help maintain my status on the social ladder—maybe even help me move up a rung or two.

It was battle getting those clothes, but hello! I was going to look awesome, so it was so totally worth it. I did feel bad for the other girl, but let's face it: I deserved these clothes after everything I had been through.

CHAPTER TWO

After trying on all the clothes and modeling them to my mom—they all fit (and looked fabulous) just like I had said—we were finally ready to go the mall.

"Mom, I can't believe I found all these great clothes. I love them and they fit perfect! Now, can we go to the mall? Please, please, please, please?! You promised, remember? You promised!"

Her face contorted into that look that she always gave when she didn't want to do something, but she had promised she would. As you can imagine, this wasn't the first time she had given me this look by a longshot. This was going to require the usual begging—maybe even crying—to get her to take me, not to mention promising to do double chores for a month.

"Penny, you just got a couple of pair of new jeans that are in great shape with a bunch of cute tops," my mom said. "Do you honestly think you need more than this? There are children in this world who would be thrilled just to have a second pair of jeans, or even jeans at all."

Oh no! Not my mom's signature "there are kids in this world" guilt trip! She could make her "there are kids in this world" guilt trip about anything: food, clothes, furniture, TVs, makeup, haircuts, good hygiene. You name it, she had used the "there are kids in this world" guilt trip on it. Once she even adapted it to being grateful for hot dogs.

"Besides," she continued "your dad and I have a meeting in the city in a couple weeks—you could come with us then, and I promise I will take you to the mall while Dad is in his meetings."

See? Clear and undeniable proof my life was so not fair.

"Mom, you promised me and you said if I had a good attitude and I found some things you would take me. Remember? You said anything under $20 and I know I can find something. I mean, I could always use a white tee. Mom, did you know that is the most important thing in a woman's wardrobe? I read in..."

"Penny, stop! You're rambling. And you are not a woman."

As if!

"Mom, listen!" I implored. "I will go to one store and we will only stay there for like 10, or 15—okay, maybe like 20 minutes, but that is it. It will only take you 30 minutes."

"I'm sorry, Penny, but it's getting late. It took a lot longer than I thought it would," my mom said. "Now, you do those double chores that you promised me that you would do the last time we went to the city, that you never did, and then we can talk."

Eye roll, arm fold, and I walked out of the thrift store in a huff. That would teach her.

"Listen," my mom said, "let's go home and get all these new clothes washed, folded and put away for the first day of school. Sound good?"

I knew it was a lost cause. It always was. Lucky for me, our shopping trip was not a complete loss. I found some amazing clothes. But it still drove me crazy when my mom promised me something and then didn't deliver. Mom's aren't supposed to make promise they can't keep. That was it. It was official. I was mad at my mom. I couldn't believe my mother—yes my "mother"—wouldn't take me to the mall. She was so frustrating and so unfair all the time! She gives my brothers whatever they want—with me, never!

Like the other day, when my older brother needed some gas money, my mom handed him a $20 bill. When I asked my mom for gas money she looked at me and said, "Penny, you don't even drive!"

"I will one day," I said, "and if you start giving me gas money now, then I can save up and I won't have to ask you when I am older and driving."

"If you are old enough to drive, then you are old enough to have a job and you can provide yourself with your own gas money."

What?! "But Mom, you just gave Patrick $20 gas money—he doesn't have a job!"

"Penny, he's running an errand for me, and he does have a job at the pickling plant."

"Whatever! I help twice as much as he does and you don't ever give me anything for it."

Then she sent me to my room. Do you see now? Do you see what I have to live with?

The ride home from the thrift store was a quiet one, obviously filled with tension. I was giving my mother my worst eye roll and glare, but she seemed to not even care or notice. In fact, she looked like she was thinking entirely about something else. How dare she! She should be thinking about me and how she was ruining my social life. I mean, these newish clothes are pretty cool, but still I need to get to the mall. Maybe I could call Olive when I get home. Olive always comes up with the best remedies.

"Penny, make sure when we get home to grab your bags and put everything in the laundry room and I will get it washed up for you," my mom said, finally acknowledging my presence once again. Sure, now she starts talking to me, but of course it is to tell me to do something—so typical!

"Fine!" I said.

"And Penny? Enough with the attitude."

Ahh, mothers!

As I walked into the front room, already carefully removing the tags off my new threads, I noticed my dad sitting on the arm of the couch looking a little perplexed. I also noticed he was holding what looked like a bill of some sort. I had seen enough bills and stuff to know what they looked like. Although, I don't know why my parents ever stressed over bills—it's not like they ever bought anything fun and cool.

"Dad, are you okay?" I asked, removing a tag. "You look a little pale. Can I get you something?" See, even if my mother didn't treat me like an adult, at least I could act like one.

"Oh, Penny!" my dad said startled, even though I was standing right in front of him. "I didn't hear you come in. How was... um…," he said, returning to his forlorn trance, looking back at the bill in his hand while rubbing the back of his neck.

"Shopping?" I said, finishing his sentence. "Well, if you want to know, Mom humiliated me—yet again—by taking me to the thrift store only to be seen by the one and only JayJ Rothefeller. I could have died, Dad, but then I saw the most amazing thing. I saw these clothes. I know I had to make them mine. But then this other girl saw them too, and we were racing. We were like two creatures fighting for our very lives, but there was this kid, who earlier had thrown a ball at the back of my head, and he—it was so awesome—he actually blocked the other girl, and then…"

"Penny," my dad said, "You're rambling."

"I know, but you're missing the point, Father!" I said. See how I did that? I let him know I was upset with him by calling him Father. It's like these people don't even know me.

"Well, what is the point?" he asked, still staring at the paper.

"The point is, Father," I said, "that my social life just may be ruined because JayJ saw me going into the thrift store with Mom, I mean, Mother. And…"

"Penny, first of all, I'm sure JayJ is a nice enough girl and I doubt she would ever be purposely mean to you. Secondly, at least your Mom took you shopping," my dad said.

"Mother!" I retorted.

"Why are you mad at your mom, or mother?" my dad asked.

"Well, first of all—wait! How did you know I was mad at Mom? I mean Mother."

"Because whenever you are mad, you call us Mother or Father. Trust me Penny, we know you better than you think. We are your parents after all."

"I know! I don't need reminding. Anyway, my mother completely ruined any chance of happiness I had left for my sixth grade year. I couldn't believe it, she's ruined everything," I said with a giant sigh. "Why can't she just let me shop at the mall?"

"Penny, I wish she could, but the factory…" my dad said.

"Well, yeah, I came in here because you look a little stressed out," I said. "Is everything okay at the factory? I mean, you can tell me, I am a girl on the cusp of womanhood you know."

"Penny," my dad said with a chuckle. "You don't need to worry about what is going on down at the factory."

"I can't wait until I get to work at the factory full-time. One day I will be Penny Picklepants, Professional Pickle Taster and International Super Star—okay, the International Super Star may take some time—but Penny Picklepants, Professional Pickle Taster. Has a nice ring to it, don't you think?" I said.

My dad gave a good laugh at that one, easing the tension in the room. Of course my mother had to come into the room just then and ruin everything.

"Penny, your dad and I need to talk," she said. "Take your clothes to the laundry and then go and clean that room that scarcely resembles a bedroom."

"Fine," I said, "but I am still mad at you, you know." I then stomped out of the room.

"Listen Penny," my mother said, blocking my way. "I am sorry about the mall, but I will make it up to you, I promise. Please don't be mad—how about I make you some cookies?"

Like I could be won over with my mom's warm, gooey, chocolatey chocolate chip cookies straight from the oven—okay, I loved cookies too, not as much as pickles mind you, but still I loved them all the same.

"Okay, but you still owe me," I said, trying to remain as stern as possible, "and I am not going to let you forget."

"For some odd reason, Penny, I am sure you won't," my mom said.

CHAPTER THREE

Dear Secret Pickle Society,

This story begins on the shores of the Mediterranean Sea on the small island of Crete, in the village of Ierapetra in the house of Pintzopoulos, home to a cruel master, a humble kitchen servant, Athena, and many others.

Athena was smart, but quiet, and only had one friend, Cucumber, whom the master killed for buying a strange plant from a stranger (I told you he was cruel). Nobody would eat such a thing because it came from a stranger and a strange land... that, and everyone really loved their broiled lamb and feta goat cheese.

The master had the plant thrown away, but Athena retrieved it and decided to grow it in secret, in honor of her friend Cucumber, which was a good thing because she was starving, and she found the fruit of this plant to be delicious. But if the master found out she was growing a strange food in secret, she would have been killed on the spot! So she checked on her plants in the middle of the night when everybody was sleeping.

One fateful night, the master's son, Achilles, saw her running across the yard. Achilles tried to follow her, but she easily slipped away. The next night Achilles waited patiently for her near the edge of the olive trees. Just when he thought she wasn't going to show, Achilles heard the sound of soft tip-toeing feet. What he saw surprised him, Athena tending a little garden outside the city gates. Achilles had to talk to her. So he jumped down from the tree.

"What are you doing?" he asked her.

Startled, Athena tried to run, but Achilles grabbed her arm.

"Please do not kill me," Athena pleaded.

"Do not worry," Achilles said. Then he kissed her.

The two were in love but how in the world of Ancient Greece was a poor servant girl supposed to end up with a prince? The two realized their only choice for happiness was to flee upon the waves of the sea. Risking death, they decided they would leave that night before sunrise. After agreeing to meet at the dock in one hour, they parted with a kiss. But Achilles never showed. Athena no choice, She left with a broken heart and seeds of her green plant.

After sailing for many days, by pure happenstance she stumbled upon a new land. In this new land, Athena discovered a weed called dill that nobody paid much attention to. The instant she smelled its sweet and tangy aroma, she knew that it would be a perfect match with her green food, which she had named cucumber after her one and only friend. With the dill and a mixture of vinegar and other tasty things, she called her creation pickles. Oh, and she married a pilgrim with the last name of Picklepants.

Kind Regards,
Penny Picklepants ♡

So back to the question: Who was this JayJ? And why would someone want to hide from her? Well, as you probably already know, any good feud starts with a good backstory, and this one was no exception.

The Rothefellers moved to Pottsville about six months ago and for some reason completely beyond me, they befriended my family. Of all the families in Pottsville, why, and I mean *WHY, OH WHY* did they have to move to Pottsville and become friends with us? They moved here from New York City. How they ended up in Pottsville, Pennsylvania from New York is anyone's guess. Nobody knew why they were here, and they wouldn't say.

JayJ's first day at our school's summer camp—a "school is starting up again soon, so let's get everyone reacquainted" weeklong day camp a month before school started—was a precursor to how mine and JayJ's friendship—okay, our loathing-ship—would develop. I introduced myself at the morning break, because I am nice like that. She made fun of me at lunch, because she is evil like that. And we were mortal enemies by the afternoon break, because life is just like that.

My mom picked me up that day from summer camp. I hopped into the van and was about to tell my mom about the new girl who was so evil that I was positive that she had been sent directly from the devil himself, when she blurted out, "We got invited to a party!" before I could say anything.

"What? What kind of party? When is it? I mean, I must start to plan my wardrobe right now. I cannot be rushed when making such fashion-related decisions. There is a lot of planning that goes into these things."

Ha! Take that evil JayJ. You won't ruin my entire day.

"We got invited to a pool party at the Rothefellers," my mom then said.

Then, all time slowed down and everything became blurry.

I think after that my mom said something like, "They just moved here from New York City—blah blah blah." And then something like, "Mrs. Rothefeller is such a nice lady—yada yada, yada." And then something like, "When we discovered that we both had girls the same age—blah, blah, blah—we both just knew that you two would become the best of friends—yada, yada, yada."

"Huh?" Did my mom just say that JayJ and I were going to be friends? The *best* of friends? And now we are going to their house for a party?

"The Rothefellers. Isn't it great? Didn't you meet JayJ today?" my mom asked. "I just bet you two are going to be great friends."

It's like my mom doesn't even know who I am. I don't remember what my mom said after that, I just couldn't stop thinking about how much fate already hated me and I was only 11 years old.

I tried getting out of it, heaven knows I tried. When I suddenly got sick on the day of the party my mom wasn't buying it.

"Mom," I said in my sick voice, lying in bed. "I better stay home. Just look at my temperature."

Please, oh please, oh please believe the fake sickness. If this works, I am so going to think about being an actress, only after I am done being a professional pickle taster and a singer on a world tour.

"Penny, the thermometer says 156 degrees!" my mom said in her no-nonsense voice. "I don't know why you don't want to go to the Rothefeller's party. It's not like everybody in town got such an invitation. It would be ungrateful not to go. Besides, it's going to be so much fun."

So much for my acting career. Maybe I should consider a career in law. I mean, my dad went to law school, for like a year.

"Mother, you cannot make me go to that party. I have certain rights you know."

"And what rights would those be?" she asked with a little bit of "here we go again" thrown in for good measure.

I think I was starting to wear her out and every kid knows you eventually get what you want when you wear your parents down.

"Well, firstly, I am pretty sure there is a law about false imprisonment, and I feel that you forcing me to go and remain within JayJ's house against my will for a party I do not want to attend is certainly a form of false imprisonment, if not kidnapping. And secondly, there is certainly a law about freedom of speech and expression, and being forced to be happy against my will at a party

I do not want to go to certainly takes away my freedom of speech and expression."

Law school here I come!

"Penny, you're going, end of discussion," my mom said, walking out my room. "And don't even start to roll your eyes at me—just a little hint, it does not work."

Judge, jury and executioner. So much for my law career.

When we arrived at the Rothefeller mansion, my staunch look of "my life is so unfair" quickly faded to a look of actual surprise. Their house looked amazing—and dare I say, fun?

Maybe JayJ was having a bad day when I first met her. Maybe, but then what would be her excuse for all the rest of the days she glared at me and said horrible things about me? Maybe she had bad days on all the days that end with y?

Of course, Parker, my little brother, who was far more perceptive then we usually gave him credit for, piped up and said, "Penny, a little more gratitude and little less attitude."

I was about to argue with him when my mom said, "That's right Parker. You're so right."

Ugh! Okay, so maybe Parker was right, at least, maybe a little bit. I could enjoy myself, right? I mean, sure, I would have to hang out with a girl that clearly hated my guts. But she had a pool! And sure, it was BYOM and my parents thought it would be a good idea to bring the processed rejected parts of a cow, aka hot dogs for us—don't even get me started on hot dogs. Did you know that the Cancer Prevention Coalition recommends that children should not eat more than 12 hot dogs per month because of the risk of cancer? My dad liked to call them "tube steaks," to which I usually replied, "You mean, the other cancer stick?" Of course, they said the same thing about french fries—and come on, everybody knows that McDonald's french fries are the most amazing thing on the planet.

After a few bites of the other cancer sticks—probably better than the tofu burgers the Rothefellers were having—and splashing in some watered down chlorine, aka the Rothefeller pool, I eventually found myself having a better time than I thought I would. Maybe Parker really was on to something about having a better attitude.

The rest of the Rothefellers weren't that bad either—guess JayJ was just the rotten apple of the bunch. In the Rothefeller family, there were Mr. and Mrs. Rothefeller—very proper, but nice—they actually looked like Ken and Barbie, so I guess that made JayJ, Skipper?

Then there was Junior. Yes, his name was simply Junior. When I asked what Junior stood for, they all looked at me like I had a strange disease. Awkward!

And then there was the oldest Rothefeller daughter, Ginger—she was 5'8" and looked like a model. I hated to admit it, but she was gorgeous. And I wasn't the only one to notice her. My older brother, Patrick, couldn't stop staring—sheesh, keep that tongue rolled in your mouth you dog—she is way out of your league anyway!

After dinner, family members started pairing off—Dad with Mr. Rothefeller—Mom with Mrs. Rothefeller—Patrick with Junior. And then there was Ginger and Patrick—surprisingly, she actually seemed to be interested in Patrick for some reason. Then there was me and JayJ.

"You don't need to follow me Penny, I already have a pet. Come on Fifi," she said, carrying a little white fur ball that fit into her purse.

Grrr! The nerve of this girl.

Luckily I found my way to the pool without following JayJ, but then I had to sit there and listen to Patrick and Ginger. Gag!

"I'm really glad I got to move to this town Patrick," Ginger said with some kind of weird southern accent. Signature eye roll! Weren't these people from New York?

"Well, I mean, yeah, it's like I'm really glad you guys moved here too and stuff," Patrick said, while doing his best to flex what little muscles he actually didn't have.

"You must work out," Ginger said, feeling Patrick's puny arms.

"Oh, yeah, you know," Patrick said, "I work out."

"Yeah, if by working out you mean playing video games all day," I said, I thought under my breath.

"Oh Penny, such a kidder," Patrick said. "I actually spend a lot of time picking up the heavy pickle barrels down at the plant."

Patrick shot me a quick "shut up little sis, or else!" look.

"Oh," Ginger said, "sounds exciting. You'll have to show me sometime." Then she put her arm through his, and said she would show him the rest of the house. I was about to say something else, but Patrick turned around and gave me another death glare from the underworld, so I didn't dare.

With the two teenage love birds gone, I could finally enjoy the sunshine sap-free and with a little bit of peace and quiet. Unfortunately, Parker and Junior kept bugging me to come and play with them in the pool. After a few minutes of constant "please Penny, please, please," and being splashed, I decided, what the heck.

Of course, they insisted on playing Marco Polo, of which I didn't have the fondest of memories playing. Whenever we would play at the public pool, I always seemed to end up being Marco 99.999% of the time. And after running into one too many fat, hairy men—hello! Ever heard of a shaver Mr. Fat Hairy Man?—I learned to hate the game.

"Hey JayJ, come and play with us too. Please, pretty please, please, please, please!" Junior asked his older sister.

"No, I am too old to be playing your silly little games, Junior."

Of course she would say that, in her snooty little non-southern accent.

"Well, Penny is playing," Parker said.

Oh cute little Parker, always coming to my rescue.

"Exactly," JayJ said.

What? What did she just say? Of course my disgust distracted me from the "not-it" contest—I guess I was it.

I was determined not to be Marco very long, which I discovered was fairly easy considering the boys kept laughing. The boys were pretty fast though, so after a while it was my turn again. I closed my eyes and started yelling, "Marco," but I could only hear Parker answering this time. Where the heck was Junior? And that is when I heard the loudest, most cringe-worthy cry of horror from, who else, but JayJ Rothefeller.

"OH! MY! GOSH! PENNY! You peed in our pool?!" said the wicked voice.

Wait! What?

"Wait!—What?—No!" I said, struggling to get the words out. "I did not pee in the pool!" I protested, utterly confused. I haven't peed in the pool since, well, never. Eleven-year-old girls, who are about to turn 12, do not pee in the pool. "I did not pee in the pool. That's totally gross!" I said, opening my eyes.

"Exactly," JayJ said. "But the dye doesn't lie Penny! The dye does not lie."

I looked down and realized I was standing directly in the middle of a watery cloud of green dye. Apparently some chemical in the Rothefeller's pool turned pee to green, and of course, I was standing right in the middle of it.

"You are so gross," JayJ said.

Did she just take my picture with her cellphone?

"Okay, I did not pee in the pool," I protested. "And this is so disgusting. It couldn't have been me, I didn't do it!"

"Oh, then who did?" asked JayJ.

"It must have been one of the boys—probably Junior—he was right next to me."

"Oh sure, blame it on my brother, Penny. He is 7 years old and plus, unlike some people, he knows better than to pee in the pool. I am so telling my parents."

"The dye doesn't lie," Junior said, shrugging his shoulders with a smirk on his face.

JayJ then turned toward the house and yelled, "MOM! DAD! Penny peed in the pool!"

I looked around trying to grasp the situation and that is when I saw Junior sitting on the side of the pool laughing his guts out staring at a twenty dollar bill.

I quickly jumped out of the pool to dry off and wipe the pee off.

Oh, so gross!

Even though I knew it was Junior who peed in the pool—just

proving the point that this family was evil—I knew my mom would take the Rothefeller's side. Why did bad things always happen to me? Even when it was somebody else's fault, I still got blamed for it!

Of course Mrs. Rothefeller and my mom came racing out of the house to assess the crime scene.

"Oh Mrs. Rothefeller I am so embarrassed. I can't believe Penny would do such a thing," my mom said. So much for loyalty.

"Oh Pam, don't even think twice about it. Kids will be kids, you know."

Whatever!

"Penny, we do have a pool house just over there. If you need to go, you can always use the bathroom in the pool house," Mrs. Rothefeller said to me, as if I were 4 years old.

"I know there is a pool house. You pointed it out to us when we came here. I would have used it if I needed to go, but I swear it wasn't me."

"As we say, the dye doesn't lie, Penny," Mrs. Rothefeller said.

Will they stop saying that! Just stay calm, deep breaths and I am sure they will believe me.

"Mom, I saw the minute it happened, it was totally her," JayJ said.

AGGHH! I! CANNOT! STAND! JAYJ! ROTHEFELLER!

"Oh, no big deal, we will just have to add more chemicals to it tonight, but for now, we will have to close it down."

Of course everybody was glaring at me as if I ruined the party. Doesn't anyone realize the party was a disaster from the get-go?

"Penny, tell Mrs. Rothefeller you are sorry for ruining their pool," my mom said through gritted teeth, while Junior turned his back so that no one could see how hard he was laughing.

I think my mom really thought I had done it and if I didn't apologize now, I wouldn't hear the end of it. "Mom, I didn't do it!" I said.

"Just apologize Penny," my mom said, trying to remain calm.

"Fine!" I said, turning to Mrs. Rothefeller, "I apologize."

"You apologize for what, Penny?" my mom said.

Oh, you have got to be kidding me! By this time, everyone was there. My face was turning beet red.

"I apologize for peeing in your pool Mrs. Rothefeller," I said through gritted teeth, but I couldn't just leave it like that, not with everyone there staring at me. "Even though I didn't do it because I know JayJ paid Junior twenty dollars to do it."

I will stand up for myself even if nobody else will!

"Penny, how dare you make such accusations," my mom said.

"Is this true Junior?" Mrs. Rothefeller asked.

Junior turned around, hid the twenty behind his back and shook his head no, and said, 'Nuh-uh!"

"I am disappointed in you Penny," my mom said.

"Don't worry Pam," Mrs. Rothefeller said, turning to me. "Now Penny, I'm sure as you grow up you will learn the importance of taking responsibility—as well as controlling your bladder," she added with an annoying giggle.

So that's where JayJ gets her annoying laugh. Then my mom had the nerve to join in having a laugh at my expense.

So there you have it, a brief glimpse into the sordid history between me and the devil's spawn otherwise known as JayJ Rothefeller. It isn't pretty, but neither is JayJ... oh, I am so totally going to use that one on her when the opportunity presents itself!

CHAPTER FOUR

The next couple of days were the same old, same old. Even though the countdown to school had begun, we still had to get up at the crack of dawn and pick raspberries, weed the garden, clean the house, and then head to the factory whenever my dad needed us. Lately, however, we were going less and less to the factory. When I asked my mom why, she would just mumble under her breath and walk out of the room. I kept feeling like something was going on, but everybody (incorrectly) thought because I was kid I couldn't handle the stress of real life.

I told my dad that my life was stressful too and that I could totally help him with his problems if he let me. But he just replied, in his gruff dad-voice, "Being an 11-year-old girl with friend problems isn't real stress, Penny. Just wait until you're an adult and then you will know what real stress is."

"But stress is stress Dad, and I handle it," I said. Just like my mom, he then mumbled something and walked out of the room. Didn't they get it? I was trying to be a responsible and mature member of the family. I couldn't wait to be an adult. Life is so much easier when you are older.

So the day before the first day of school finally arrived. I couldn't believe I would be a sixth grader come tomorrow morning. Sixth grade was so cool! Unlike the other grades in elementary school, in sixth grade you had multiple classes, each with their own teacher.

The sixth graders had a whole wing of the school all to themselves. And the best part? We got to have our own lockers! I mean, yeah, we had to share it with somebody, but the point was that we had lockers. I guess they figured they were getting us ready for middle school, which I was so ready for like yesterday. I think the real reason was that they realized that at least some of us were on the cusp of maturity. I was so excited. I had to call Olive.

"Hey Olive. What's up?" I asked.

"Nothing. What are you doing?" she replied.

"Nothing. So, I just have to tell you, my parents are acting so weird lately. I don't know what their deal is. I tell them I can help more with the factory, and they just treat me like I'm a little kid. They are acting so weird lately."

"Your parents have always acted weird Penny," Olive said. "They own a pickle factory for heaven's sake."

She had a point.

"So how are the new spicy pickles?" Olive asked.

"They are delicious, of course!" I said. "I keep telling my dad to put a picture of me with two thumbs up on the label with a caption that reads 'Penny Picklepants: Professional Pickle Taster,' but he just laughs and says 'You know that is Patrick's job,' and walks off. There's a bottle of them downstairs. Why don't you come over and see how delicious they are yourself."

"I'll be right over," Olive said.

As I waited for Olive, I started to think how I could convince my dad that I am ready to do more at the factory. I don't think he fully appreciates my dream of becoming the factory's youngest professional pickle taster. But there's a tradition in our family that the job always goes to the oldest son. It's so unfair! When I try to convince him that it is time to shake things up at the factory, he just laughs. "It's been done like this the last 50 years and it will stay that way for the next 50," is what he always says. He doesn't realize it just gives me that much more determination to revitalize the factory one day. One day, however, felt like forever sometimes.

Two minutes later the doorbell rang.

"It's for me," I yelled down. "I'm in my room."

Five seconds later Olive appeared at my bedroom door, looking short of breath.

"Hey," she said, walking in.

"Took you long enough," I said with a laugh.

"I ran the whole way," she said. "Besides, what are we doing in your room when there are delicious spicy pickles to be eaten downstairs?"

"Oh, yeah," I said. "Okay, but first you have to help me plan out my first-day-of-school outfit."

"Penny!," Olive said, "I didn't run all the way over here to help you and your fashion dilemmas."

"It will just take a second though," I said. "Come on, just help me."

"Okay. Shoes, pants, and a shirt. There! We're done. Now let's go eat some pickles."

"Olive, Olive, Olive," I said, shaking my head, "if only it were so easy. You can never over plan for a once-in-a-lifetime event like this. How many times will I have a first day of school in the sixth grade after this? Never! You can never take it back once it's gone. You need to prepare for these kinds of things if you want them to be spectacular."

"Ugh!" Olive groaned, sitting down on my bed. "Okay, wear those shoes right there," she said, pointing to my so-last-year tennies. "With those jeans," she said pointing to my Saturday-only jeans. "And that shirt in the laundry basket."

"You mean my little brother's Pokémon shirt that somehow

ended up in my laundry basket?" I said pulling the gross little shirt from my basket.

"Penny," Olive said, "A shirt is a shirt. Just pick something and let's go eat some pickles!"

"Olive!" I bemoaned, "It's the last day before school starts. This is no time to kid around. Just help me, please."

"Fine!" Olive said. "Can you at least narrow it down for me?"

"Okay," I said, with a big smile on my face. "I've narrowed it down to just 32 different combinations."

"32?!" Olive said, incredulously. "You drive me crazy!" Olive then got up from my bed and marched out of my room. "I'm going downstairs to have some pickles. I'll see you down there when you are done, if you ever will be."

"Fine!" I yelled, "I guess I'll just figure out the most important outfit of my elementary career all on my own, and you'll have to wait until tomorrow to find out what it is."

"Oh no!" Olive yelled back, going down the stairs, "The anticipation is killing me."

There was no point in spending any more energy in picking out the perfect outfit now. Talking with Olive had thrown a monkey wrench into the gears of my fashion mojo. I guess there was no other choice than to join Olive in eating the new Picklepants Spicy Pickles, which wasn't such a bad alternative—trust me!

"I can't believe that tomorrow is the first day of sixth grade," I said, chomping on a deliciously crisp Picklepants Spicy Pickle. "We are getting so old so fast."

"What? We're kids, Penny. It's not like we're starting college."

Ugh! Olive, my best friend of all people, didn't get it. She still had so much growing up to do before the seventh grade.

Even while Olive and I talked and ate the pickles, I was trying on and pondering what outfit I would wear. I don't know what it was, maybe the pickles, maybe the conversation, but suddenly my fashion senses were firing on all cylinders.

"Wow!" I said, "I am so glad we came down and had these pickles. They've totally put my fashion mojo back in line. I now know what I'm going to wear to school tomorrow," I blurted out.

"Oh brother!" Olive said, "I'm outta here. See ya tomorrow."

"See ya, Olive!" I said, "Remember to meet me at the flagpole in the morning."

"Like we have every year since the first grade," Olive said.

Good old Olive. She may have been my only friend, but she was the best friend a friend could have.

I finally decided on my first-day outfit. First, my new Vans. Yes, my mom finally took me to the mall. But instead of jeans, I bought a new pair of white Vans that I oh so loved! Together with my perfect fitting pair of jeans and my cool new tee… okay, so the tee wasn't exactly brand new. It was one of the many I bought at the thrift store, but it was so cool. I just loved it. I am going to look so good. JayJ won't even know what hit her.

As I inspected myself in the mirror for the last time, I heard my mom yelling up to me to stop trying on my clothes and to get to bed. Something about getting enough sleep to be ready for the big day. I yelled back that I would and carefully folded my new clothes. I placed them on my chair so when I woke up, they would be ready.

After tossing and turning in bed for the next hour I was starting to get a little irritated with myself. I just couldn't fall asleep. Maybe a cup of warm milk would help, I thought—something my dad taught me. He has his moments of genius.

As I walked down the stairs to the kitchen, I could hear my parents talking quietly, which made me stop. What were they talking about so late at night? My parents never stayed up late. The latest I had ever seen my parents stay up was for New Year's, and that was usually only until 10:30. Tonight, it was well passed 11:00. What the heck were they talking about?

"Then what are we going to do Peter?" I heard my mom ask.

"I don't know," my dad said. "The factory just isn't generating enough. We obviously pinned a lot of hope on the new spicy pickles line, but our sales have been lackluster at best. Some are saying that it's not the product, it's the way the economy is going. There have been some factories that have gone under. And I think, we're just lucky to be still producing a product at this point. I don't know how much longer we can go on like this, however."

Remaining still, I swallowed nervously, trying to process everything my dad was saying. I couldn't believe it. But when I started to put all the pieces together of how my parents had been acting lately, it all made sense. I continued to strain to hear the rest of what my dad was saying.

"I know what I want to do," my dad said, "but sometimes what we want and what we should do are two entirely different things. I used to think that I could never sell the plant. It's been in the family for a hundred years. My great-great grandfather started this plant from scratch. He would turn in his grave if he ever found out I sold the plant. I just don't think I could ever do that."

"Well," my mom said, "what about taking out another mortgage?"

"That's the thing," my dad said, "there's already a second mortgage on the factory."

"What do you mean?" my mom asked, "I thought it was all paid off."

I heard my dad exhale a big sigh. "There was a mistake with the mortgage that the bank caught. That's who was calling when you and Penny left. He apologized, but said there was nothing he could do about it. He said a title search picked it up when they were closing out the loan. Apparently my dad had taken out an additional mortgage on the factory and the house, which was supposed to be combined with the one paid off. Now I have to get it paid off in the next six months, or the balloon payments set in. I just can't believe I got dumped with all these problems. Of all times."

I knew I had to do something to help my dad save the plant. My big dreams of one day becoming "Penny Picklepants Professional Pickle Taster" depended on it. I had to have a pickle plant to fulfill my dream. Now granted, I also had dreams of marrying Taylor Lautner, becoming a famous fashion designer and having a country named after me, but that is beside the point right now. Right now I need to help save the factory. I just couldn't imagine not having the factory in our lives. Then and there, I made a pact that I would do anything and everything to help my parents. Only problem was, I had no idea what to do.

I slowly turned around and quietly tip-toed up the stairs so my parents wouldn't hear me. I knew where all the squeaks in the steps were so I tried to avoid all the creaking of the old wooden stairs the best I could, but then: CREEEAK!

Could you get any louder, steps?

"Who's there?" I heard my dad call.

"Penny?" I heard my mom say. "Is that you?"

Oh crap, oh crap, oh crap. What should I do? Should I do the right thing and answer my mom and tell her I had heard everything and that we are a family and family sticks together? Yes, that is what I should do. So instead, I stood real quiet and held my breath hoping she wouldn't hear me.

"Penny? Penny!" my mom said.

Again, I should do the right thing. I now have a second chance. So instead, I sucked in my stomach, and didn't move a muscle.

"Penny, I know you are on the steps," my mom said. "Go to bed, it is too late! You need to get to bed."

Okay, if I stop breathing and hold in my stomach and shut my eyes there is no way they will know I'm here. Maybe I should grunt and then she would think it was one of my brothers. Yes, that is what I will do, the old grunt and blame. Man, I am so good at this espionage thing—maybe I should consider a career with the CIA.

"Penny," my mom said, "just because you are holding your breath, sucking in your stomach and closing your eyes, doesn't mean we don't know you are there. Now go to bed this instant."

"Fine!" I said, relaxing my stomach and letting out a huge breath.

As I laid in bed thinking about the pickle my parents were in… Ha! I just crack myself up, I mean, even in times of hardship, I can still make myself laugh. Anyway, I knew I had to do something to help them. I went through every scenario that I could think of from asking for a loan from the bank, to getting a job. I doubt, though, an 11-year-old girl, even as sophisticated and mature as I was could get a job. I mean, the only job I was qualified to do was to give fashion advice and somehow I doubt that old women, like 30-year olds, would take fashion advice from me—their loss! Anywho, I figure if these ladies didn't get fashion by the time they were

30 they would never understand it. I mean by the time you are 30 your life is pretty much over anyway.

I decided my best option was to go to the bank after school and ask for a loan. Yes, it would be perfect. I figured I would walk in, explain the problem, explain how I would completely revamp production, and then they would give me the loan.

CHAPTER FIVE

The next morning came quickly—a little too quick if you ask me. I was tired, but I couldn't help but be excited for the first day of school—I mean, I was going to look good. And the first day of school was always the best, seeing what everybody else was wearing and catching up on all the summer romances. And of course, I loved hearing about my friend's fabulous vacations, and figuring out who came back with the best tan and most importantly, who had the best hair, and shoes, and accessories.

I could hardly wait to get out of the car and find Olive. Olive had been my best friend for as long as I could remember. She was the funniest person I knew because she always laughed at my jokes. We were as different as night and day, but I figured that is what made us such good friends. She didn't really care about fashion, although I had told her on numerous occasions that if she was going to be my friend, and best friend at that, that she would have to care about fashion. Truth is, she never really believed that ultimatum, or any other for that matter. All that mattered was that we always had a blast together, and at 11 years old—almost 12—what else did you need in a friend?

As I waited for Olive at our usual spot by the flag pole, JayJ's group spotted me and started to walk over. I turned my back hoping this would deter them. Hopefully, they would find somebody else to prey upon, but once again, my stealth skills proved to be not quite as stealthy as I would have liked them to be.

"Penny," I heard JayJ say.

I really hated the way that girl said my name.

"Oh Penny Picklepants!" she said.

Think fingernails, think chalkboard, combine the two, and there you have JayJ's voice.

I needed to make myself invisible. What a perfect time to hone my stealth skills. Obviously turning my back didn't work, and holding my breath, sucking in my tummy and shutting my eyes didn't work for me at home. But what else could I do? I had nothing left. And maybe it would work on JayJ. So I did what any good spy would have done, I shut my eyes, sucked in my tummy and held my breath.

"Penny?" I heard JayJ say, but now she was in front of me. "Why are closing your eyes, sucking in your stomach, and holding your breath? Do you actually think I can't see you when you do that?" All the girls with her laughed.

"Oh, JayJ," I said, opening my eyes. "No, I wasn't hiding from you."

"Then what were you doing?" she asked.

"Oh, that?" I said, trying to stall. Was that first bell ever going to ring? And where was Olive? "Oh, that, um, I was just…" Oh man! I had to think fast. Problem was, whenever JayJ was around, my mind just went to mush. "I was just… meditating."

"You were meditating?" JayJ said, laughing, which meant everyone else in her group had to laugh.

"Yeah, so what?"

"You are so weird Picklepants," JayJ said, shaking her head, "but at least you're always good for a good laugh." Of course her drones laughed and laughed. This girl was so annoying.

"Wow, so, where did you get your outfit, Penny?" JayJ asked.

"I went to the mall, just like you JayJ," I said. Which was true, I mean, I got my Vans there at least. Where the heck was Olive?

"Really?" asked JayJ. "That's kinda funny, because those jeans you are wearing are from last year's line. In fact, I had a pair just like them that I left at the thrift store."

Oh crap! It couldn't be. Please, oh please, oh please, don't tell me it's true. But it all made sense. Those perfectly cute clothes at the thrift store were all JayJ's! Oh life, just when I think you've finally dealt me a much deserved break, you go and set me up for the greatest humiliation of all, and at the hands of JayJ of all people.

"And not only did I have a pair of jeans just like that," JayJ continued, "but I had a top just like the one you are wearing."

Maybe if I gave her my death glare she would just, poof, go away. Come on death glare lasers, do your job. It always worked on my little brother. Why aren't you working on JayJ?

"In fact," JayJ said, "I can prove that shirt you are wearing was one of the shirts I donated to the thrift store."

"What are you even talking about? I got this shirt at a store in the mall," I said. Cue eye roll, ready, set, and action. Sheesh! Even my infamous eye roll didn't faze her? I swear she is from another planet. And did I just blatantly lie to her? I think she brings out the worst in me.

"You see Penny, that shirt you are so proudly wearing and lying about where you got it from is mine. I gave it to the thrift store to help poor people and I know it's mine because it had a stain on the back of it, which you obviously didn't notice when you bought it, hence why I gave it away." Snicker, snicker, snicker. Pointing, pointing, pointing. My first day of school was not going according to plan.

Okay, so I had been caught lying. But the worst of it was that I had been caught lying by JayJ wearing JayJ's hand-me-downs that

JayJ donated to the thrift store. I had to get out of here. Where was Olive? I couldn't wait any longer. I had to think of an exit strategy. I could:

A. Go politician on her, i.e., sit here and deny, deny, deny. But the stain was an obvious give away, which by the way, the next time I went shopping with my mother—yes we were back to calling her mother—I was so inspecting every article with a fine tooth comb.

B. I could try and come up with a witty comeback. But my brain's witty comeback storage unit had been completely depleted in light of present circumstances. I'm so mortified, I can't even think of my middle name. Do I even have a middle name?

C. I could run away and hitchhike to a new city, change my name and start a new life. But then again, I didn't even know where the bus station was or if we even had one.

D. I could start talking to her in Spanish. I mean, I pretty much spoke el Español. Who knows, maybe in times of great distress my hidden language skills would kick in like a shot of adrenaline—I am waiting hidden language skills… any time now… ugh! How did you say dang it in Spanish?

E. I could wait for the bell to ring… *RING* Oh my gosh! The bell—it was ringing. I was literally saved by the bell!

"Whatever JayJ," I said, hopping down from the flagpole base. Not much of a witty comeback, but it will have to do for now.

"Hey Penn—just got here. What the heck happened?" Olive said, slightly out of breath.

Olive! She made it. I don't think I had ever been so happy to see Olive than at that moment.

"Where have you been?" I asked.

"Sorry!" Olive said. "My mom, she made us a really big breakfast for the first day of school, and then she made me a really great lunch, and then…"

"It's fine," I said, "but I'll tell you what's not fine! One little conversation with JayJ has just ruined my entire 6th grade social life. In fact, I think it may just have ruined my entire 6th grade year!" I wanted to cry, but there's no way I am going to give JayJ the satisfaction.

"What happened?" asked Olive.

"Long story short. I'm wearing JayJ's old clothes," I said.

I could tell by the look on Olive's face she knew how big of a deal this was to me, although I could also tell she wouldn't have cared a single bit if she had been the one caught wearing JayJ's hand-me-downs.

I was so rattled that I was shaking. I forgot to tell Olive what I was going to tell her right when I saw her, which was that the pickle plant was in trouble. By the time I remembered, class had begun and we were shushed to silence by Mrs. Shushems. It will just have to wait until lunch.

The rest of the morning dragged on as we got our new books and went over the rules of what we could expect and what Mrs. Shushems expected of us. Why do they think they need to go over the rules? The rules never change. Be nice, don't talk out of turn, if you need a potty break, wait until the designated potty break times. I guess the only thing that had changed since kindergarten was the fact that it was no longer called a potty break, but using the restroom.

Finally, lunchtime arrived. Olive took her lunch very seriously. She wanted to be a food critic when she grew up. Practically everyone knew that Olive's mom was the best cook in town. She was even contemplating opening a restaurant. I loved going to Olive's house because her mom made some seriously good food and the desserts she made were out of this world. I kept hoping that Mrs. Oliverson would tell my mom that orange Jell-O with julienned carrots was not considered a dessert, but so far, no such luck.

"Olive, you will never believe what I heard my parents talking about last night," I said.

"Um," Olive said between bites of her sandwich, "they finally confessed that you were adopted?"

I gave Olive my friendly "haha, very funny" eye roll, the one where my smile neutralizes all of the eye-roll's potency. "No," I said, "apparently there are problems at the plant, serious problems."

Olive just sat there and stared at me, eating her sandwich. The good thing about talking to Olive during lunch was that most the time she just sat there listening while she ate, but you could tell she was thinking about what you would tell her. But this couldn't wait, I needed her advice. This was an emergency.

"So what do you think we should do Olive?" I asked. "Should we get a loan from the bank?"

"First of all Penn," Olive said, finishing the last bite of her sandwich, and washing it down. "What do you mean by 'we'?"

"I mean, you and me, silly," I said. "We need to figure out how to save the plant. This is serious. I can't do it all on my own."

Olive just sat there and stared at me, now eating her chips.

"You do realize," Olive finally said, "that in order to get a loan, you have to have a job. The bank isn't going to give a loan to an eleven year old girl, cusp of maturity or not, thousands of dollars to help save a factory. If you want to save the plant, you will need to come up with a way to make the money on your own."

"I know," I said, "but it was the best thing that I could think of at 11:30 last night. And now not only am I worried about the plant, I am worried about my clothes. It's just so embarrassing that my mom makes me shop at the thrift store. When I found all these great clothes I was so excited and I never thought in a million years that they would be JayJ's. I swear, I think my mom is trying to kill all hopes of a social life for me by making me shop at the thrift store, and..."

"Penny!" Olive said, "you're rambling."

"Sorry! You're right. I'm just so stressed. Anyway, you mean, we will have to come up with a plan, right?" I said. "And you really think I'm on the cusp of maturity? You are such the best friend!"

"Penn, back to the point," Olive said. "Trust me, the bank thing is not going to work. And if I am going to help you, it is going to be based on certain conditions."

"Okay, like what?" I asked.

"Well, for starters, under no circumstances will we be using hairspray nor any other flammable beauty product for anything except its intended purpose; under no circumstances will we be using, nor will you ever mention the word Nair (more on this later); there will be no harming of animals (probably in reference to the Nair incident—just keep reading); you are not allowed to call me at 2 o'clock in the morning to tell me that you have had a vision in which Karl Lagerfeld, whoever that is, has told you he wants you to start your own fashion line, and I repeat, Karl Lagerfeld neither was, is, nor will he ever be your close personal friend; we will not start nor will you suggest that we start a fashion hotline; and lastly, and this one is important as it often slips your mind—whatever we do, it must be legal."

Wow! It was as if Olive had planned on making that speech for a long time now.

For the rest of the day I felt like my head was swimming in a haze of gray. I was having a hard time zoning in on school. All I could think of was the Picklepant's Pickling Plant and how I was going to save my future.

The last hour of school we were separated into our special one-day-a-week class. The boys went to Wood Shop and the girls went to Home Economics, but everybody just called it Home Ec. When I pointed out to Olive that it seemed a little sexist that they would send us to Home Ec. and the boys to Wood Shop, she just looked at me and said, "I happen to like cooking."

Sometimes I wonder why I even bother.

CHAPTER SIX

Mrs. Smith, the Home Ec. teacher, seemed fairly normal for having such a weird last name. I mean come on, her last name was Smith! She definitely wasn't from around here, making her highly suspicious. I mean, why would anyone want to teach a bunch of 6th grade girls how to cook? When I raised my hand to ask her why we needed to learn how to cook she just laughed and said, "Because the joy of cooking is something everyone deserves to experience." Huh? When I pointed out that the boys in the wood shop didn't have to "experience" it, she smiled and said politely, "Well, I'm sure many of them would love to learn how to cook, but tradition is tradition."

Instead of wasting an entire semester on the woe of cooking, I felt our time would be better spent learning the important life skills like how to apply make-up, and how to mix and match one's wardrobe—you know, the really important stuff, like fashion sense and the joys of accessorizing. When I told Olive that I should write a letter to Principal Q that such classes should at least be offered to us, she just rolled her eyes at me and told me to stop talking and to pay attention. Sheesh, she sounded like my mother.

After Mrs. Smith had explained that we would be applying basic cooking principles both in class and on our own time, Olive got so excited. By basic I hoped she meant stuff like bowl+cereal+milk or bread+toaster.

"I can't wait to start cooking! I have so many recipes that I found on the internet that I am dying to try," Olive whispered.

"I am dying that you just said that Olive!" I snapped.

"I happen to like cooking Penny," Olive said, raising her voice.

"And just because it has nothing to do with fashion does not mean it does not matter."

"Do you have something to share with the class Miss Oliverson?" asked Mrs. Smith.

"No ma'am," Olive said.

"Then I suggest you pay attention," Mrs. Smith said.

That certainly wasn't the first time that I had got Olive in trouble for talking during class. Olive gave me one of her death glares. I had to admit, Olive had developed quite the mean death glare—I mean, nothing on par with mine—but not bad, and definitely an improvement from her dreadful fifth-grade death glare.

I didn't really have time or the opportunity to explain to Olive that cooking so wasn't cool, but flunking out of Home Ec. was even less cool so I figured I better step it up.

"In addition to applying the basic principles of cooking," Mrs. Smith continued, "you will also be tasked with creating and keeping a journal of your cooking adventures."

Did she just say cooking was an adventure? Who was this lady?

"The school's webmaster," Mrs. Smith continued, "has been kind enough to set up what he called a cooking blog for our class. Each of you will be able to set up your own page where you can post pictures, post your recipes, and share with the class your experiences."

Ugh! This class just kept getting worse by the minute.

"You have the choice," Mrs. Smith said, "of either going it alone or partnering with a fellow student. But no more than two per team. As they say, 'Too many cooks spoils the broth.'"

Then the bell rang. Freedom at last!

"So," I said turning to Olive as we walked to our locker, "what are we going to call our blog?"

Olive then turned a deep shade of purple, which by the way, is so not a good color on her, and so last season!

"Well, I kind of," Olive said as she squirmed searching for the right words, "I kind of, I mean, I was sort of thinking I wanted to do it alone."

I could not believe what I was hearing. I mean, Penny and Olive were like Peanut Butter and a really fancy, fashionable Jelly. We were like Macaroni and a perfectly aged, really expensive French Cheese.

"I mean just this once," Olive said. "But you know any other projects we can do together. I mean you are my best friend, but I know that you…" she trailed off.

"Olive," I said, with pleading oozing all over each of my words, "I cannot do this without you. I mean you are the brains and I am, well, the comic relief. I guess in this case you are the pans and I am, um, like, the stuff you put in the pans." Could she not hear in my words how I could never do this without her?

"Ingredients?" Olive said.

"Right! I am the ingredients! See? We finish each other's sentences. I could never do this without you. You and I," I said, gesturing back and forth between us with my thumb, "have never done anything without YOU. Besides, it will be so much fun. I'll totally stay out of your way. You can do all the cooking and I will do all the writing. It is a win-win situation."

Olive let out a big sigh, the kind she usually does when she, as usual, sees things my way. "Okay," she said, as if she had always known she would be saying it, "but no funny business. We will figure out a name for our blog later."

With school over and a 7:00 P.M. phone call to Olive scheduled for that night to discuss everything that had happened at school, and what we were going to do save the pickle plant, and what we were going to name our blog, and other important things like that, I was already exhausted. My parent always said, "You will know exhaustion when you work 10 hours a day," but I doubt they ever had to deal with something like JayJ Rothefeller all while come up with a plan to save a pickle plant, on top of creating the perfect name for a cooking blog. Seriously, sixth grade was shaping up to be a very stressful grade.

My mom finally arrived to get me and Parker like after we were practically the last ones left at school.

"Sorry," she said, "I got distracted making bread."

"You're making bread?" I asked. All was instantly forgiven. I loved my mom's homemade bread.

My mom smiled. "I figured it would be a nice after-school treat after your first day," she said.

My mom so understood me. Well, at least until I tried explaining to her what a monster JayJ was. It was like trying to teach a samurai warrior about fashion. Actually, when you think about it, samurai warriors were quite fashionable. Anyway, you get the point. It was pointless.

When we walked in, I could smell the freshly baked bread cooling in the kitchen. I raced Parker to the kitchen, handily beating him. All of the loaves were untouched. I loved being the first one to cut a slice. I slathered on the butter and devoured the piece of warm, melt-in-your-mouth goodness. I then, of course, did as any fine connoisseur of fine foods would do, and chased it with a perfectly dill-pickled cucumber, because everything tastes better with a dill pickle. Just as I was finishing my snack and thinking life was going to be okay after all, my mom broke my Zen moment by asking me to take one of the loaves to a neighbor.

"Penny," my mom said, with that I-have-a-favor-to-ask look on her face, "I have a favor to ask of you." See? What did I tell you! "Do you know the Frankincense home on Piquancy Street?"

"Not really," I said.

"It's at the end of the street, the lovely Victorian home." Well, at least she had good taste in homes. It couldn't be all bad I supposed. "I believe her house number is 2728, but you can't miss it," my mother said.

I was just about to point out that I had had a rather stressful day at school, as well as my general disinclination towards the elderly (anybody over 35), when I noticed my mom was giving me that look.

And then she said, "The poor thing, her husband passed away some time ago. She's all alone." Oh, great, here comes the guilt trip. "And I just bet," my mom said, "she could use a visit. She is a lovely lady Penny. I know you would love her if you got to know her."

"But mom," I said.

"Penny," my mom said with an awkward silence following it, finally saying, "just go."

I had no choice. It was one of those "you know it's the right thing to do" versions of "just go."

"Oh, and Penny," my mom said as I was walking out the door, "be sure to tell her I would like to pay her visit, so ask her when would be the best time."

"Okay," I said, begrudgingly walking out the door.

I walked down Piquancy street slowly to house number 2728,

staring at the sidewalk most of the way. I was trying to think of ways I could just drop off the bread off without talking to this Frankenstein lady. It's like, if my mom wanted to visit this lady so bad, then why didn't she go and deliver the bread herself? I mean, I had enough to deal with in my own life already as it was. It wasn't like I could go take on other people's problems on top of everything else.

As I approached the house, I stopped in my tracks. It was the old creepy house that everybody avoided on Halloween night. Not even Patrick would go there to get free candy, and boys will do just about anything to get free candy. It wasn't that it wasn't kept up and nice. Actually, it was a really neat house. It was just that there were so many creepy stories and everybody knew to avoid it. Nobody, through the history of kids, had ever seen kids there. Some said that kids would go in, but they would never come out. I was not about to overlook all the stories for the time being.

Afraid for my very life, my trembling hand let go of the bread on the doorstep. I rang the doorbell, and then I ran like I had never run before. Our PE teacher, Mrs. Funda, would have been so proud to see me, Penny Picklepants, run an entire block without even stopping once.

I made it home with five minutes to spare before my scheduled phone call with Olive to discuss the big topics of the day. I sat down at the computer in the kitchen and called her a few minutes early. But after spending an hour rehashing the day's events, we were nowhere closer to coming up with a solution to the pickle plant problem than we were with coming up with a name for our blog.

I swear we were just about to have a breakthrough when my

older brother Patrick barged into the kitchen and told me my time was up because he needed to use the computer. Now, I know what you are thinking. Why would I need to get off the phone if Patrick needed the computer? And I can answer that by saying that my mom is el ultro cheapo—man, I am so ready for Spanish class—I mean, my mom actually refuses to pay for normal internet because we can get dial-up for free. As the French would say, "Tres annoying!"

"Olive, I have to go," I said. "Patrick needs the computer."

I think I heard Olive snicker. "Okay," she said. "Let's just figure it out tomorrow at lunch. We just really need to get started on the blog, name or no name. I don't want to get behind."

"Olive, seriously," I said, "don't worry about it. We only have to cook once a week. We will be fine."

I hung up the phone and gave Patrick my best, well, worse, depending on how you look at it, eye roll.

"Penn seriously," Patrick said, "I need to look up some details on the internet and then call Ginger. We are making plans for the weekend."

Patrick connected to the internet. Remember those funny noises from dialup? Yeah, I don't have to remember them. They are a daily occurrence in the Picklepants home. Patrick then looked up some things about restaurants and movie times.

"Patrick," I said, "why don't you be like a normal teenager and text her or something? Don't all teenager just text?"

"Well," he said, "I would, but Ginger prefers to be called on the phone. She's a very traditional girl. She likes everything to be formal and proper, and I'm just doing whatever it takes to make her happy."

"She is so weird," I said. "And what is the deal with that accent?"

"I'm ignoring you," he said. "Now leave!"

He then disconnected from the internet and called Ginger.

I took my time going up to my room. My spy skills may not have worked on my mom, or JayJ for that matter, but Patrick wasn't the sharpest knife in the drawer. I doubt he would even pick up that I was still in the kitchen.

"Hey Ginger, it's Patrick. Yeah, hi. Just a minute," he said in the sweetest voice. Then he covered the phone with his hand, turned to me, and using the meanest voice said, "Beat it Penn! This is a private conversation!"

Dang it! How do spies do it?

CHAPTER SEVEN

Dear Secret Pickle Society,

It all started when a southern chef named Doug H. Nuts the Fifth, from a long line of Nuts who were the specialists of their day in all things deep-fried, started a revolution that would continue to this very day, and a very tasty revolution at that. Just as today, in Doug H. Nut's day everybody knew everything tasted better when it was deep-fried.

However, Doug had so far failed to make any lasting impressions in the deep-fried field, not that Doug wasn't good at the family profession. Doug could whip up a batch of donuts, hush puppies, or funnel cakes like nobody's business. But Doug yearned for more. So one special day Doug deep-fried a pickle, thus making deep-frying history. They became an instant hit in town, then the county, and soon the entire state was craving the deep-fried salty goodness of Doug's deep-fried pickles.

Of course, Doug's batter recipe was a secret and he placed it in the secret compartment of his family's recipe cabinet. And there it lay in a glass bottle for a hundred years, until a girl, on the cusp of maturity I might add, who hailed from Pottsville, Pennsylvania, discovered the secret compartment of her family's recipe cabinet and read the recipe herself. I'll share that recipe with you, but shhh! It's a family secret.

Ingredients
* 1 egg, beaten
* 1 cup milk
* 1 Tablespoon all-purpose flour
* 1 Tablespoon Worcestershire sauce
* 3/4 teaspoon salt
* 3/4 teaspoon ground black pepper
* 3 1/2 cups all-purpose flour
* 1 jar (32 ounce) sliced dill pickles, drained
* 1 quart vegetable oil

Directions

1. In a small bowl, mix together the egg, milk, Tablespoon flour, and Worcestershire sauce. In a separate bowl, stir together the remaining flour, salt, and pepper.

2. Dip the pickles into the milk mixture, then flour mixture.

3. Place the pickles carefully into hot oil (350 F) in small batches. Fry until pickles float to the surface, and are golden brown. Remove with a slotted spoon, and place on paper towels to cool. Eat and enjoy!

Sincerely,
Penny Picklepants ♡

P.S. It was actually my great-grandma Nuts that discovered the hidden recipe, but just like her, I too am on the cusp of maturity.

At school the next day Olive and I put our heads together to finally come up with a plan to help the plant. I came up with a list of things, but for some reason Olive did not like a single one of them.

HOW TO SAVE THE PLANT:
1. Go to the bank and ask for a loan.

"Are you absolutely sure the bank won't give us a loan?" I asked.

"Penny," Olive said, "You are 11 years old! You don't even have a job. How in the world are you going to pay back the bank?"

"I do have a job, Olive," I said. "It's called looking fabulous 24-7!"

Olive then gave me her best impression of the Penny Picklepants eye roll. I have to admit, that one stung just a little bit. Maybe there was hope for her after all.

HOW TO SAVE THE PLANT:
1. ~~Go to the bank and ask for a loan.~~
2. Start a babysitting company.

"Okay," I said, "I've got it. The Penny and Olive babysitting company."

"Do you even know how to babysit?" Olive asked.

"Um, yeah!" I said, "You turn on the TV for the kids while you talk on the phone and eat junk food. I babysit Parker all the time."

Olive than gave me a long and exaggerated sigh.

This is proving harder than I thought. Maybe I should get a new business partner!

HOW TO SAVE THE PLANT:
1. ~~Go to the bank and ask for a loan.~~
2. ~~Start a babysitting company.~~
3. Start a professional pet-sitting company.

"Okay, let's not panic," I said. "Maybe the sitting of babies just isn't our thing. But what about the Penny and Olive professional pet-sitting company?"

"You do remember the last time you tried something like that, right?" Olive said. "You ended up using Nair on Mrs. Natkip's cat to get rid of its flees!"

"Hey, that was a great idea and you know it," I said.

Olive then gave me the eye roll and long, exaggerated sigh combo.

Okay, it wasn't THAT bad. Olive seriously exaggerates everything. Last spring I read an advertisement in Vogue for a fashion camp. It was all about unlocking your inner-fashion diva! How could I resist? All fashion campers would spend a week in New York City learning about the ins and outs of the fashion industry. We would be given backstage access to fashion shows and we were even going to meet a famous designer. Granted, I couldn't tell you who the designer was, much less tell you how to pronounce his name, but whatever, he was a famous designer for crying out loud.

The camp cost $1,000 if you registered early, and $1,500 if you registered after May 30th. When I asked my parents for $500, they both looked like they were gasping for air choking on chicken bones. I explained to them it was a matter of life and death. I needed $500 to pay the early-registration fee. That way I would save them the $500 late-registration fee. It was like I was practically giving them $500 in exchange for their $500, but they just didn't see it that way. The final $500 payment had to be paid before June. When they finally decided to breathe again, they sternly said, in unison, "No!" Over the next week, no matter what I tried, I made no headway. I even waited until they were apart to try the classic "Mom said it was okay if you say it's okay" trick on my dad, as well as on my mom, but they wouldn't budge. When I asked my mom why she wouldn't let me go she told me that it was too expensive.

"What if I paid for it all by myself," I said, "then would you let me go?"

"If you can come up with a thousand dollars in a matter of two weeks," my mom said, "then by all mean you can go."

Hmm, and they say I don't have any negotiating skills.

I had to make money and I had to make it fast. But how in the world was I going to get $1,000 before May 30th? As I was riding my bike the next day, I saw a flyer stapled on a telephone pole for a woman who was looking for somebody to take care of her cat while she went to Europe, or something like that. When the flyer said it would pay $500 I tore off one of the tabs with her phone number.

She gave me the job. I couldn't believe it. She said that she would be dropping of the cat, Mr. Nat, the day after tomorrow. Yes! My first job, and the best part, I would be able to pay for the first half of camp. I figured I could worry about the other payment later.

The first few days went really well. I fed him, played with him, made sure he was using his litter box. I even let him sleep in my room. I could look past Mr. Nat's franticly biting himself and the shedding. I could even look pass the constant grooming—this cat was more worried about his looks than I was!—however, I couldn't look past the little black dots that seemed to move all over his skin.

I didn't want to say anything about it to my parents because my dad reminded me that he hated cats and my mom wasn't all that happy about the cat hair everywhere. My only option was to turn to Olive, so I gave her a call. She was the smartest person I knew and friends always help friends when in need.

"Hey Olive," I said, "Whatcha doin?" I was using my overly-friendly, overly-interested voice.

"I'm doing my nails," she said bluntly.

"Really?" I said. "Am I rubbing off on you? I am so impressed! Are you doing your finger or toes?"

"Umm," she said, in a "duh" kind of way. "If I was painting my fingernails, don't you think it would be a little hard to answer the phone?"

"You make a good point," I said, although I knew, being such a pro, that I could easily talk on the phone while doing my nails.

"So what color are you painting your nails with?" I said.

"Red #55, I think," she said.

"I find that #55 sometimes clashes with some of my red shirts," I said. "So I have been using Red #57. It looks better on me, anyway. However, sometimes I find that Red #58 works better, and so…"

"Penny!" Olive said.

"Sorry, getting off the point," I said. "The reason I was calling was because I think something is wrong with Mr. Nat, and you're the only one that can help."

"Uh huh," she said, paying more attention to her nails than my problems.

"Well," I said, "he's shedding real bad, and he's irritable, and he keeps biting himself, and then there are these little black things."

"Penny," Olive said, "Mr. Nat has fleas!"

GROSS!

"Where do fleas live?" I asked.

"Um, I think in the hair, on the skin, or something," Olive said.

"Huh," I said. "So how do you get rid of them?"

"I think they shave them, but I'm not sure," Olive said.

"So to get rid of the fleas we just need to get rid of Mr. Nat's hair? And to get rid of Mr. Nat's hair we just have to what?" I said.

"Well my mom uses a razor to get rid of the hair on her legs," Olive said. "But sometimes she puts this lotiony stuff that smells really weird on her legs if she is in a hurry. I think it's called something like gair, or jair, or nair… Yes! That's it. It's called Nair."

"Are you sure, it's called Nair?" I asked.

"Yeah," Olive said, "But… wait! No Penny! Are you crazy?"

"Gotta go, see ya!" I said. No time to waste. Poor Mr. Nat was suffering.

By the time I had gotten home from the store with a bottle of Nair Extreme—"Best for the Worst of your Hair Problems" it read on the bottle—Mr. Nat was going crazy in his carrier. I wasn't sure if it was the fleas or he was excited to see me. Regardless, he was just itchin—get it? I so crack myself up sometimes—to get out. I had to get rid of the fleas as quickly and quietly as possible, without my family finding out. I hadn't told my parents yet, because, well, they'd probably make me take the cat to the vet or something, and then I would lose the money for sure. But if I could help Mr. Nat myself, maybe Mrs. Natkip would give me a little extra.

When I approached the door of the carrier, Mr. Nat started to hiss at me. Seriously, doesn't this cat know I am trying to help him? Sheesh! Talk about ingratitude. And why is he arching his back? I wondered. He must be stretching, I figured. The hissing was getting louder as I got closer. Maybe a treat would calm him down. It always worked for me.

I pushed the treat through the door and he stopped hissing. But then, when I opened the door on the cage, he bolted like he had super human speed. Lucky for me, I had closed the door to my room, which was the size of a small box, so really the only place he could go was under my bed, which didn't give Mr. Nat much room. When I looked under the bed, I couldn't see him. I started moving everything out from under it. Finally, I found him curled up in the far corner, hissing at me.

"Come here Mr. Nat," I said. "Good cat, come here you flea infested cat."

Of course, I was using my sweet-even-though-I'm-totally-bugged-with-you voice. But still he hissed.

"Fine!" I said, "if you hiss at me, I will hiss at you." HISS! HISS! Okay, so it doesn't sound as scary when he did it, and it was getting me nowhere.

After 10 minutes, 12 treats, and 15 scratches later, I got Mr. Nat to come out. Now I just had to get him downstairs without my mom hearing me or the cat.

"Penny?" my mom called. "Your Dad and I are going to run some errands. Would you like to come?"

Phew! Something finally going my way.

"That's okay," I yelled. "I will just stay and de-flea... I mean play, yes play with Mr. Nat."

"Okay, we will back in about an hour," she said.

Sweet! I had an hour to get this cat flea-free. That should be plenty of time.

When I heard the car leave the drive way, I raced downstairs to put Mr. Nat in the kitchen sink. It was big and Mr. Nat could look out the window, which I thought would make him relax. It would be like a cat spa. Unfortunately, Mr. Nat didn't see things my way. He did not like the sink, did not appreciate the view, and I am pretty sure he did not like me.

"Don't worry Mr. Nat," I said. "The feeling is mutual."

I tried to put him in the sink, but he kept spreading his legs and arms in every possible direction. This cat was thrashing and flailing and splaying its limbs like it was getting electrocuted. I just couldn't get him to relax. What was this cat's problem?

"This is like a spa you dumb cat," I said, "Don't cats like spas? Don't you guys like pampering?"

I started to use my entire body to get him to go into the sink. My legs, believe it or not, came in quite handy in this situation.

When I finally got him in the sink I suddenly realized I had left the Nair up in my room. "AHHH! I hate cats!" I screamed.

I couldn't let him go, so I carried him upstairs, grabbed the Nair, and headed back downstairs to begin again. But this time I put the oven mitts on. Brilliant, I thought. But have you ever tried to put oven mitts on while holding an angry cat infested with fleas?

After getting the mitts on and successfully get Mr. Nat in the kitchen, it was time to put on the Nair. I briefly glanced at the instructions and saw the word "thick" and "5 minutes," which I interpreted as putting on a thick layer for 5 minutes then washing it off. I poured the entire contents of the bottle on Mr. Nat and started to rub it in. I don't know how long I had been rubbing the Nair in when I realized I hadn't turned on the timer. With one mitted hand holding Mr. Nat down in the sink, I reached over to the microwave with the other mitted hand. Unfortunately, Mr. Nat must have sensed that my single mitted death grip was a little less deathly than I thought because he bolted out of the sink like I would from a Bon Jovi concert. Sorry Bon, but were not even halfway there.

"NOOOOOOO," I screamed.

Oh great, oh great, oh great. Where did he go? Where did he go? The Nair must have increased his already super human speed because within nanoseconds he was out of the kitchen and no-where to be found.

"I don't think this could get any worse!" I said to myself.

Then the doorbell rang.

"You just had to open your mouth didn't you," I said, again to myself.

I was hoping against all hope that it would be Olive. She, of all people, would know what to do in a situation like this. But no, it wasn't Olive. It was Mrs. Natkip. It just had to be Mrs. Natkip.

"Hi Penny," she said, letting herself and her fancy hat and purse, into my home. "I came back early from my trip because I missed my Mr. Natty britches so much."

"I… huh! You and… you're back… and the cat is," was about all I could manage to get out.

"I know what is worrying you," she said.

"What? You do?" I guiltily asked.

How did she know? Am I that easy to read? Could she smell the Nair on the oven mitts? Holy cow! The oven mitts! Just put them behind your back and act normal, Picklepants.

"You are worried about getting paid after I came home early," she said, "but don't worry about that. I will pay you the full amount. I am very fair when it comes to my Mr. Natty-patty. Speaking of, where is Mr. Natters? I know he will be very excited to see me. Come here Mr. Natter-fatters."

Sheesh! Did she give this cat a nickname for every one of its nine lives?

"I… huh… will, um… be right back," I managed to get out.

Wow, Mr. Nat's super human speed must have worn off on me because I tore up the stairs like a banshee. Hoping beyond hope, I checked again under my bed. Actually, I just followed the clumps of hair, and they led directly underneath my bed.

"Come here, Mr. Nat," I said. "Come here, you stupid cat."

Luckily I had learned from the last time how to get him. This time, I got him in record time, but he still had Nair all over him and

I needed to wash it off pronto.

"Penny is everything okay?" I heard Mrs. Natkip call from downstairs. "You are certainly taking your time up there."

"Yes, Mrs.—ouch! Stupid cat!—I mean, yes Mrs. Natkip," I yelled. He had scratched me again. Seriously, how did this cat find the one patch of open skin?

"'Just give me a minute. I want Mr. Nat to look good for you." At least, hairless anyway.

I took him into the bathroom to give him a rinse. But it was just as much of a struggle to get him to sit still in the bathtub. There was only one thing to do. I hopped in the tub with him, turned on the water, and proceeded to wash off the Nair, all while completely drenching myself. By the time I got out of the tub, he looked like he had got in a serious fight with the trimmers and the trimmers had won handily, at least mostly. He looked like a polka-dotted cat with anger issues, most of his hair missing, except a few patches here and there. It wasn't pretty.

I threw him in the cage, gathered up his toys, and came down-stairs. I was done with this cat. I just wanted my $500 and to be done with this cat for good.

"Here you go Mrs. Natkip," I said, as I came down the stairs.

"Oh my Mr. Natty-poos! I can't wait to see you," she said. "And Penny, I left your money on the table there, dear."

"Okay, great!" I said, as I escorted Mrs. Katnip out the door. "Thanks for letting me watch your cat. I had a blast. See you later. Okay, bye now, see ya."

I was pushing her out the door before she could get a good look at Mr. Nat.

"Penny," she said, "Don't forget your money is on the table."

Then she stopped and looked at me incredulously.

"For heaven's sake, Penny why are you all wet?" she asked.

Then I just shut the door.

I had successfully gotten Mrs. Natkip out the door when I sat down to collect my thoughts as well as my money. I took off the oven mitts, as equally drenched and covered in Nair and cat hair as I was. That was the hardest $500 I had ever earned, but at least now I could pay for the first half of fashion camp.

"Fashion camp here I come!" I said. But then I counted the money. Three tens, a five, and fifteen ones. I counted it again, and then again. I then pulled the side table away from the wall. There was nothing else. I could hardly believe it.

"Fifty-bucks!" I screamed. "I just went through all of that for $50 bucks!"

My parents came home to find clumps of cat hair everywhere, a clogged drain, and a flea infested home. By the time I explained to my parent's what had happened, paid for new oven mitts, ointment for all my cat scratches, not to mention the emotional distress that I had to endure, I figured I had made a negative $327.76. In short, I didn't make it to fashion camp that year.

"Okay," I said, "so pet-sitting is out of the question."

HOW TO SAVE THE PLANT:
1. ~~Go to the bank and ask for a loan.~~
2. ~~Start a babysitting company.~~
3. ~~Start a professional pet-sitting company.~~

"Whatever happened with Mrs. Katnip?" Olive said, doing her best to keep from laughing out loud. "Did she ever call to ask why her cat looked like a polka-dot?"

"Yes," I said. "When I told her Mr. Nat had fleas when she dropped him off she hung up the phone and never called back. Anyway, getting back to the issue at hand, how about a pickleade stand?"

"A pickle what stand?" asked Olive.

"You know," I said, "a pickleade stand, like lemonade, but pickleade. The pickle plant has plenty of it. And we could even make pickle popsicles and sell them too."

"That is disgusting!" Olive said. "Who would ever pay to drink pickle juice, Penny? And a pickle popsicle? Have you completely lost your mind?"

"Hey!" I said, "Don't knock it until you've tried it. Pickle pops are the best frozen treat there is. Besides, I read that professional athletes will drink pickle juice to recoup after a hard workout, so it's healthy. I've never heard of professional athletes drinking lemonade after a hard workout."

"Yeah," she said, "because Pottsville is just teeming with professional athletes, isn't it?"

HOW TO SAVE THE PLANT:
1. ~~Go to the bank and ask for a loan.~~
2. ~~Start a babysitting company.~~
3. ~~Start a professional pet-sitting company.~~
4. ~~Pickleade stand.~~

We were still nowhere closer to figuring out how to save the plant when we found ourselves in Home Ec.

"Oh my gosh!" I thought to myself. "HOME EC!"

We had been so focused on coming up with a plan to save the plant that we hadn't even had time to discuss a name for our blog.

"Correction, Penny," Olive said, "You have been so focused on coming up with a plan to save the plant that YOU haven't had time to discuss a name for our blog. Remember, you are doing the blog. I am doing the cooking."

Some best friend Olive is turning out to be. And how did she even know what I was thinking?

As Mrs. Smith started to go around the room to ask who would be going solo and who would be partnering up, I had to force Olive to say we would be partners.

"Is that right, Miss Oliverson?" asked Mrs. Smith.

Olive gulped and then just sat there. She looked at me, Mrs. Smith, and her internet recipes, then back at me, and so forth. A bead of sweat rolled down her forehead. I had to act fast. I first gave her my "you will love being partners with me" look—it's all in the eyes—but that didn't seem to be working.

"I'm waiting, Miss Oliverson," Mrs. Smith said. "Are you and Penny going to be partners?"

Why wasn't my first look working? There was no time to figure it out. I had to bring in the big guns. So I resorted to my "you will so regret not being my partner forever" look—it's all in the pursing of the lips—a low trick, I know, but drastic times call for drastic measures.

"Miss Oliverson, I need an answer, and I need it now," Mrs. Smith said. By this time the whole class was looking at Olive.

"Yes," Olive said, "Penny and I will be partners."

Phew! That was a close one. Luckily, my second look finally broke through, after sending it no less than six times. Olive was the best friend ever.

Then Mrs. Smith walked away.

"I will be your partner Penny," Olive said. "But remember that you have to write everything down and put it on the blog, like a cookbook."

"Oh my gosh Olive!" I said so loudly the whole class looked at me, including Mrs. Smith with her furrowed brow. "Sorry," I said to the class, blushing. I then gave Olive a big hug, as Mrs. Smith continued getting the solo or partner answers from the other classmates.

"That's it," I said in more hushed tones, "A cookbook! We'll start a cookbook and then sell it on the internet. It is genius! And all the recipes have to include pickles from the Picklepants Pickling Plant, making people want to buy them."

HOW TO SAVE THE PLANT:
1. ~~Go to the bank and ask for a loan.~~
2. ~~Start a babysitting company.~~
3. ~~Start a professional pet-sitting company.~~
4. ~~Pickleade stand.~~
5. Pickle Cookbook.

Who knew that Olive could be so smart? Okay, we all knew, but still sometimes I had to remind myself just how smart she was.

"What?" Olive said, thumbing through her recipes. "Adding pickles to everything? Gross! You honestly think a cookbook that a couple of 11-year-old girls from Nowheresville could ever save the plant? Love the enthusiasm, Penny, but I'm afraid like all your other plans it's just not going to work."

Ouch! So maybe the whole cookbook thing wasn't the only solution for the plant, but how fun would it be to cook all our food adding something picklely to it! When Mrs. Smith reminded us that we needed to name our blogs and create our first entry that night, I blurted out, "That's it Olive! The Twenty-Pickle Pie!"

Mrs. Smith gave me another of her furrowed brows.

"Sorry, our blog, the name of our blog, that's the name," I said.

"Got it, Miss Picklepants, but one more outburst from you, and…"

But before she could finish the bell rang. Ahh! Saved by the bell again! This day just kept getting better by the moment.

CHAPTER EIGHT

"Twenty-Pickle Pie? TWENTY-PICKLE PIE?!" Olive said, raising her voice slightly more than usual. "Are you insane?"

So Olive wasn't exactly excited about having a blog called "Twenty-Pickle Pie" or about adding pickles to all our recipes. But I knew she would... eventually. Well, I hoped for eventually.

"Olive," I said, "just give it a chance, it will be fun!"

"Penny, fun is getting an A. Not fun is getting an A minus. And this has A minus written all over it."

"How about this—I will stop pestering you about fashion if you agree to cook with pickles."

Hello negotiation skills. They say that those actors who can sing, dance, and act are considered to be a triple-threat. Perhaps "Penny Picklepants, Negotiator" could round out my triple-threat—Penny Picklepants: Professional Pickle Taster, Fashion Designer, and World Renowned Negotiator.

"Actually," Olive said, "I don't mind when you talk about fashion, I just tune you out."

Hmmm, so much for "Penny Picklepants, Negotiator."

"How about I sweeten the deal and we can watch that Bollywood film that you rave about, for our next sleep over. As well as, as well as..."

She was giving me that look of "you better be upping the ante."

"As well as going to the museum of your choice for the next two..."

I don't think two was going to cut it.

"Three"

Still not doing it.

"Okay, the next four Saturday's? Final offer."

Things were looking up. "Penny Picklepants, Negotiator" is so back on!

"I can live with that," Olive said. "But" she said, stopping me with her finger, "you better not flake out on me this time."

"Olive," I said. "Come on, it's me you're talking to."

"That's what worries me," she said.

Well, I guess she had a point. I mean, a museum? On a Saturday? For a month? Maybe if it was a museum on malls and fashion!

So began the cooking adventures for Olive Oliverson and Penny Picklepants. I was super excited, but Olive seemed to be having second thoughts about the pickles in everything, even after all my expert negotiating.

"Penny, I'm just not sure about the pickles in everything. I mean who has heard of adding pickles to, say, oatmeal? It sounds pretty disgusting!"

"Olive, pickles are nature's food, and should be added to everything because it's natural. Just think of it as adding color—think of the beautifully green tint our food would take on. And don't forget the salt. Every recipe calls for salt. Besides, remember our deal?"

"I know you are going to totally flake on me. Besides, you have never cooked in your life—how would you even know whether every recipe has salt in it?"

"I've watched my mom cook a lot, which by itself ought to be enough for an A in this stupid class, but irregardless..."

"Irregardless isn't a word," Olive said.

"What?"

"Regardless and irrespective are words, but not irregardless."

That's another thing about Olive. She thought she was the

Queen of Grammar. I'm sure she's right most of the time, but come on—give it a rest already.

"Well, neither's ain't," I said, "but people ain't about to stop using it. Besides, if you know what I mean, what difference does it make?"

"I'm just saying."

"Well, REGARDLESS," I said, overemphasizing the word. "Every recipe I've seen my mom make calls for salt. We will just add pickles when the recipe calls for salt. Trust me, it will totally work. How about this, you get to pick the first thing we cook."

"Okay, how about spaghetti."

Sounded easy enough to me. Open a can, broil some noodles, heat some sauce up, add some diced pickles and voila, Spagickles was born.

"Perfect. Come over to my house as soon as you can and then we'll get started."

Olive arrived just after I finished eating my after-school snack—a pickle of course. After an entire day of school, the last thing I wanted to do was cook. Luckily, Olive would be doing most of it.

"Ready to get started?" Olive asked.

"I guess, if we have to," I said, smiling.

Surprisingly enough, things started out pretty well. Olive got a big pot full of water going, just waiting for noodles to be dumped in once it started boiling… Olive says it's called boiling, not broiling. I've heard it both ways.

I had the pickles diced and ready to add to the sauce. I could at least handle the pickles. Olive decided that making homemade spaghetti sauce—who knew it could be made at home?—would be a bit too much for our first day of cooking, so she brought over a thing of bottled sauce. We got the pot out, cranked the nob and dumped in the sauce.

With a little time to spare, I jotted down a few notes about our cooking adventures thus far. However, we started to get a little bored waiting for everything to cook. The water seemed to be taking forever to boil and hearing Patrick and Ginger cooing, and giggling with each other—making us nauseas and we hadn't even eaten yet—we decided a quick bike ride was in order.

As we started to pedal, we of course had to make fun of Patrick and Ginger. In my best Ginger impersonation, "Oh Payt-rick, y'all are so cuh-yoot wee-uth yer whee-ut and yer good looks and all," aka, "Oh Patrick, you are so cute with your wit and your good looks." And Olive, in her best Patrick impersonation, "Oh Ginger… hee hee," aka, "Oh Ginger, I am a total geek and I can't believe a girl like you would date a guy like me but I will do anything to make you happy. Now can we make out?"

By now we were laughing so hard that I wasn't really paying attention to where we were and I certainly wasn't paying attention to the sidewalk. In my best Ginger impersonation, "Oh Payt-rick, I think y'all are so..."

"PENNY, LOOK OUT!"

Just as I was about to ask Olive why in the world she was screaming at me, I happened to look forward to see a mailbox three feet in front of me. Now two. Now one. Now zero—now who's the genius that went and put a mailbox in the middle of the sidewalk?—WHAMO!

Everything then went to slow motion. I saw my front tire hit the post of the mailbox. My bike stopped with a thud, but I didn't. I kept going in the same direction, up over the handle bars, my face slamming into the big red box with white lettering that spelled "JAMS" on the side of it—oh please, oh please, oh please, do not let this mailbox have any connection to one Jiminy Jams, the boy who is my soul mate, even though he may not realize it just yet.

After the side of my face slammed into the mailbox, my body twisted and contorted like a professional diver, except slightly less graceful, and with a slightly less watery landing, that was more on the hard grassy side—actually, whatever I landed on was more like nice and soft rather than hard and grassy.

Dazed and confused, I just laid there. Had I died? Where was the tunnel of light? I heard a slight muffled sound and wondered if that was what the angels of heaven sound like.

"Ggggg fffff mmmmmmmeh," came the sound.

Wow! If that is what the angels of heaven sound like, I'm going to need some practice to learn their language. It was going to be way harder than Canadian.

"Gggg fffff mmmmmmeh," came the sound again.

Seriously where is that coming from?

"Geeethh offffff mmmmmmeh!" it came again, a bit more English-like this time—the language was becoming clearer to me—then, out of nowhere, the nice and soft thing that I landed on started squirming.

"Penny," came a voice from the general direction of the nice and soft thing that I landed on, "I hope you're okay—if you are, could you please get off me?"

Wow, this angel that is asking me if I was okay looked exactly like Jiminy. I mean, of course he would look just like Jiminy. It wouldn't surprise me if all the angels look exactly like Jiminy.

"Oh my gosh, oh my gosh," came another voice, sounding

just like Olives. "Penny? Penny! Penny, are you okay? I was like—'you're going to hit the mailbox'—and then you were like looking at the mailbox—and then you hit the mailbox—and it was like, so crazy. Seriously, are you okay? Should I call 911? Don't move…"

Okay that's weird? This angel that is talking to me not only sounds exactly like Olive, but looks just like her.

"Olive?" I said, groggily.

"If you move you may become paralyzed," came the voice just like Olive's from the person that looked just like her. "And I don't want to have a cooking partner that can't cook. I mean, I'm going to be doing all the cooking, but still, you are my best friend."

Okay, that is definitely NOT an angel—so much for going to heaven.

"Olive?" I said, still a bit groggy. "Is that you?"

I looked around and saw Olive looking back at me. Then I saw Jiminy Jams looking at me. Yeah, he wasn't an angel either, yet still soooo good looking. I could just sit here and look at that face two inches away from mine all day long. Then it finally hit me that I could also hear laughing.

"Oh my gosh!" came the most un-angelic voice ever. "Could you be a bigger nerd Picklepants? That was like the funniest thing I have ever seen. Luckily I got it all on video and I am so going to put it on the internet!"

JayJ! Why does she always have to be around to turn even the highest points of my life into the lowest?

"JayJ, just go in the house—Penny, are you okay?" asked Jiminy.

Jiminy Jams knows my name? Could this day get any better? BEST DAY EVER! Wait! Why was JayJ going into Jiminy's house? WORST DAY EVER! Should I ask him why? I mean, we are practically besties now that I landed on him and he knows my name, right?

Oh my gosh! I landed on Jiminy Jams! Worst of the worst days ever. No, I mean, best day ever. Wait! Which was it?

"Yeah, fine I am." I said.

Did I just say that backwards? What's going on?

"Thanks, for landing my breaking," I said, with a sheepish smile. "Oh my gosh, you broke my landing. I so sorry am! Are you okay?"

"Oh, no problem," Jiminy said, with the most beautiful smile one could ever imagine.

I was ready to fall into his arms then and there. Well, fall into his arms again, except slightly more graceful this time. And what was with my words coming out backwards?

"I'm just glad that you're okay," he said. "I was getting the mail and then next thing I know you are heading towards the mailbox and then you were on top of me."

He's blushing. Oh my gosh I just made Jiminy Jams blush!

"Yeah," I said, "Fine totally I am."

There it is again. What's going on?

"I bike will just grab," I said. "Or left what is of it."

Oh my gosh! What was going on with my speech?

Jiminy helped me up—hee hee, he touched my arm! I am so not showering for a week—okay, maybe not a week, I'll leave the never showering up to Parker—but I am not washing that arm. I was still a little bit woozy, but I couldn't tell if it was from the crash or the fact that Jiminy was still holding onto my arm.

"Penny, are you sure you're okay?" Jiminy asked. "I bet my mom would give you a ride home."

And what a gentleman!

"No, fine I am, thanks anyway but."

"Okay, if you say so," Jiminy said with a chuckle.

Oh my gosh, why is everything coming out backwards?

"Jiminy, I am waiting..." came the very un-angelic voice again. Seriously, does JayJ always have to ruin my moment?

"I'm coming," Jiminy said.

I swear I heard a, "Whatever," coming from JayJ, but I had to stay focused on the fact that Jiminy still—yes STILL—hadn't let go of my arm.

"Are you sure you're okay Penny? Really, I don't think my mom would mind giving you a ride home."

"Yes," I said giggling, looking at his hand holding my arm. "Fine I am."

Jiminy walked me to my bike, holding onto my arm, which didn't let go until he picked up my bike.

"Nice very you are," I said. Ugh! I had never had a problem talking—now, in this perfect moment, I start talking like a little green guy from some movie my older brother obsessed about—which, by the way, so did NOT have good fashion. What was going on?

I straightened my bike out the best I could and began walking. And like that, Jiminy left me for JayJ. I had a feeling that it wouldn't be the last time that that happened.

Olive and I walked home with what used to be my bike—a tad bit harder than I thought it would be. My front wheel now had a big flat spot on it making the handlebars go up and down as I pushed it. And now the wheel wanted to go to the right while my handlebars were twisted all the way to the left. Talking about Jiminy the whole way home certainly helped the situation, though.

"Do you think it was destiny that I landed on Jiminy?" I asked.

"Wow! Are we back to speaking in normal sentences again?" Olive asked. "Oh Jiminy, so hot are you. How strong you can't I believe are. Jiminy me kiss. Me now kiss," Olive said making a smooching sound.

"Hey!" I protested. "Real nice—make fun of the person that just did a somersault off her bike and bumped her head."

"Yeah, right onto a soft, fluffy Jiminy pillow," Olive said, cracking herself up.

I couldn't resist and had to laugh too, which sort of hurt, but laughter is the best medicine, and medicine hurts sometimes, right? Anyway, laughs aside, we had to get down to business.

"Well, hilarious or not, why in the world do you think JayJ was over at Jiminy's house?"

"Ohhh," Olive, said, pursing her lips. "Really couldn't tell ya."

"I think I have an idea," I said.

"What?"

"Well, seeing that JayJ is such a jerk, I bet JayJ's parents are paying Jiminy to be her friend."

Olive just looked at me and raised her eyebrows.

I had a feeling it wouldn't turn out to be the reason she was over there at all, but unlike most things in life, wishing was free.

"Penny?" Olive said, now quite seriously, as we turned the corner onto my street. "Where is that smoke coming from?"

Suddenly we smelled burn, a whole lot of burn.

"Oh my gosh!" I said, with the distinct whining of a smoke alarm in the background

"Our Spagickle!" we screamed in unison—although, it sounded like Olive said, "spaghetti." We dropped our bikes and ran into the kitchen.

With my bike accident and thinking about Jiminy, and JayJ, and Jiminy and JayJ, but mostly just about Jiminy, we had forgotten about our cooking assignment. When we walked into the kitchen, the sauce was everywhere except for in the pot. Since when does sauce know how to jump? It was on the ceiling, the walls, the floor. And if I looked hard enough, I bet it was even in my bedroom. The pot we had the water in to cook the noodles was now the smoking pot of blackness.

"Oh my gosh," I said. "My mom is going to kill us!"

"Us? You are the one who wanted to go on a bike ride, landed on Jiminy, and started talking funny around him."

Oh no she didn't!

"Are you kidding me? I almost died today Olive! And all you are worried about is our stupid little assignment!"

Of course while we were fighting my mom got home and walked into the kitchen. Oh great here it comes.

"What on earth happened in here?" she said, with the one vein on her forehead that always appears when she's really angry starting to bulge. "And my new pot?!" she screamed. "What were you thinking? You could have burned down the house!"

"Well, in my defense..." I said.

"I don't want to hear it Penny!"

Why do parents always do that? They demand an explanation and then when you are about to give them a perfectly good explanation, they cut you off. Parents are so confusing.

"Just clean this mess up before your father gets home," my mom said, with what looked like tears welling in her eyes.

"Well, where's Patrick?" I said.

"What does that matter?" she said.

"He was here when we left. He should have smelled the smoke."

"Apparently Patrick left after you did. In any case, it doesn't matter. This is your mess, so you clean it up."

My mom started to walk out of the kitchen, but then stopped and turned back around.

"And from now on, I'm sorry to say this, at least for your sake Olive, but you are no longer welcomed to cook in my kitchen. You will need to find yourselves a new kitchen to cook in."

Oh great! Now where are we going to do our assignments?

"Does that mean I don't have to help with dinner anymore?"

Of course I had to push it. I took a step back when my mom gave me the death glare. Wow, when did my mom learn the death glare like that? It was so deathly and so glarey.

"Clean it now!" she said, with pursed lips, and walked out of the room.

Of course, in the midst of being yelled at, Parker came bouncing in from outside with DS in hand. "Huh?!" he said, stopping in his tracks. "Whoa, cool! This looks just like one of my video games after I've blown everything to bits."

Grrrrr! Olive and I then proceeded to rid the kitchen of tomato sauce from ceiling to floor. We wiped off tomato sauce from the door to the garage all the way to the door on the fridge, from the fan blades on the ceiling fan, to the bottom of the legs of the kitchen table. As far as my mom's poor new pot, I think it might just be a goner, but only time will tell.

Eventually Olive had to go home, and my mom needed her kitchen back to cook dinner. Rather than risk any further contention I went straight to my room. I had hoped that in the next few days the Great Picklepants Kitchen Fiasco (GPKF) of 2012 would blow over and my mom would forget about it. I mean she forgets stuff all the time. Like doctor appointments, why she went to the grocery store, and really important stuff like what I wore 3 weeks ago. But she didn't forget about the GPKF of 2012. When I asked her if it would be okay do our cooking assignment as long as she supervised us, she just laughed and said, "Not a chance."

Dang it!

When I told Olive that we had no other choice but to do the cooking assignments at her house, she reminded me just how OCD her mom was about her kitchen.

"Penny, my mom reminds me every chance she gets that she has waited 35 years for a kitchen like hers."

"Well, where else are we going to do it?" I asked.

"I don't know." Olive said.

I sat there in silence hoping that the only obvious option would force Olive to say the inevitable.

Ten seconds. Eleven. Twelve. Thirteen. Fourteen.

"Okay," Olive said.

Fourteen seconds! That's how long Olive dragged her feet. Man, Olive can be so stubborn some times.

"If we do it here Penny, we have to be so super careful. We can't leave sauce on the stove and go for bike rides. I mean, we can't even let the sauce splatter out of the pot at all for that matter."

"I know, I know," I said. "My bike is totally ruined so why would we go on a bike ride?"

"Penny! You know what I mean."

When I reassured Olive that nothing bad was going to happen, we decided that we would try our hand again on a pasta dish. They were hard to screw up (barring certain, recent circumstances), and usually tasted pretty good. Olive had an easy pasta recipe that was from her Grandmother that she thought would be perfect for us.

"It's my Grandma's recipe that she got when she married my Grandpa. On the bottom it says 'be creative and have fun.'"

"Sounds great," I said. "Just as long as we can add pickles."

"Penny, I don't think adding diced pickles to my grandmothers Alfredo sauce is what she meant when she said be creative and have fun."

"Oh, count air my fair. That is exactly what she meant."

Olive burst out laughing.

"What did you just say?" Olive asked.

"I said you know that's what she meant. What's so funny?"

"It's 'au contraire mon frère'" she said, still laughing.

That's what she was laughing about? My Spanish? Oh no she didn't!

"Olive, I happen to speak Spanish pretty well, so I think I would know whether oh count-air my fare was Spanish."

That ought to put the little Grammar Queen in her place.

"Oh Penny," Olive said, finally controlling her laughter. "What would I do without you?"

Now that's more like it.

"Look Penny," Olive said. "I just don't think Alfredo and pickles are such a good match. Truth be told, I think it's probably going to taste disgusting."

"Well how would you know if you have never tasted it?" I said, with a deductive, lawyerly flair. Maybe the whole lawyer thing will work out after all. If we were in front of a court of law, I would have the jury eating pickles out of my hand.

"Well, have you ever had Alfredo and pickles?" Olive asked.

Opposing counsel's point taken, but not so fast.

"No, but that's beside the point that everything tastes better with pickles. How about this. We make the sauce as is, and then to be creative and have fun we will add the diced pickles as a topping."

Wow! Negotiating skills coming through like a champ. But maybe I should stop thinking about what career would complete my triple threat. It's getting rather confusing keeping track of so many options.

"Like a condiment?"

"You don't want to add pickles, but you will add a condiment? Okay!"

Olive slapped her forehead with her hand. "Penny, a condiment is..."

"Whatever Olive. Let's just put diced pickles on top so you can save the integrity of your precious granny's recipe."

All this and we hadn't even started cooking yet!

Before we started on our Alfredo and Pickles concoction, Olive reminded me that I needed to take notes—as if I never do—and that my job was to read her the recipe so that she could concentrate on the cooking.

"And I repeat, we will not take a bike ride while waiting for the water to boil," Olive said.

"I know," I said. "And I repeat, my bike is ruined so how would we even be able to take a bike ride?"

We then had a good laugh, saying everything with "And I repeat" in it. The thing with me and Olive is that no matter how much we get on each other's nerves, in the end we always end up laughing.

When Olive handed me the recipe the first thing I noticed was how old and wrinkly it was. I was about to say, "And I repeat, this recipe card is just like your grandmother, old and wrinkly," right when Olive's mom walked in the kitchen. Phew! Dodged that bullet.

"Now, I trust you girls won't burn down my kitchen," Olive's mom said, with a smile. "I just have a few errands to run so I'll be back in 20 or 30 minutes. But seriously, not too big of a mess, okay?"

"Okay Mrs. Oliverson," I said, with my sweetest smile. "We promise."

Olive's mom paused and gave me a concerned look. What was that all about? I turned to Olive only to find her giving me the exact same look.

"We won't make a mess," I said. "Now let's get started. Sheesh!"

"We have the water for the pasta on the burner," Olive said. "And so we will now start with the sauce. What's the first ingredient?"

"Looks like butter," I said. "We need to melt 1/4 cup of butter over medium heat."

Check and check. Doing good so far.

"Okay, what's next?" Olive asked.

"Let's see, next we need to add 1 cup of cream," I said. "And we need to let that simmer for five…" The card was too wrinkly to see what it said next.

"Five what?" Olive asked.

"I'm not sure," I said, squinting my eyes. "I can't read it very well."

"Most likely 5 minutes," Olive said.

I was beginning to think our second kitchen expedition was off to a raging success, old wrinkly recipe card or not. We were going to do it, we were actually going to make Alfredo sauce without it ending up everywhere except for the dinner plate.

"Okay, what's after that?" Olive asked.

"Let's see," I said, "now we need to add the garlic and cheese. So add one clove of garlic and then it looks like, um, I think 13 cups of par-mee-san cheese."

"You mean parmesan cheese?" Olive said, with a laugh.

"Oh. Well, I've usually seen it spelled the other way," I said.

Olive just laughed. Things were going pretty well.

"Wait a minute," Olive said. "Did you just say *thirteen* cups of parmesan? We do not have 13 cups of parmesan. I don't think Pottsville even has 13 cups of parmesan. Are you sure you read that right?"

"Olive, remember the arrangement. I read the card, you cook the food."

"Can you just double check it, Penny, because 13 cups is a lot of cheese."

"Okay, let me check. Let's see, yep, pretty sure it says 13 cups of parmesan cheese."

"Pretty sure?" Olive asked. "Pretty sure doesn't sound very sure to me. Here, let me just see it Penn."

"Olive, I think I know how to read a recipe card. It would be a hard thing to screw up reading 13 cups of cheese by mistake."

"Exactly! That's why I want to see the card."

"Olive, it says 13 cups of parmesan cheese. We can just put some other cheeses with it if you don't have enough."

"Do you even realize how much 13 cups of cheese is Penn?"

"Do you?" I asked.

"Yes, I do," Olive said. "I help my mom cook all the time."

"Well, so do I, at least until she kicked us out of her kitchen, that is."

"Exactly," Olive said. "That's why I think I should read the card."

"What do you mean exactly?" I asked.

"I mean," Olive said, "you got us kicked out of your mom's kitchen. Let's don't have a repeat of GPKF of 2012 and get kicked out of my mom's kitchen. Let me just see the card."

"No," I said. "You put me in charge of reading the card, and I have read it. Now you need to cook and do what I say."

"Penn, there is no way that I am going to put 13 cups of cheese into that pot. It won't even fit for crying out loud."

"Well, there is no way that I am going to let you read this card. Until we are finished, it's my card."

"That is not your card!" Olive said. "It's my grandma's and it belongs to us. Now give it."

Olive then lunged towards me to grab the card. Of course, I was too fast for her.

"Nice try," I said. "But you've got to be a little bit faster than that to catch Penny Picklepants."

"Give it here," she said, lunging again. "Penn, this isn't funny. We need to make this recipe right."

"I know," I said. "So just do what I am telling you and it will be right."

Olive screamed a sound of frustration. "Penny Picklepants, you drive me crazy!" Olive said, walking towards me while I backed up. "Just give me the card."

Olive lunged again for the card.

"Not so fast, Olive Oliverson. I'm the reader, you're the cooker. Now cook!"

"Penny!" Olive said. "I'm warning you."

"Oohhh, I'm so scared," I said.

And then suddenly she started to chase me. I ran out of the kitchen into the living room, through the entry room and dining room which led back into the kitchen. I checked for Olive behind me as I came tearing back into the kitchen, when I suddenly ran smack dab into Olive. I then proceeded to fall down on my rear end—déjà vu, a la thrift store and JayJ. Man I need to watch where I am going. I then noticed that the recipe card was missing. It was in Olive's hand now.

"Penny!" Olive said. "This says 1/3 cup of parmesan cheese, not 13!"

"Well, how am I supposed to know? And I repeat, that thing is as old and wrinkly as your grandma!"

"What is going on in here?" said a voice just like Olive's mom.

It was Olive's mom.

Oh great. Olive's mom was back and I had just insulted her mother right in front of her face. What's more, I had just noticed how smoky the kitchen was becoming. And no sooner had I noticed this, the smoke alarm went off.

"I leave you for 20 minutes," Olive's mom said, raising her voice over the smoke alarm, as she placed her dry-cleaning down on the kitchen table and walked briskly to the stove. "And I return to find you horsing around in my kitchen, apparently oblivious to a pot of burning butter on the stove?"

Olive's mom removed the pot from the flame and turned off the burner.

"I am highly disappointed in you girls," Olive's mom said. "Now open some windows to air my kitchen out."

Olive looked at me with a death scowl, as we each opened some windows.

"You ladies get this cleaned up at once, and then you can excuse yourself from my kitchen. My kitchen is closed for the day, don't make it closed for good. Now, I forgot to pick something up for your father, Olive, so I'll be back in 15 minutes. When I get back, I want this kitchen spotless."

Olive's mom then left in quite a huff.

Olive gave me a searing "way to go Penny Picklepants" look.

I gave her my "it's not just my fault" look.

We got to work on cleaning up the kitchen, which was in much better shape than the last cooking disaster. At least it was an improvement in disasters. I mean, progress is progress, right?

Olive and I hadn't said a word the entire time we had been cleaning her mom's kitchen. You could have cut the tension in the air with a butter knife. I had to do something to ease the tension. And I knew just the trick.

I took the spray bottle of water and squirted Olive in the face "by accident." She was not amused, at least not until she squirted me back with hers. Before we knew it, we were engaged in full-scale spray bottle battle, in her mom's brand-new kitchen.

Most importantly, by the end of it we were on laughing terms again, not to mention pretty soaked. Although our Pickalfredo—you know, Alfredo with a dash of pickle—ended pretty much like our first cooking expedition, at least we had fun cleaning up. Who knew that cleaning burnt Pickalfredo—Olive has yet to embrace the name—would lead to the best in-house water fight ever.

"Best in-house water fight ever! Who's up for round dos?" I asked, holding up my spray bottle in spraying position.

"That was fun, I admit" Olive said. "But there is no way we can have my mom come back with us and her kitchen soaking wet. We have to make this place spotless before she gets back.

"No worries Olive, I'll start with the counters, you do the floors."

I moved everything, including her mom's cookbooks that she left out on the counter.

"Why the heck does your mom leave her cookbooks on the countertop?" I asked. "Seems like a strange place for a cookbook."

"Well, not really," Olive said, "she collects vintage cookbooks and likes to display them. She even has one that's older than my grandma."

"Old people and their old stuff," I said, shaking my head.

As soon as everything was wiped down, cleaned and re-cleaned for good measure, we had to amscray so that Olive's mom wouldn't find our soaking-wet selves in her kitchen.

"Well, I guess we'll try again tomorrow," I said, shrugging my shoulders.

"We'll see," Olive said with a little laugh.

"I'll go home and update our blog first thing," I said.

After a pause at the door, I turned and said, "See ya."

"Bye, Penny," Olive said, with a smile.

When I got home I found a note from my mom.

Penn,

Ran to the plant for a minute. Made some more bread— please take a loaf down to Mrs. Frankincense. And this time, don't just buzz the doorbell and run off!

Love,
Mom

"Fine!" I said to myself. "I'll just drop it on her doorstep and leave without ringing the doorbell."

Is talking to myself normal when no one else is around? And what about asking myself a question about talking to myself when no one else is around? Just like me, life could be so deep and complex.

CHAPTER NINE

Dear Secret Pickle Society,

My name is Penny Picklepants, and I love pickles. I have dreams of becoming the youngest Professional Pickle Taster (aka Professional Pickle Taster Extraordinaire) at my family's pickle plant. The plant was given to my dad by his dad, who in turn received it from his dad, who got it from his dad, or so the story goes. Each received special training, to become the official in-house pickle taster before eventually taking over the business. Unfortunately for me, I have an older brother, Patrick, who is being groomed to become the official in-house pickle taster.

The problem with this is that Patrick doesn't even like pickles. I, on the other hand, couldn't survive without pickles. I wouldn't even know what to do if we lived in a world without pickles. Unlike Patrick, I have been blessed with the refined taste and appetite for all things pickled. But my father won't take my suggestion to be named the official in-house pickle taster seriously. I have a plan, however. See, if you made me a member of your society, thus catapulting me into the realm of being taken serious, I believe that then, and only then, my dad would have no choice but to take me seriously. So please, oh pretty please, make me a member of the Secret Pickle Society.

Sincerely and Seriously,
Penny Picklepants ♡

Not that I wasn't running late already as it was. "Penny Picklepants," my mom yelled from downstairs. "If you are not down here in 5 seconds, you are walking to school young lady."

Ugh! What I wouldn't give to have a mom that understood and appreciated fashion. I had already tried on three different pairs of jeans four different times each, but such are the demands of fashion. Of course I went with my favy jeans. I mean, I knew all along I was going to end up wearing them. But I just had to make sure.

"Penny, I mean it. Five, four, three…"

"I'm coming!" I yelled, running down the steps. "Sheesh. I'm here, let's go."

"Don't forget your smoothie," my mom said.

My mom had read that the best way for kids to get their vitamins wasn't from colorful vitamin pills shaped into cartoon characters, or more recently, from vitamin-packed gummi bears, but straight from fruits and vegetables. So ever since, she's been making us drink a breakfast smoothie. You name it, she puts it in this smoothie, from soy milk and spinach, to kiwis and all different kinds of fruits and berries. She even puts in seeds, like wheat germs (germs? Gross!), and get this, chia seeds. Yes! Just like the kind you use on your chia pet. So far I hadn't started growing chia hair, but that didn't mean I wasn't checking on a regular basis.

I grabbed the smoothie and took it with me in the van. There was no time to drink it at home. And of course, Parker was already sitting in the front seat.

"Move Parker!" I said.

"I was here first," Parker said with a giant grin. "Snoozers, losers."

"No, I was here first, like five years before you!" I said. "Now move it."

"Penny!" my mom said. "There's no time. Get in. I am leaving."

"Mom!" I said, betrayed once again by my own mother that could not understand the significance of the front seat to a sixth grader. "I cannot let everyone see me getting out of the back of the van with my little brother in the front seat. It's humiliating."

"More humiliating than walking to school and showing up late?" my mom said. "Penny, I'm leaving this instant. Either get in or start walking young lady."

My mom then put the van in gear. She meant business.

Ugh! Why does my mom have to be so difficult all the time? Can't she see how difficult my life is without her adding to it? I think she enjoys moments like these.

My mom pulled out of the driveway a little faster than usual.

"Mom, we'll be fine. The Dunderheads leave this late all the time, and usually even later."

"That's fine for the Dunderheads, Penny, but Picklepants are not tardy."

My mom was really big on punctuality. I don't think she had a clue what being fashionably late was all about. I feared that she was tragically and utterly doomed to remain among the fashionably illiterate forevermore.

We were making pretty good time actually, my mom keeping it just above the speed limit.

"Mom! Watch out for that squirrel!" Parker said.

My mom had been too preoccupied with our potential tardiness to notice that a squirrel had just run into the middle of the road, directly in our path. She swerved to miss it just in time, at least I think she did. I didn't feel any small thump or hear any cracking of tiny bones. Unfortunately, I did suddenly feel an icy substance splatter all over my favy jeans.

"Mom?" I said slowly, so as not to upset my favy jeans. "I think we're going to have to turn around."

"What? What are you talking about?" my mom asked. "It was just a squirrel. You don't have to stop if you hit one."

"No, mom. Look," I said, staring down at my favy jeans.

Come on favy jeans, hang in there. Everything is going to be okay. We've just got to remain calm and everything will be just fine.

"Penny, I can't look—I'm driving."

Parker then peered his head around the front seat.

"Uh oh!" Parker said, accentuating the "oh" an unusually long time.

"What is it?" my mom said, turning her head halfway back without taking her eyes off the road, and then adjusting her rear-view mirror.

"Oh Penny, what did you do?"

"Me?" I protested. "I was just about to take a sip from your disgusting veggie smoothie that you force us to drink when you, due to your maniacal driving, had to swerve to miss a poor innocent squirrel."

"Penny, we are only two minutes away," my mom said.

What was she suggesting? That I just take a few of the napkins among the thousands my dad kept stored in the glove box for emergencies such as this?

"Mom," I said, "there is no way I am going to school in these jeans. It would be cruel and unusual punishment, and that is against the law."

Chalk one up for Penny Picklepants, Esquire, lawyer extraordinaire. Do you think in the history of lawyers there's ever been a pickle lawyer? But I digress.

"Fine, Penny," my mom said. "But first I am dropping off Parker. There's no excuse for two Picklepants being late on the same day."

"Yeah," I said, "besides needing to get home on the double before your smoothie stains my favy jeans permanently. Parker, pass me some more napkins."

When my mom dropped Parker off, I saw Olive waiting for me by the flagpole. I wanted to get out and tell her I would be back, but I couldn't let the entire school see me in this condition.

"Just drive mom!" I said. "And fast!"

My mom actually made it home in record time and pulled into the garage. I bolted out of the van and ran into the laundry room, which was directly between our garage and our kitchen. I took off my favy jeans and proceeded to rinse them in the laundry sink, while my mom went to fetch me some new jeans. That's when I heard someone whistling a cat-call whistle.

"AHHHHHHH!" I screamed.

Right then and there Tyler Dunderhead and his little brother were walking by on our sidewalk with a direct view into our laundry room with its door left wide open where I was standing in plain sight in my little pink undies. "Nice pink undies," Tyler yelled, his little brother giggling in agreement.

"AHHHHHHH!" I screamed again, slamming shut the door. Wait! Did Tyler have his cellphone? Did he just take a picture of me standing there in my pink underwear?! "AHHHHHHH!" I screamed the third time.

"What is all the racket about, Penny?" my mom said, coming into the laundry room. "They're just a pair of jeans. They can be replaced."

"Tyler Dunderhead and his little twerp brother just walked by with the garage door open and the laundry room door wide open with me standing here in nothing but my pink undies! And I think he just took a picture with his cellphone!"

"Well, at least your top matches," my mom said, with a grin.

I shot my mom a death glare.

"Oh, Penny, it's not that big a deal," she said.

"Mom! You have no idea!"

How could my mom, my own supposed flesh and blood, have no idea what this could do to me?

"Here, just put these on," she said handing me a new pair of jeans, pushing me out the door. "Let's let the others soak for a while and I'll wash them when I get back."

"Mom!" I protested. "The garage door is still open!"

"There's no one there. Just cover yourself with your jeans and put them on in the van."

My mom zoomed out of the garage, carefully checking the sidewalk of course, and then peeled out as she zoomed down our street.

"Go mom!," I said, impressed as I pulled up the second leg of my jeans.

That's when I realized there was a problem... again.

"What?" I said. "What are these? What did you grab, Mom? I had two other pairs sitting on my bed. What are these?"

My mom had grabbed one of my old, no-longer-worn pair of jeans from the to-be-taken-to-the-thrift-store pile of clothes.

"I grabbed the first pair of jeans I saw," my mom said.

"Mom, I cannot wear these! They don't even fit, and, AND they are like so two years ago!" I protested.

"Penny, you are just going to have to make them work," my mom said. "We are not going back. Just tell everyone they are capris."

"Mom! Everyone knows you don't wear capris after Labor Day.

I bet Karl Lagerfeld's mom never made him wear capris after Labor Day," I said.

"Karl Lager-who?" my mom said.

Ugh! My life was so difficult. Why couldn't I have been born to
Heidi Klum?

"So do you really think my smoothies are disgusting?" my mom
asked.

"No, Mom," I said. "Actually, they taste a lot better than they
look on my favy jeans."

My mom laughed.

Most people would be mortified if they spilled the entire content of their 16 ounce green smoothie on their favy jeans only to
have their mother rush them back to their house, make them drop
their dirty jeans in the laundry room, stand there with only their
pink undies on only to realize that the laundry room is in an area
of the house that the neighbors can see into from the garage, only
to have the Dunderheads walk by at that very moment and take a
picture of me, only to have their mom grab the entirely wrong pair
of backup jeans—aka too small, too tight, can you say high-water-
floods that can't even be made into cute capris—only to have their
mother make them put the wrong pair of jeans on in the car on the
way to school, again, only not to have enough time to tie their shoe
laces in the car because their mother is freaking out that they will
be late, only then to trip on their shoelaces right in front of their
mortal enemy, only to have that mortal enemy be the one and only
JayJ Rothefeller, only to have JayJ say "Guess what picture Tyler
Dunderhead just sent me from his cellphone?", and then only to
have JayJ show me a picture of me standing horrified in my pink
undies. Yes, most people would be mortified if this happened to

them. I just call it a Tuesday.

For our next cooking adventure Olive and I had decided, during lunch recess, that we were going to keep it simple with some scrambled eggs and toast—and of course diced pickles.

"Penny," Olive said. "Not even you could screw up scrambled eggs and toast. I mean, it's scrambled eggs and toasted bread for crying out loud."

"I'll just let that one slide. And, don't you mean scrambickled eggs and toast?" I said with a grin. "Get it? Scrambled plus pickles equals scrambickled. Scrambickled eggs. Don't you love it?"

Apparently, she did not see the humor.

"Sure," she said. "Just meet me at my place and I'll butter up my mom to make sure she lets us use her kitchen again."

As I walked to Olive's house, after school (and homework… blah!), I realized I was starting to get really excited about our blog. I never knew it could be so fun to write, and about the adventures of cooking, of all things. Granted we were nowhere close to being chefs, or even cooks for that matter, but we were having a lot of fun in between all the mishaps. I mean, who wouldn't want to read about the greatest in-house water fight ever?

When I knocked on the Oliverson's front door, Olive answered and then pushed me out onto the porch.

"You will never guess what happened," Olive said.

So much for hello, how are ya.

"Umm," I said. "The government is finally admitting to an alien conspiracy behind area 51?"

I knew it! I knew it was only a matter of time.

"What? What are you talking about? Penny, we have discussed this a million times, the government is not trying to hide anything alien on area 51. They keep it under wraps because they are breeding talking dolphins. I saw a special about it on TV. Anyway, back to the point. The point is, when I asked my mom if we could use her kitchen, she told me that one of her vintage cookbooks was water warped and moldy. It was one of her oldest ones. She is freaking out. The cookbooks must have gotten wet when we had our water fight."

"Best in-house water fight ever!" I said. "Wait! How does she know it was us?"

"Well, she doesn't. But I am an only child and my dad never goes into the kitchen, and she says the book was fine the last time she used it. Anyway long story short, she told me her kitchen is no longer open to us."

What to do, what to do.

"Well—" I said, "did she say it was closed to you? I mean, she may have closed it to us, but if she will still let you in then you could do the cooking, which you're going to do anyway, and then you could just tell me about it."

Chalk one up for Penny Picklepants, Professional Problem Solver.

"Yeah, just one problem. She said I wasn't allowed back into the kitchen for one month. We're going to have to find somewhere else until then."

"Okay," I said. "I'll take one for the team. I will go in there and I will apologize to your mom. If that doesn't help, then I will beg, drop to my knees and beg like I have never begged before."

"I tried begging, Penny," Olive said. "My mom told me a lady does not beg."

"But I beg all the time."

The look on Olive's face did little to dispel the feeling I had that I held very little respect in the Oliverson home. But now wasn't the time to ponder the complexities of Mrs. Oliverson's dislike for all things Penny Picklepants. I had to come up with a solution to our kitchen dilemma and it had to be fast.

"I've got it," I said. "We'll talk to Mrs. Smith and see if we could use the kitchen in the Home Ec. room."

"Mmm," said Olive, with a hint of "I'm impressed" mixed in.

Penny Picklepants, Professional Problem Solver is there no problem you cannot solve?

"Well, I don't know, but this is a matter of life and death," Olive said, flaying her hands around as if she tried hard enough, she would take flight.

"Olive, it's just school," I said. "I think we will be okay."

I guess I am the level headed partner.

After some deep pondering, more flailing and realizing that no matter how hard she would flap her hands, she wouldn't fly away, Olive said, "Okay, before school tomorrow let's go talk to Mrs. Smith. Wait! Penny, she has been reading our blog, she knows that we have been screwing up—she will never let us use the kitchens now!"

Oh great, the flailing has started again.

"Okay, so I have a little confession to make." Well, that got her attention. At least she isn't flailing her hands any more.

"What? What is it?"

"So, umm…" I said, pausing, but not for effect so much as trying to figure out the best way of breaking this to Olive. "I have kind of, just sort of—trust me it isn't a big deal, but I have been putting that our cooking fiascos are more like cooking miracles, for dramatic effect."

Olive appeared to be on the verge of achieving flight.

"Artistic license?" I said, shrugging my shoulders and then shutting my eyes in case of—well I wasn't sure why I closed my eyes. I just figured it was an effect of the guilt.

"WHAT?!" Olive said. "Penny, I'm not going to lie. Ugh! I knew I shouldn't have been partners with you."

Ouch! After a few minutes of more flailing and crusty looks directed at me, Olive again stopped the flailing.

"Well, what have you been writing?" Olive asked.

"Well, I just sort of write what I think is going to happen, which actually ends up being what actually happened, and then I write what really happened, which actually ends up being what I had hoped would happen."

"What?" Olive said. "You completely lost me between your reals and actuals and happens."

I swear, it's like nobody understands what I am saying anymore. Am I not speaking English, people? Am I starting to speak so maturely that no one can understand me anymore?

"Olive, it's like this. For our first cooking adventure of Spagickle, I wrote that we hoped that we wouldn't forget about the water, ruin my mom's new pot and that the sauce wouldn't end up all over the wall and in places where the moon don't shine. I then wrote that our pasta turned out amazing and that Spagickle was going to take over the world. Ya got it now? I mean, it's all for dramatic effect, artistic license. To be honest, I didn't think it would be a big deal, I didn't write it like that to lie, I mean, this blog is as much about saving your grade as it is about saving the plant. I can't just write the plain, awful truth and expect that to save the plant.

I've got to embellish it and then give it a happy ending. That's what sells, Olive."

"I get it, Penny," Olive said. "But I don't like it."

"Well, if I hadn't done it like that then we would really be without a kitchen."

The truth of the situation seemed to be sinking in on Olive.

"Listen, Olive," I said, "tomorrow we'll just tell Mrs. Smith that both of our kitchens are currently unavailable and ask if we can use one of the school kitchens this week. Then we'll tell her it was so much nicer working at the school that we would like to do all our cooking there from now on. What could go wrong?"

A simple look from Olive answered that.

CHAPTER TEN

The next morning Olive and I met at the flag pole. We then headed straight to Mrs. Smith's class. So far, the meeting was going fairly well.

"So what do you say, Mrs. Smith? Can we use one of the Home Ec. kitchens?" I asked.

"Now," Mrs. Smith said, long and drawn out, her nose buried in some notebook in which she was taking notes, "why exactly are both of your kitchens unavailable?"

I was afraid she was going to ask that.

"Well," I said, turning and staring at Olive for some form of inspiration, Olive turning and staring at me to lend some form of moral support. "It's because both our mom's..." I said, fishing for the right words, "thought it would be best if we... took a break." Yes! A break. What nicer way of saying we were kicked out of our kitchens? "Yeah, a break from, from our kitchens." I probably should have stopped right there. "They thought it would be good for us to have experiences in different kitchens." It was the best I could come up with on the spot, and wasn't really lying. It was more like a version of the truth.

Mrs. Smith stopped what she was doing and looked up at me with a confused look. Not good. Splitting her concentration between her paperwork and our request was to our advantage. We didn't want her to think too much about it, but now I had raised a flag. Her concentration was now focused solely on us.

"Mmm," Mrs. Smith said. "Well," she said, her attention turned back mainly to her notebook. "Okay."

I looked at Olive with a big smile. She gestured with both her hands palm down to remind me to keep it calm.

"Okay, we can use the Home Ec. kitchen? Or okay,…" I said, trailing off, leaving Mrs. Smith to fill in the blank.

"Okay, you can use the Home Ec. kitchen. But there's just one rule," she said, looking up from her notebook with the most attention she had given us yet. "Do not burn anything."

She then offered a half-hearted smile before returning full attention back to her notebook as a sign that we were dismissed.

Oh sure make that the one rule. Guess that meant our food as well.

There was actually one more rule, or condition. We had to cook during our lunch break. Mrs. Smith left right at the end of school, and she locked the kitchen when she left. I was fine with cooking during recess, though. At least that way JayJ wouldn't be around.

As we walked out I turned to Olive.

"I can't believe she is going to let us use the kitchens," I said, in my so-excited voice. "I mean, what I told her was basically the truth, it was just that there was no way I could tell her that we had been kicked out of both our kitchens."

"I know," Olive said, with some regret in her voice. "But we cannot let anybody find out. If Mrs. Smith finds out we were banned from our kitchens then she is sure to ban us from hers as well. And then where will we go? I cannot fail this class Penny, no matter what. I have never failed a class and I am not about to fail this one."

"Olive, nobody is going to find out," I said. "And you are not going to fail this class. Trust me, it will be our little secret."

I made sure that we brought all our ingredients for scrambickled eggs and toast the next day. And for once, everything went well, from start to finish. And the scrambickled eggs were quite delicious. Even Olive agreed. The pickles added a nice flavor to the eggs.

"Olive," I said. "Can you believe it? We actually have a success. Our first success. We did it. We are cooking extraordinaires."

"Well," Olive said. "I'm not sure if Scrambled eggs…"

"Scrambickled eggs," I reminded her.

"Right," Olive said reluctantly. "I'm not sure if scrambickled eggs qualifies us to be cooking extraordinaires, but at least we didn't burn anything."

And that is when everything crashed and burned.

Mrs. Smith pulled us out of class to tell us that a student (who else, but yours truly, JayJ Rothefeller—you should have seen the smirk on her face) had overheard us talking about how we had made up the story about our mom's wanting us to take a break from their kitchens and in fact we had been kicked out of both kitchens. She went on to say how disappointed she was. Olive started to cry and blamed me. I started to cry—well, at least I tried—and blamed JayJ. Mrs. Smith then kicked us out—the kitchen, not the class—and said we were no longer allowed to use the school's kitchen for our cooking assignments.

The more I thought about it, the madder I got. Not about getting kicked out of the kitchen. I was mad at JayJ.

The bell then rang. Class was over.

"That's it Olive, we are getting her back. I can't stand it any longer. She is such a… a… a JERK!"

"That's all you can come up with?" came a voice that was the most grating voice you will ever hear. "Calling me a jerk? I would think that with all your "skills" you could come up with something a smidge more creative." JayJ then walked out of Home Ec. Then she stopped and turned back around. "Oh and by the way, the videos of you peeing in the pool and of you crashing your bike are in the top 50 most viewed videos on YouTube. Millions of people from all around the world thank you for making their day just a little brighter. Can't wait to see what the reaction will be to you standing in your little pink grannie panties."

She turned, and proceeded to walk down the hall with all her cronies laughing hysterically. She didn't even give me time to think of a witty comeback.

"Yeah well, the jerk store called and... and... and they want you back! Cuz you are a jerk!"

Ha! I showed her.

"Penny," Olive said. "She's already around the corner. She can't hear you."

I really hate when Olive points out the obvious.

"Come on," I said. "We need to come up with something quick or you are going to fail Home Ec."

"Do you really think she put those videos of you on the internet?" Olive asked.

"No," I said, hoping against hope that even JayJ wouldn't stoop that low. "She's just showing off for her goon squad."

For the rest of the day I had a hard time concentrating. I just kept thinking about whether or not JayJ had really put those videos of me on the internet. The fact that every time I walked by JayJ and her friends they would spontaneously start to laugh made me wonder. I was seriously beginning to really, really not like this girl.

When I got home, I ran to the family computer—yes, remember we are one of those families that only has one computer? I know, so lame right? Miraculously, both the phone and the computer were available. I had to see if JayJ really had posted those videos. I nervously sat and waited as the modem made those funny noises.

"Come on already," I said to the computer. A person with a normal computer and internet could have checked for the videos and watched them three times by now.

Finally, the internet connected. I then went to YouTube and waited for the page to load at dial-up speeds. It was like watching finger nail polish dry. Actually, with the perfect shade of red, watching finger nail polish dry was rather enjoyable.

The page loaded enough to show the search box. I started to wonder what would be the best words to search for, when the rest of the page began to load. My eye was instantly drawn to a video entitled, "The Dorky Pickle Strikes Again." Then a still-frame of me in the pool loaded in the video box. I looked at the number of views. 1,309,215 views. I swallowed. And then I began to cry. I couldn't even read the comments if I had wanted to. Did you know you cannot read and cry at the same time? Who knew such a thing was physically impossible?

As I turned to leave the computer room, Patrick and Ginger walked into the house, their lovey-dovey arms around each other and their lovey-dovey eyes looking at each other being all lovey-dovey—so annoying, and of all times to show up.

I tried to get around them without them seeing my puffy and blood-shot eyes, but Ginger must have noticed and asked why I had been crying.

"Well golly-gee-willikers Penny, why have ya'll been cryin' and such?"

Okay, it wasn't quite that bad, but it might as well have been.

What I really wanted to say was, "Your stupid, devil-spawned, jerk of a sister is stupid, and dumb, and a jerk, and I hate her and I think that everything about her is stupid and dumb and I think that her name is stupid and dumb and I think everything about her is stupid and dumb. Did I mention I think your sister is stupid and dumb?!"

What I really said was, "Nothing."

And then I ran upstairs to my room.

I threw myself down on my bed to ponder the deep, dark questions of life. Why did life need to be so unfair? Why did JayJ have to pick on me and why did she want to make my life so miserable? Why couldn't she pick on somebody else for a while, and when I say a while I mean forever?

I sat on my bed for what felt like forever. Okay, so it was like 20 minutes, but still, it was a long time for me to ponder the deep questions of life.

There was a knock at my door.

"Penn?" came my mom's voice just outside the door. "Can I come in?"

Why do parents ask if they can come into your room as they are opening the door and already coming into your room? I guess it is one more question on my list of unanswerable questions.

"Why are you asking when you are already in my room?" I snapped.

"Penny, no need to get snappy. I just came to see why you were so upset."

See that? Of course my mom would turn this around on me. She has no sympathy! Like she would even know what it is like to have a mortal enemy who is out to get you at every twist and turn. I mean she is a grown up and they don't have to worry about anything and plus it was like a bazillion years ago since she was in school. And when she was, she never had problems like this. Everything was so much simpler in the olden days. Like they even had enemies way back then.

"Did something happen at school?" my mom asked.

"Yes mom," I said, not expecting her to understand. "That something is called JayJ Rothefeller!"

"Penny," my mom said. "JayJ really is a nice girl. I think maybe you're just not giving her the chance to prove it to you."

After giving my mother the death glare of a lifetime, although she couldn't see it with my face buried in my pillow—and yes, after that little comment I am officially not talking to my mom until I am old and 35—I turned my back to her and made a pouty "hmph" sound.

"I think what you need is a little time thinking about others. That always cheers me up." What in the heck was she even talking about? "I just baked some fresh pumpernickel. I bet our neighbor would love it if you dropped some by, and this time actually say hi."

Was she seriously asking me to take another loaf of her stupid bread—okay, it was delicious, but under the circumstances—to that old lady down the street?

I sat up and looked at my mom in disgust.

"Why do you keep asking me to take bread to this old lady who lives in the creepiest house ever?"

"Penny," my mom said.

But I wasn't finished.

"Do you know if she even eats it? Does she even want it?"

"Penny, I think—" my mom said.

But I still wasn't finished.

"How do you know whether she likes pumpernickel? She could hate it. Or worse, she could be allergic to the pumper or the nickel, or even both. Did you ever stop to think about that?"

"Penny, you are—" my mom tried to interject.

But I was still far from being finished.

"And why don't you bring her the bread. Why do I have to do it? She's obviously your friend, not mine!"

"Penny, she asked if she could talk with you," my mom said.

"And plus I am not talking to you until I am old and 35 so I am declining your wishes."

I then buried my head back into my pillow.

Wait, what did my mom just say?

"Wait, what did you just say?" I asked, my head still buried.

"I said she wants to talk with you."

I pulled my head back out into the open.

"She wants to talk with me?" I asked.

"She does."

"Why?"

"I'm not sure."

I tilted my head and raised my eyebrows as to suggest she wasn't telling me the whole story.

"Really, she didn't say," my mom said. "She just said she would like to talk with you, but she told me not to say anything. I guess the cat's out of the bag."

I sat there and stared at my tear-stained pillow. For some reason, knowing this made me feel better already.

"Just talk with her, Penny," my mom said.

I guess just talking to her once wouldn't hurt.

"Plus," my mom added, "I really think you'll have more in common than you think."

"Yeah," I said, with a laugh. "And you think JayJ and I should be friends."

My mom smiled. "If you talk to her, then maybe we could go to the mall on Saturday for an hour or two."

Okay, maybe not talking to my mom until I am old and 35 is a little dramatic. Maybe I will just give her the silent treatment until Saturday, just in time to go to the mall, but I am still mad at her.

"Thanks mom," I said, feeling better already, and not just because the trip to the mall. "I'll go over to this lady's house after I do some homework. I promise!"

Okay so much for the silent treatment until Saturday.

After a little hug—I guess we've made up—and a little smile, she looked at me.

"I love you Penny," my mom said, with a tear glistening in her eye.

"I love you too, Mom," I said.

After writing on the blog about our first true success, scrambickled eggs and toast, the creative juices were beginning to flow. I wrote about how my mom keeps making me go to this old lady's house and how old people smell weird. I mean seriously have you ever smelled an old person's house? It is totally weird. Then to add to the fact that this smelly, old lady lives in a haunted house is beyond the limits of what a child should have to bear, albeit a child on the cusp of maturity.

I was taking my sweet, old time going to the Frankincense's

house of smelliness and hauntingness. I mean, I wasn't entirely sure if her house was smelly or not, but from the haunted looks of it, it seemed like a safe bet. Olive and I had seen the ghost in the attic window lots of times. Actually, a lot of people had. Even Patrick had seen it, and until he started dating Ginger, I had trusted Patrick's judgment above just about anyone's.

When I got to the door of the Frankincense home, I stood there for a moment and tried hard to think about what I was going to say. What do you even say to old people? Did they even speak the English that I know and love? Maybe I should just say hi, maybe a comment about the weather, and then run. I mean, my mom didn't say I needed to have a long conversation with her, she just said I had to "talk" to her, whatever that meant.

I rang the doorbell and waited. Nobody answered. I allowed myself to breathe. I guess she wasn't home. I put the loaf of bread by the door and turned to leave. Then I heard the craziest thing ever. I mean it, it was crazy.

"I love your blog, Penny," came one of the mildest, sweetest voices I had ever heard. "You are very funny."

Wow, with that one little sentence Mrs. Frankincense had dispelled the long-running rumor that old people didn't know how to speak English. Oh wait, did I start that rumor?

"I love hearing about your adventures in the kitchen," continued the voice. "With your friend Olive, and how you add pickles to everything. It's genius."

And they had senses of humor too? Who would have guessed that old people could appreciate great humor?

I slowly turned around and said what any young author would say when they were getting a compliment on their work.

"Huh, thanks," I said. Then I ran away not knowing what else to say.

Who's the one that didn't know English again?

CHAPTER ELEVEN

Dear Secret Pickle Society,

Pickles are universal. They can be found around the world in their various forms. In India, they prefer their pickles on the spicy side of things (sounds delightful). In Germany, you can find your pickles sweet or sour. In Mexico, they pickle jalapeños (spicy!). In China, they pickle radishes. And pickles come not only in a variety of flavors, but a variety of names. In Korean, "kimchee" literally means pickles. In Russian, you call pickles "rassol." No matter where you happen to call home, one thing is for sure: pickles are universal.

Sincerely,
Penny Picklepants ♡

Mrs. Frankincense reads my blog?! Nobody was really supposed to read our cooking blogs, except for our teacher, Mrs. Smith. I mean, sure they're on the internet for anyone to read, but they're just cooking blogs—still, I had to admit, ours was pretty darn funny. I mean, look who wrote it after all.

I had a smile on my face the whole way home. I was going to tell my mom first thing how Mrs. Frankincense reads my blog when I realized that…

HOLY COW! Mrs. Frankincense reads my blog! SHE READS MY BLOG!!! OH! MY! GOSH! I just wrote something totally horrible about her… well, old people. I mean, how should I know whether her—and every old person's—house smelled? Besides, how could her house be stinky if she reads my blog, right? All I know is that I have to take down my newest blog entry, and PRONTO!

I flew through the front door and ran straight for the computer... and of course, Parker was on it, doing absolutely nothing.

I was totally winded after running down the rest of the block as fast as I could.

"P... Pa"—deep breath—"Pa... ark"—deep breath—"Parker!" I said.

"Huh?," Parker said, remaining completely calm and completely oblivious to anything but his game.

"Parker, I"—breath—"I need the com"—breath—"puter. Get off!" I yelled.

"Uhh," said Parker, long and slow.

"Parker," I said, gaining back most of my breath. "Listen, I don't have time, I need the computer, I need it now."

"Uhh."

"PARKER! I need the computer now! Now get off before I tell mom."

"Uhh."

AGGH!

"Parker! Get off the computer before I make you get off."

Maybe it's that little 7-year-old boys don't understand English.

"Uhh," Parker said. "Wait, you had the computer when you got home from school, so it's my turn."

Okay, I am going to pause our story for just a minute to explain our cuurent computer situation. Yes, the Picklepants live in the 21st century, it's just that we don't live like it's the 21st century. Instead, my parents insist that we live like we are stuck in the 18th century. They think that only having one computer, on dial-up mind you, is plenty enough for our needs. Now, most of you are asking yourselves "What the heck is dial-up?" And you have no idea how bad I wish I didn't know either. So, there was once a time when high-speed internet did not exist—I know, it's hard to believe. People had to have these things called modems that make funny noises when they connect to the internet. And they are SOOOO slow. When I bring up the point that the factory has wireless internet and has computers everywhere, again, all I get is the eye roll. And my mom wonders where I get it from! Anyway, the point is my parents think we need to live like we are in the 18th century. Except, I am sure people even way back then had at least two computers per household, but whatever. And because my parents also insist on only having one computer, we have to share the computer. We each get one hour per day to be on the computer. Now back to our story.

"MOM!" I yelled. "Parker won't let me use the computer and I need it like now. I mean like, RIGHT NOW!"

"Why do you need it?" my mom asked, walking in. "I thought you finished your homework before going over to visit with Frannie, which by the way, how did it go?"

"Well, it went really good. But right now, I really need to get on the blog and fix an entry I wrote about Mrs. Frank..."

Wait, my mom would freak out if she knew that I wrote a blog entry about how smelly and old Mrs. Frankincense is, was, but isn't, never was. Anyway, I will get into so much trouble and then most likely she won't take me to the mall on Saturday.

"You wrote a blog entry about Mrs. Frankincense?" my mom asked.

Oh great, that look of, "Am I going to be disappointed?" was starting to creep over her face.

"No, no I said Mrs. Smith, my Home Ec. teacher. I said that

she smelled like rolls, yeah, yeah, like rolls. And Olive and I should make rolls. Um, rolls that have pickles in them. Yeah, that's it... and, and... we should call them pickolls, you know, like, pickles and rolls mixed together make pickolls. Get it? Pickolls."

I certainly hope she was buying this because I know I wasn't.

"Oooh-kay," my mom said. "I think you are just going to have to wait your turn because Parker has it for the next 30 minutes and then Patrick said he needed it for some homework after that."

Of course my mom would be diplomatic about it. She never takes into consideration that my needs are greater than my brothers. "Just stay calm," I kept telling myself. I mean, I just posted the newest entry today. I really doubt Mrs. F. would have read it by now or in the next hour and a half. I will just wait until Patrick is done with his homework, get on the blog and delete the blog entry, and write another one. Yes, it will all work out.

"Fine," I said. "But the minute Patrick gets off, it's mine!"

Sometimes I wonder if JayJ and my mom are part of some ultra-secret pact sworn to ruin my life.

After what felt like forever, Parker got off the computer.

"Hey buddy," Patrick said. "Time for you to stop killing aliens."

"Oh man!" Parker said. "Okay, but lemme just finish off the queen's hive."

"No way!" Patrick said. "You are already at the queen's hive?"

Boys and their video games. What's the big deal? It's not like it's fashion or something.

A few minutes later, Parker was off the computer.

"All yours, big brother," Parker said.

"Patrick!" I implored, walking into the kitchen after eavesdropping from the next room. "You don't understand. I have to get on the computer right now."

"Penny, mom said you had to wait until I was finished. I have a paper and…"

"Patrick! You don't understand. I have to edit my blog. I have to change something I wrote. Every second could be too late. It will take me two seconds."

"Okay," Patrick said. "You have two minutes, and you owe me."

"Whatever," I said. "And thank you."

Luckily, the internet was still on from Parker using it, so I didn't have to go through that whole rigmarole. What the heck is a rigmarole anyway?

I was finally on the blog. All I had to do was delete today's entry and rewrite it sans old people, old people smell, and old people haunted houses. I don't know why, but I was shaking. I guess I was a bit freaked out that Mrs. F. had already read the blog. But there was little chance she had read the post yet. I mean, I posted the blog entry just before dropping off the bread. She was probably waiting for me to bring the bread, so she couldn't have read it on my way over, and then she was probably fixing herself a piece of bread and sitting down to enjoy it, and thinking of what a charming young woman I was.

A delete button popped up on the screen. Naturally, I clicked on it. A window came up and asked me if I was sure. I clicked on YES. Then the same thing happened, and then happened again. So I just kept clicking on DELETE and clicking on YES.

"Hello? Just delete the entry already," I said to the computer.

Finally, it was deleted. And finally, after a lot of clicking, something that had started out bad was working out for me. Maybe this was a turning point, or perhaps THE turning point in my life. One day, when I am a famous pickle taster, slash international singer, slash fashion designer—still working on how best to round out my triple threat—and a journalist is asking me at what point my life turned around, I am going to say this moment, right here, right now.

I was so happy that was done, I figured I would just write the new blog entry tomorrow. Besides, Patrick was breathing down my neck.

"All yours," I said. "And Patrick, thanks!"

"No problem, sis," Patrick said.

I guess Patrick was alright… sometimes.

"Oh, you didn't need the internet, right?" I said.

"No, I do need it."

"Oh, sorry, I logged off, forgot to ask sooner."

"It's alright," Patrick said, although I could tell he was a little perturbed.

Then the telephone rang.

"Penny!" my mom yelled from upstairs. "It's for you."

"Great!" Patrick said.

"Sorry," I said to Patrick. "I'll be quick."

If this really is my turning point, then maybe Jiminy is calling to express his undying love for me. What? It's at least within the realm of possibility.

"Hello?" Please be Jiminy! Please be Jiminy!

"Penny what are you doing?"

Dang it! It was only Olive. And she sounded a little stressed. But there is no way she had a more stressful day than I had had.

"Olive, you will never guess what happened to me today. So I was writing on the blog about…"

"So you were on the blog today?" Olive asked.

Seriously, what is Olive's problem? I am trying to tell her a story. Do I really need to rethink this whole best-friends thing, because a best friend does NOT cut you off when you've had just about the worst day in your life.

"Yes," I said. "I was on the blog, which I was trying to tell you if you would let me. So remember when JayJ..."

"Well, where is it then?" Olive asked.

Okay enough is enough!

"Olive!" I said. "Seriously, stop interrupting me. It's getting tres annoying. Like I was trying to say before you interrupted me..."

"Penny, it's not there."

"I know Olive, that is what I am trying to tell you. I wrote the blog entry today after school, but I wrote about my neighbor, you know Mrs. Frankincense, and I wrote some kind of mean things, and so I had to remove that entry, so I deleted it, but tomorrow..."

"Penny, you don't understand," Olive said, interrupting me for the fourth time. Yeah, I was counting. "The blog is not there Penny. It's gone."

Huh? Okay, don't panic. She's got to mean today's blog entry.

"I know Olive," I said with my calm voice. "That is what I am trying to tell you, I deleted the blog entry and I will write a new entry tomorrow."

Sheesh, what's her deal?

"Penny," Olive said with her calm voice. "The blog is not there. You did not delete today's entry. You deleted the entire blog!"

Say what?

"No I didn't!" I protested.

Did I?

"Are you sure?" I asked.

"Well, I'm pretty sure that when you get on the blog system, it says our blog has been deleted."

This cannot be happening! Not on my turning-point day.

"This is why I never wanted to be partners with her in the first place. Not only have we been kicked out of three kitchens because of her and her total disasters and her lies, but now we don't even have a blog. Seriously, why am I even friends with her?"

"Olive?" I asked. "Who are you talking to?"

"To my imaginary therapist. My parents won't take me to a real one, so I have to make one up. Trust me, being friends with you requires an imaginary therapist."

Wow! That was revealing.

"But that's beside the point!" Olive said, back on the warpath. "The point is you have ruined everything. Our friendship, my life, and worst of all, you have ruined any chance I had of getting an A after I agreed to be your cooking partner. Yes, you heard me, you have ruined my A. I have never gotten anything below an A except for a single A minus, thanks in part to Miss Hues because she didn't like my paintings. I mean, half the class didn't even know what chiaroscuro was let alone tenebrism."

"Olive," I said. "No one knows what the chiaro-whats-it or the ten briskets thingy you just said are. But that is beside the point. The point is, I really doubt that I deleted the entire blog. That would be insanely crazy."

"Penny Picklepants. News flash! You are insanely crazy—insanely crazy at ruining things!"

The more I thought about it, the more my stomach dropped to the floor—actually I think it was half way to China by now.

I started to think Olive could be right. There sure were a lot of "Deletes" and "Are You Sures." I was so worried that Mrs. F. was going to read the entry, I must have hardly paid any attention to what I was doing.

"Penny, I am done and tomorrow morning I am telling Mrs. Smith I am working alone. Got it? You are on your own, I'm done!"

Click. Dialtone.

"Olive? Olive? Did you just hang up on me?" I asked.

"Good," Patrick said. "Now maybe I can get on the internet."

"You did not just hang up on me," I said, still on the phone. "You just hung up on me. Well fine, I will hang up on you now, even though technically you are no longer on the phone."

I slammed the phone back on the hook.

Life! So seriously not fair.

That night, my dreams were invaded with the unraveling of my life. JayJ was a virus living in my computer. The more I tried to delete her, the more copies of her were made. Jiminy's left hand was a loaf of bread and his right hand was Mrs. Frankincense. He kept asking his right hand, Mrs. Frankincense, if his left hand, the loaf of bread, smelled funny. All the while Olive was a badger and was yelling at me, but all that came out of her mouth were clicks and dial tones. After a few hours of this real-life induced dream craziness, I called it good and woke up to get ready for the day.

When I went downstairs to get some breakfast, I noticed my dad was sitting in his office. And that is when it hit me how many more problems I had then just the deleted blog, a best friend that was now my ex-best friend, and a mortal enemy bound and determined to ruin my life and doing a mighty fine job if I had to say so. I had to watch, in silence and in the shadows, as my parents worried their little hearts out about the plant.

"Hey Dad," I said, more chipper than I was feeling. "Watcha doin?"

"Hi Penn," my dad said, checking his wristwatch. "What are you doing up? You are usually sound asleep at 6:00 in the morning. Come to think of it, you are usually sound asleep until 8:00, at which time your mother usually has to resort to dragging you out of bed."

Why do parents always point out the obvious?

"Yeah, I couldn't sleep—I guess a lot on my mind."

"Mmm," my dad said, letting out a sigh. "I guess I know how you feel. What seems to be troubling you?"

I then proceeded to tell him all things stressful in my life, with the exception of the plant. I didn't want him to know I knew because if parents know that you know what they know, they get all weird, you know?

Anyway, he just sat and listened and he didn't even say anything when I said that JayJ was the offspring of the devil. "Dad, I seriously think JayJ is the offspring of the devil." I then paused a brief moment, expecting a reprimand. But he didn't say a word. After I spilled my guts for the next 30 minutes, I had to admit, I felt a lot better.

"Well Penny, there certainly seems to be more than your fair share of trouble troubling you, but if there is one thing I know about you," my dad said, smiling, which by itself seemed to induce confidence, "you will make everything right, you always do in the end."

I gave my dad a great big hug, and forced myself not to cry.

"Now, I need to get back to finishing these papers for work. Go get some breakfast."

"Okay," I said. "Speaking of work how is the plant doing?" Oh great, why did I have to say anything? Now he'll know that I know.

"Oh, everything's fine," he said, less than convincingly. "I'm going to have lunch with Mr. Rothefeller today. Do you want me to ask him if they adopted their daughter from the devil?"

Well now we know where I get my sense of humor from!

"No Dad," I said, laughing. "I don't need any more proof. The red horns protruding from her head are proof enough."

That got a chuckle from my dad.

I then began walking out of the room.

"Oh Penny," my dad called. "I thought your mom said that you had been writing everything down for your blog in a notebook?"

"Oh my gosh! Dad you're right. Why didn't I think of that? I must get my genius genes from you. Thanks Dad!"

Now I knew everything would be okay with regards to the blog. I would just have to go over my notes and make new entries for the days we attempted to cook and with nobody up, I could get all the entries finished before school and then Olive and I will be friends again, best friends again, and all before 9:00 in the morning.

Two hours later, I got everything caught up on the blog, but now I was exhausted.

"Mom, I need some coffee stat—I am exhausted."

"Well for starters, your father and I don't drink coffee, and if we did, you would not be allowed to drink it, but I will pour you a glass of orange juice."

Well, orange juice was a pretty good substitute.

"And why are you so exhausted?" my mom asked. "You don't look like you just woke up."

"Wait! What does that mean? You think I look horrible when I've just woken up?" I swear my mom knows how to ruin every moment, like what had been a perfectly good morning.

Of course Parker piped up. "Yes, she does think you look horrible when you wake up. She's just afraid to tell you, but I'm not."

I threw my piece of toast at him, but he ducked and it hit my mom instead.

After giving me a stern look of "there's no throwing your breakfast in this house," she actually scolded Parker.

"Parker!" my mom said. "That is not true. Now apologize to your sister."

"Sorry," Parker said, in a most insincere manner.

"Penny," my mom said, "don't read so much into what I'm saying. I'm just saying that you look like you've been up for a while. That and I heard you getting ready at 6:00, and now it's... oh my gosh! It's 8:30. Time to go. Let's go. You can tell me on the way what you've been doing."

On the way to school I told my mom what happened with the blog. I kept out, of course, the part of why I had deleted the blog in the first place. I didn't think she would appreciate it very much. By the time I was finished, we were pulling up to the school.

I saw Olive, but she wasn't at the flagpole. I quickly got out of the car, did my usual "yeah, yeah, you too" routine with my mom, and proceeded to shut the door when my mom yelled something like, "It may be fate, I have to bake the car to get the soil ranged." Huh? But when I turned around she had already left—oh well, whatever. I had more pressing matters to attend to.

"Olive!" I yelled, but she did not respond. "Hey Olive," I said, walking up behind her.

She turned around slowly.

Then in unison we both said, "I'm so sorry!" And then we hugged.

"Remember how you insisted on me keeping notes?" I said. "I found my notebook with all my notes and got everything updated so we are good to go on the blog. I will explain to Mrs. Smith what happened and why there are so many entries that have the same date. What do you think? Are we partners again?"

I was standing there with my hand out ready for a shake, a fist bump, a high five, anything to seal the deal of our partnership.

"Penny, I am sorry I flipped out on you and I appreciate that you got the blog updated, and we will always be best friends, but I've made up my mind. I really just want to work by myself on this one."

So this is what it feels like when supermodels trip on the runaway and fall on their face.

"I talked to my mom last night," Olive continued, "and she said that I could use her kitchen again just as long as I am alone. My mom also called Mrs. Smith last night and explained what had happened and that I would work really hard to get caught up, but that I would be working alone from now on. Are you mad?"

What I wanted to say was, "Am I mad? Am I MAD? Of course I am mad, how could my best friend in the world ditch me at the first sign of trouble and still be my best friend? I got up at 6:00 in the morning to fix this, granted I got up because I was having the strangest dreams ever, and my dad was the one who pointed out that I had the notebook with all the notes I had taken, but that is beside the point, because I took that notebook and I fixed the blog and I fixed everything. I fixed it! And you have the nerve to ask me whether I am mad?! YES! I AM MAD!"

But this is what I really said, "Me, mad? At my best friend? Of course not! I am fine working by myself. Totally and completely fine… to work… all by myself. It will give me the opportunity to cultivate my culinary talents."

Did that sound convincing? Because I wasn't sure who needed more convincing, me or Olive.

"Oh great," Olive said. "Besties again. Now we can focus on—"

"Coming up with ways to save the plant?" I interrupted.

"Well, I was going to say school, but I guess we can look into that as well. But for now, we just need to hurry, because today is PE."

After Olive and I got ready for PE and walked into the gym, we instantly realized something was wrong. Mrs. Funda, our PE teacher, was nowhere to be found.

"What's going on?" I asked Belinda Galinda.

"I guess Mrs. Funda is out with a cold," Belinda said. "Coach Shoe is teaching both the boys and the girls because of the short notice."

What's Spanish for "Aggh!"

I hate PE! Okay, I don't always hate PE. I like PE, when our regular PE teacher, Mrs. Funda, is in charge. She only teaches the 6th grade girls. We always have lots of fun. She never yells at us— says it's bad for the vocal cords. She always cuts our runs short— says we need to have more than 5 minutes to do our hair. And she lets us play as much basketball as we want—the one game that I can play without inflicting harm or injury to myself or others.

But Coach Shoe as our substitute? Are you kidding me? Even though we had never had him as a substitute, we had heard the horror stories. Most the time the boys look like they are on the brink of death by the end of PE. If he's as bad as they say, Coach Shoe must be the worst PE teacher ever.

And get this, his first name was Jim. Yes, a PE teacher whose first name was Jim and whose last name was Shoe—Jim Shoe! With a name like that, I wonder how he ever made it through the military, let alone middle school.

Coach Shoe never married. It had been passed down over the years, from grade to grade, that he had supposedly been engaged at one time. But he called it off because she couldn't run the mile in under 8 minutes.

He drove me crazy. He thought he was still in the army with his "Men, hit the showers!" and "Men, give me 20." And my personal favorite (not really) was how he gave the boys a pep-talk before every PE class.

Olive and I fell into line, as Coach Shoe stood at the front with his back turned towards the class.

"Men," Coach Shoe finally said.

Uh, hello? Girls here too!

"I am here to make you into something you are not. To mold you. To show you what you are made of. To make you all that you can be."

I then raised my hand. I was going to ask how PE could possibly make me a better professional pickle taster.

The boy to my right quickly grabbed my hand and pushed it down. When I looked at him to give him my worst crusty, he looked at me and shook his head nervously with a fearful look on his face and whispered, "Don't do it."

Well nobody tells Penny Picklepants what to do!

I again raised my hand, giving the boy my best "I will do whatever I want" look. But this time I raised my left hand.

Next thing I know the boy sitting to my left (where did Olive go?) quickly grabbed my hand and said, with a shake of his head, "Dude, don't do it, for the love of humanity—do not raise your hand."

What? Fine, I will just ask the question WITHOUT raising my hand.

"And men," Coach Shoe continued, "in order to be all you can be, you must..."

"Coach Shoe?" I yelled out. "Coach Shoe, will you please explain muh meh mumow..." Next thing I know both of the boys to my left and my right covered my mouth with their bare hands. Gross! Get those dirty paws off my face.

Coach Shoe then slowly turned around to face the class. A very menacing looking vein seemed to be popping out of his forehead that I didn't recall seeing before and his face seemed a shade more red than usual.

"Who dares interrupt the Shoe?!" he boomed in a ticked-off drill sergeant sort of way, with a half-smoked, unlit cigar planted in the side of his mouth. Is that even legal? Under the circumstances, I think I will let that question slide.

Suddenly the entire class shifted to my left and to my right, leaving me all alone in the middle.

"No one interrupts the Shoe! Especially, during his motivational speech, the very speech that could one day just save your very lives!"

Wow! This guy took his speeches pretty seriously.

JayJ snickered, causing Coach Shoes to shoot JayJ a look something akin to armor-piercing lasers, instantly stopping her in her tracks. At least something good came out of this mess I just put myself into. Coach Shoe had put JayJ in her place within a nano-second of his gaze. I must admit, deer in headlights is a good look for JayJ if there ever was a good look for her. Somehow, I need to figure out a way to hire this guy to look at JayJ with that same gaze whenever she's comes around me. But for now, I've got to figure out how to get myself out of this.

Coach Shoe slowly raised his hand and pointed his finger at me.

"You!" he shouted. "Name and rank soldier!"

Um, what? Soldier? Okay, let's see. I figured I had two options. I could: (A) lie and tell Coach Shoe that my name was JayJ Rothefeller. Hmm, problem with that was JayJ was standing two feet away. I doubt she would let that one slide. On the other hand I could, (B) tell Coach Shoe who I was and that my rank was pure awesomeness—sounded pretty good, actually. I guess there was a third option as well. I could, (C) hope that my shaking legs could register as an earthquake on the Richter scale causing Coach Shoe to tell everyone to seek immediate shelter in the nearest foxhole.

"Um, my name is Penny Picklepants, sir, and, um, I guess my rank is 6th grade," I said, with much less confidence than I was aiming for.

Coach Shoe just sat and stared at me for what seemed like an eternity. But I held his gaze—mostly because I didn't know where else to look. He finally broke his gaze and looked at the rest of the class surrounding me on my left and my right. Then he looked back at me.

"That," boomed Coach Shoe, "was the most treasonable, most demoralizing, unpatriotic act of cowardice I have ever witnessed in my entire military career!"

After a moment, Coach Shoe began pacing back and forth, surveying the class, the vein on his forehead nowhere close to retreating. "What," demanded Coach Shoe, "is the first rule of every soldier, soldiers?"

There was a pause. I had no clue. Maybe friends don't let friend wear camo after the fall? But somehow I didn't think that was the answer he was looking for.

Then the boys finally chipped in, albeit with lackluster enthusiasm, "Leave No Soldier Behind!"

"I did not hear you!" Coach Shoe shouted.

"Leave no soldier behind, sir!" the boys shouted, this time with a little more gusto.

"Now, for this act of cowardice," Coach Shoe said, somewhat regaining his cool. "You will run four laps."

There was a collective groan among the "soldiers."

At first I thought he meant for me to run four laps. Oh well, so much for asking for help with my future. I put my head down and tried to make my way through the wall of classmates to begin my run of shame.

"Not you Picklepants," Coach Shoe said. "It is your lackluster brothers in arms who disgracefully call themselves soldiers that will be running those four laps in your honor."

What the? Oh no!

"Now run you maggots!" boomed Coach Shoe.

There was a collective moan again from the entire class, except now every eye was fixed upon me, countless dagger-filled looks all aimed squarely at me.

With the rest of the class on the first of their four laps, Coach

Shoe turned to me. "To stand there," Coach Shoe said, "and not flinch a muscle, under fire, while you were left behind by your fellow soldiers, that…" Was that a tear glistening in his eye? "That right there was one of the bravest acts of heroism I have witnessed in my 25 years of service." What was going on here? "Excuse me," Coach Shoe said, turning his back to me. "I seemed to have got something in my eye."

As I sat there on the bleachers not knowing what to do, I started to sense a low grumbling that sounded something like "thanks a lot Picklepants" generally emanating from the running mass of students from my class. I had an odd feeling that the class really wasn't running so much in my honor, as in my derision. I had to do something. I had to run with them.

"Coach Shoe, sir?" I said.

Coach Shoe, sniffling, then turned and faced me again.

"Sir, I can run. I don't have to just sit while…"

Coach Shoe then turned his back to me again and seemed to be wiping something from his eye.

"Spoken like a true soldier, soldier!" Coach Shoe said. He cleared his throat, and said, "I've seemed to have got something stuck in my eye again. Run soldier. Run and show this brigade what a true soldier is made of."

Um, okay.

I started to run with the rest of the class, but I'm not sure how much it helped. The entire time I ran, Coach Shoe reminded them what a bunch of sissies they were by yelling things like "Look at Picklepants. That soldier has more heart than this entire brigade!" and "I wouldn't want a single one of you with me in a foxhole, except for Picklepants!" and "Without Picklepants on your side, you wouldn't last a day in battle!"

Needless to say, my running did not stop the death glares, but Coach Shoe eventually told us we could leave. "You have 5 minutes to shower soldiers! Now move out!"

I was a little leery of what was going to happen in the locker room. I figured I would first apologize to Olive since she was my best friend. "Olive, listen I am so sorry that you had to run laps, I didn't think the entire class was going to get punished." I was so worried that she wasn't going to let this one go.

"Well, at least you ran with us, eventually. But honestly, I wanted to ask him how PE was actually going to make me a better adult, much less save my life one day."

See? Olive totally got me. No wonder we were best friends. "I know right?" I said. "I mean, really, how is running around a track going to make me a better professional pickle taster?"

"Especially when the plant won't be your family's anymore and your poor, sad, pathetic dreams of being a professional pickle whatever will be dashed," JayJ said as she came up from behind me and Olive.

Leave it to her to make matters go from bad to worse.

"How do you... what is... it isn't even..."

What was my deal around this girl?

"Having a hard time talking there, Picklepants?" JayJ asked. "Don't worry. Nobody listens to you anyway."

Of course all the girls started laughing. I swear she pays her friends to laugh at the perfect times.

"Whatever! I'm out of here," I said.

That's it? That's all I could come up with?! What is wrong with my brain when I get around this evil person? It's like all my witty comebacks desert me, only to return when nobody is around.

Of course laughter erupted after Olive and I walked out of the locker room. I am sure JayJ was telling the girls of the 6th grade all sorts of things about me.

"Penny," Olive said, "don't worry about her, she is such a jerk and the only reason those girls are laughing is because they are afraid of her."

"Thanks Olive. I just wish I could get back at her. I hate it that she always wins and makes me look stupid in front of everybody every time. I should just start small, you know like, turn her pool into Jell-O. How many packages of Jell-O do you think we would need to do that?" My mind was starting to swirl.

"Penny, don't even think about it."

"Olive, you know that I am just thinking out loud. I would never do something like that." At least I think I wouldn't. Would I? "But perhaps we could do something on more of a smaller scale." I said.

When I got Olive's slow nodding of approval with that far off look in her eye, I suddenly liked where this was going.

CHAPTER TWELVE

Even though I was having huge, ginormous, dare I say even grandiose thoughts of getting back at JayJ for everything she had ever done, was doing, or ever would do to me, I had bigger fish to fry—hold that thought: fried fish and pickles is totally going to be mine and Olive's next cooking adventure—granted, we still had yet to master boiling water—okay, *I* had yet to master boiling water—but Olive always took care of that. Then it occurred to me. Olive and I were no longer cooking partners. I had no kitchen. I had no partner. I had no hope.

When I got home from school still pondering how to fix the whole cooking debacle, my mom handed me yet another loaf of bread and told me to take it to Mrs. F. Seriously, how many loaves of bread could one woman eat? But since my finding out that Mrs. F. was actually reading my blog, and what more, actually enjoying it, I figured that perhaps I could start being a little nicer to my blog's one and only reader. Well, besides Mrs. Smith that is. Ha! I was so excited. My blog had a non-obligatory reader. But then I remembered that I might need to apologize to Mrs. F. for my comments. I was really hoping she hadn't read my blog before I deleted it, and that she was as forgiving as Olive was. Ugh! I hate apologies.

Upon ringing the doorbell my stomach hit the floor. Mrs. F. opened the door. I had my apology ready for my smelly and old comments, but first I took a good whiff of her home. Yup, no smelly old smell.

With a huge smile on her face, Mrs. F. greeted me. Well, if she was mad at me for my stupid comments, she certainly didn't show it.

"Hi Mrs. F... rankincense, I just wanted to..." I said, smiling back.

"Well, Penny," she said, "you look upset."

I did?

"Won't you come in and have a piece of your mother's bread? It is so good with melted butter and a sliced pickle."

I really didn't want to come in. I mean we could just chat every now and then, and just on her porch, and then... Wait! What did she just say? Doth my ear deceive me?

"I do that too Mrs. F... rankincense," I said.

She smiled and said, "You can call me Frannie. Won't you come in?

I guess it wouldn't hurt, especially if she was offering fresh, hot bread with pickle slices.

"Sure," I said.

Wow! This home was beautiful. I just stood there, mouth fully agape, taking it all in.

Frannie had started to walk towards her kitchen, then stopped and turned around when she noticed I wasn't following.

"Are you coming, dear?" she asked, with a smile.

What was it with that smile? It was so warm and inviting. I don't think a perfectly hot, hot chocolate on a cold winter's night could have warmed me up any better than that smile did.

"You have a lovely home, Mrs. Frank..., I mean, Frannie."

"Why thank you Penny," she said. "What say we go into the kitchen for a slice and find out what else we have in common?"

I took a seat at her kitchen table while she prepared the bread and pickles. Her kitchen was just as beautiful as her living room. I kept wondering to myself, how could a haunted house be so beautiful inside? I was starting to think all those stories were the product of the overly-active imaginations of children, children whose imaginations were so not like mine.

"Is there anything I can do to help?" I asked.

"No, dear, you just sit, and tell me all about yourself."

How cool was this? It was like I had just found out that I had a secret grandma that I got to keep all to myself—my very own, personal grandma. How cool was that?

Then I took a bite of one of her pickles. Best pickles ever!

"Holy cow! What is this?" I asked.

"What is what?" Frannie replied.

"This," I said with my mouth full of another bite, barely able to get the words out. "This, what I am eating."—another bite—"It's one of the most delicious pickles I have ever eaten."

"Oh, they're just from my homemade batch of pickles. I'm glad you like them," Frannie said.

HOME! MADE! PICKLES!

"These things are incredible," I said. "You have got to show me how to make these."

"Yes, one day I shall," Frannie said.

I then proceeded to tell her all about the complexities of my life. I felt like I could tell her anything, even about the pickle plant. "Of course nobody will talk to me about it because they think I am too young! How crazy is that?"

Frannie's answer: "So very crazy."

How cool was that?!

I told her all about Jiminy. "I just can't figure out why he would be with JayJ!"

Frannie's answer: "I know, right?"

How cool was that?!

I even told her about JayJ. "I am positive that that girl is the spawn of the devil."

Frannie's answer, "Totally!"

How cool was that?!

I even told her about how I didn't have a kitchen to cook in. "I mean, who knew you were supposed to stay IN the kitchen when the water is boiling? We never covered that in class!"

Frannie's answer: "Well, why don't you just cook here?"

WHAT?

"I could be your cooking partner and besides I think putting pickles in everything is pure genius."

Seriously, HOW COOL WAS THAT?!

Could this lady get any cooler?

"Are you serious?," I asked, practically jumping out of my chair. "I could cook here? In this amazing kitchen? With you? I mean, I will totally do all the cooking and I will take all the notes." There was just one problem. "But you're not a student in my class. I'm not sure if Mrs. Smith will let us be partners."

"Well, I figured what Mrs. Smith didn't know wouldn't hurt her." Frannie said.

Yes, this lady could get cooler!

"Okay then, partners?" I said, holding out my hand.

After shaking hands I wasn't sure of what to say.

"So, do we start now?" I asked awkwardly, "or just wait until another time?"

"A wise man once said, 'Do not dwell in the past, do not dream of the future, concentrate the mind on the present moment.'"

"Huh," I said, a bit confused what to say next, or what she even meant.

"Yes. Let's start now," she said with a big grin and a hearty laugh.

"Great!" I said enthusiastically. "But I didn't bring anything to make. I could run home and grab something."

"Heavens no," Frannie said. "We have plenty here. What do you say we start with something simple? And then we can work our way up from there. I have some chicken strips in the freezer. Would that be a good starting point?"

"Perfect," I said, thinking how amazing it was that here I was with an older person who actually respected and asked for my opinion. Then I just stood there, not sure how to proceed.

"The refrigerator is there," Frannie said, pointing to the fridge behind me, "and the stove there. As you said, you will make everything, and I'll be here to simply lend moral support as well as a helping hand where I am needed."

"That's the plan," I said.

And then I got to work familiarizing where Frannie kept everything in her kitchen as well as figuring out how to set the temperature and timer on her oven. As the chicken baked, we had some more time to talk.

"All I know," I said, "is that I have got to find a way to get back at JayJ. It's starting to consume my every spare thought."

Frannie, smiled at looked down at the table where she still sat.

"Penny my dear, in time I think you will come to realize that such things usually have a way of working themselves out on their own. It may even surprise you how it all works out."

"If by 'working out' you mean having all of JayJ's hair fall out and her finger nails turning green, then yes, I totally agree."

"No," she said, with another hearty laugh. "That is not what I meant."

I wasn't so sure.

It was getting late. We said goodbye and I hurried home. I was so excited to get home and write on my cooking blog about my raging success with Frannie. We had successfully made chicken strips with sliced pickles. Anyone up for Penny Picklepant's famous Chickle Strips? Get it? Chicken and pickles... Well, anyway, they were delicious, easy, and the fact that none of it involved smoke, water, or the fire department meant it was a raging success. I knew throwing some chicken strips into the oven wasn't exactly a culinary sensation, but it helped boost my confidence. Beef Wellington, here I come! Or shall I say, Beef Pickleton?

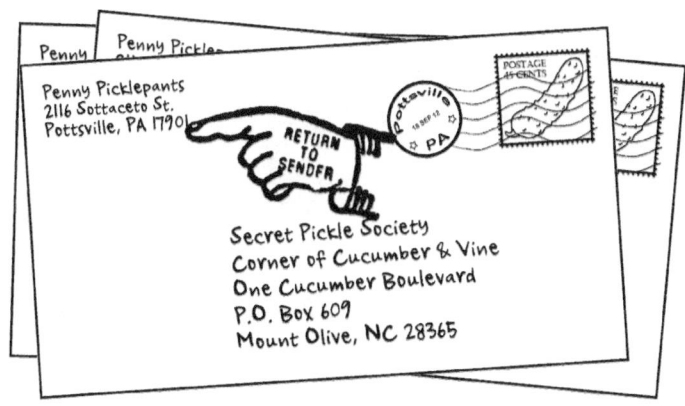

CHAPTER THIRTEEN

Seeing that my life was already just about as unlucky of a life as one could have, I figured I didn't need to push what little luck remained by including a Chapter Thirteen. Consequently, the chapter has been permanently deleted from this book. But don't worry—all you're missing is more embarrassing moments for me and more gloating by JayJ. Oh, and then there was the talk my mom gave me—you know, "the talk." Yeah, as you can imagine, it went over just about as well as Conan O'Brien in jeggings.

CHAPTER FOURTEEN

Dear Secret Pickle Society,

P is for always having Plenty of Perfectly Piquant Pickles.
I is for Insanely and Incredibly Irrepressible Pickles.
C is for Considerably Crunchy, Capably Crispy Pickles.
K is for Konsummately Kippered Pickles fit for a King.
L is for Ludicrously and Luxuriously Luscious Pickles.
E is for Exquisitely and Enticingly Enjoyable Pickles.
S is for Scrumptiously Spicy, ever so Sweet Pickles.

Sincerely,
Penny Picklepants ♡

P.S. You so want a Picklepants Pickle right about now, don't you?

When I got to school the next day, I had been so excited about the night before (with the exception of "the talk" I had with my mom) that I had forgotten that we were going to have a school assembly just for the 6th graders. It's the same thing every year. Basically, it's a slide show presentation of all the great things you can expect in junior high—like basketball, football, soccer, student government, and of course cheerleading. And then at the end of the slide show there's always a part of what not to do when you get to junior high. It was usually just totally goofy, made up things, and it was there to just make everybody laugh.

Like I need anything more to get me excited about junior high, I mean it's junior high! I was so excited to go to junior high that I had already started to compile a list of why I was so excited. Here's my list so far:

1. I won't have to see JayJ all day, every day.
2. Because none of my classes will be with JayJ.
3. But all my classes will be with Jiminy.
4. And Cheerleading! I will make the perfect cheerleader.
   Plus Jiminy plays basketball, so in addition to all our
   classes, we will be at all the games together.

Okay, so I had only gotten four reasons on my list so far. But seriously, how can you not be excited for 7th grade? We would finally be emerging on the scene of society and be taking our places in the hierarchy of popularity. I assumed I would be near the top, I mean, being a cheerleader and all!

As we all filed into the gym, Olive and I took our place on the bleachers, right behind Jiminy, with JayJ nowhere in sight. Best day ever! Jiminy even turned around and looked right at me—yes, I know it was right at me, because Olive told me so, like a hundred times—oh, and did I forget to mention that he smiled? Of course I didn't forget to tell you, silly. It's called dramatic effect, duh! Can you believe it?! HE SMILED! And he smiled right at me! It was practically like an engagement. Okay, not really, but still, it was pretty awesome.

Suddenly the lights dimmed, the music started blaring, and the slide show started. It was going so great and from the energy in the gym, you could tell everybody was equally excited about junior high next year.

After showing all the cool things about junior high, it was time to show the "what not to do in junior high" segment. Then I stopped breathing. Not because I was laughing so hard that I lost my breath like everybody else in the auditorium was about to do. Rather, it was because the picture that JayJ had taken of me when I had supposedly peed in her pool came up on the screen in full

Technicolor glory for the entire 6th grade class to see on the auditorium's giant movie screen. I looked like a deer in head lights sitting in a pool surrounded by green dye. In big bold letters the caption read, "Rule #1: Don't pee in the pool. But if you do, don't get caught." The auditorium erupted in laughter. The next picture was of me crashing on my bike. "Rule #2: Watch where you are going." More laughter. The next was of me standing in my pink underwear in our laundry room. I didn't even read its caption.

I was so humiliated that my instincts to run kicked in. I stood up and started to run. But being in a dark gym and totally forgetting I was sitting in bleachers, I fell right on top of Jiminy, followed by more laughter, as well as a muffled voice that sounded just like Jiminy's when I landed on him after crashing on my bike.

"Penny, are you okay?" Jiminy asked. "If you are, could you please get off me?"

Not again! Seriously, not again! This boy was going to have some serious PPTSD—you know, Post-Penny-traumatic stress disorder—if I didn't stop falling on him.

Somehow I managed to get myself off of Jiminy, said sorry a thousand times, found the steps, and I ran. I ran out of the gym, out of the school, and I ran straight home. I must admit crying and running as fast as you can was a lot harder in real life than how it was portrayed in the movies. I had made it home when I lunged for the front door, only to have grabbed it so hard that when the door didn't budge, I fell on my bum. I tried again and again and the handle wouldn't budge. Fine! If I couldn't turn the knob, I will just pound on the door until my mom opens it for me. After pounding for what felt like a million years, I realized that my mom wasn't home so I did what any respectable woman in my position would do. I sat down on the front steps and started to cry even harder.

I had no idea how long I had been crying when I heard my name.

"Penny? Is that you?"

I was about to yell "go away" when I looked up and through my puffy and tear-stained eyes I saw Frannie standing in front of me. "Frannie!" I stood up and threw my arms around her and gave her the biggest hug I could muster. I'm sure I looked like a mess, but it felt so good to be with somebody who wasn't laughing at me.

"Well hello to you too, dear," Frannie said, my hug nearly knocking her over. "Is everything alright?"

"No," was all I could say, before I started crying some more.

"There, there dear," Frannie said. "How about I take you home, fix you something to eat and we will talk about why you are so upset."

After having a sandwich, with one of Frannie's amazing home-made pickles of course, I told Frannie what had happened at the assembly.

"I know it was JayJ who put those pictures in the slide show," I said. "Nobody else would stoop that low and plus, she was the one who had taken the pictures in the first place, at least the first two. Why is she out to get me Frannie? Honestly I have never done anything to her. Nothing! And she has hated me from the minute she met me. I hate her, hate her, hate her."

"Penny, I am so very sorry that you had to go through that today. She really does sound quite despicable."

"See? Now do you see why she is the offspring of the devil?"

Frannie handed me another tissue and I blew my nose and wiped my eyes, although not so much in that order or with the same tissue.

"I know that you think revenge isn't the answer," I said. "But if I could, I would. And then…" And then my mind went blank. "Ahhhh! I'm so mad I can't even think of plans of revenge."

"You could sneak into her house, cut her hair, and dye it green?" Frannie said. Huh? Did Frannie just give me an idea for revenge? "Or, you could turn her pool into a big pool of Jell-O. You could toilet paper her house and fork her lawn. Or you could put red paint on her seat at school."

I was feeling better already.

"Frannie," I said. "Are you thinking what I am thinking? That we should do all five?" Please say yes, please say yes, please, say yes.

"Oh Penny, I am just giving you something fun to think about. In reality, revenge only ends up hurting you. Trust me. For as long as I have lived, I have yet to see a plan of revenge work out to any-one's favor. It usually ends up hurting worse the person seeking the revenge. Look at me, Penny."

I wiped my eyes and looked at Frannie.

"Promise me that you will not try to get back at JayJ."

"I promise that I will not do anything to JayJ that she wouldn't do to me."

"Penny, that isn't promising much."

Ugh! "Okay!" I said begrudgingly. Could she tell I was crossing my fingers behind my back? "I promise that I won't take revenge on the devils spawn, otherwise known as JayJ Rothefeller."

"Good. Now let's go home and see if your mom's come back. I'm sure once you talk to her you will feel even better."

Mmm… somehow I doubt that. Anyway, I ended up crossing my fingers behind my back when I promised Frannie I wouldn't seek revenge. Truth was, I just couldn't make a promise I wasn't ready to keep yet. What JayJ did to me was far more than humiliating and nothing short of horrible. I had to get her back. Even if it was just one time, I had to make her know what it felt like.

When I got home, Mom and Olive were sitting on the front steps, talking no doubt about what had happened. When I saw them and the concern they had on their faces, it made me start crying all over again. I am sure we were a sight to see—four girls (okay two girls and two old ladies—yes my mom is old)—standing on the sidewalk crying and hugging. They say misery loves company—I couldn't agree with them more. And the best part? My mom didn't even try defending JayJ, not even once.

When I woke up that next morning and thought about the previous day's events, my stomach dropped with anxiety. There was no way out of it. I figured, if ever there was a day to play sick, this was the day.

Breakfast made me feel a little better, that is, until Parker opened his mouth.

"Guess what they're calling Penny at school?" he said.

"Parker, we don't need to hear it," my mom said, as she cooked some eggs. But Parker must have chosen not to hear her.

"Well, for starters, some are calling you Penny PeePeepants."

"Who is?" I asked.

"The Kindergartner's," Parker said.

"They're calling it the Great Penny Peed in a Pool Fiasco of 2012."

What? Oh great, even the Kindergartner's knew about my greatest embarrassing moment. But why did they have to pick the pool incident—which by the way, I did not do! Why couldn't they have called it the Great Penny Crashed on a Bike Fiasco of 2012?

"Others are calling you Penny Wizzed-her-pants."

"Parker, that's enough," my mom said, though still more interested in her eggs not burning.

"And still others are calling you Pees-in-the-pool Penny, Penny Tinklepants, and there are a whole lot more and also some about your pink underwear." I blushed, but he could care less, his nose buried in his DS. Then Parker said, with a sigh, "I think our last name just makes it a little too easy for them—I'm really sorry, Penny."

And I knew he was.

"It'll be okay little buddy," I said, giving him a reassuring smile, knowing full well it would be anything but okay.

To get out of school for the day, I had to fake being sick again. But this time, I would skip the thermometer and go with stomach cramps. I had heard once that the key to faking out the parents was the clammy hands. I bent over, moaning and wailing, and that's when I licked my palms. I have to admit, it felt a little childish and stupid, but then, so is JayJ. When I showed my mom my hands, she said, "Nice try Ferris. Now go get dressed."

Huh? Ferr... what? How did she know? Sometimes I wonder if my mom really does possess superhuman powers.

"Penny, I know that you are embarrassed, but you have to keep your head held high," my mom said. "Trust me, it will all blow over sooner than you think."

Sure it will, except she wasn't the one being ridiculed by the entire elementary school, and she didn't have to go to school with these ruthless nicknamer-ers. And then there was JayJ herself!

I would like to report that the day after wasn't that bad and after a day of texting, videogames, YouTube, and other mindless entertainment, the school had entirely forgotten about what had happened to me in full Technicolor glory. But this is my life and well, if you've been paying any sort of attention you would know that nothing ever goes right in it. After being pointed at (about a bazillion times), laughed at (about a gazillion times), and hearing all the whispering—pss pss, Penny Tinklepants... pss pss, Penny Peepeepants... pss pss, Penny Pees-in-the-Pool—I had had it.

"Olive, I can't take it anymore. I am getting back at JayJ and it is going to happen today. We have to come up with something quick and something fast before the end of the day. By the end of the day, I want people talking about and pointing fingers at her!"

So during lunch we came up with a perfect plan. It involved flour, dumping said flour on JayJ, humiliation, covering JayJ in said humiliation, a camera, and taking a picture of JayJ totally covered in flour and humiliation. By the end of the day I would be drinking the sweet nectar of revenge.

I figured our plan was fool-proof—cue Mission Impossible theme track... now! Upon our arrival in Home Ec., we would receive our cooking assignments for the day. Mrs. Smith would then proceed to bury her nose in that notebook of hers, as she does every time right after she gives us our assignments, removing any complications she would otherwise pose to the mission. I would then proceed to the cupboard to get all of the required ingredients. I would come back to our cooking station and say to Olive, in my greatest acting voice, "Oh goodness me, I have forgotten the flour." How would I know whether we would be using flour that day? I didn't. But we always used flour. Always! So I did... know that is. I would then gracefully return to the supply cupboard to collect the flour. The flour would be collected in a large Tupperware container provided to us for just such a purpose, and I would fill it to the brim. With the flour collected, I would then proceed in the general direction of our cooking station, while simultaneously removing the lid from the Tupperware container in a very stealthy, spy-like fashion. Just before reaching our cooking station, I would then proceed to "trip" while holding the Tupperware container, now without the lid, but still completely full of flour, which would accidentally—yeah, right!—end up all over the devil's spawn, aka JayJ. Upon "accidentally" spilling the completely-full Tupperware of flour all over JayJ, I will then say, "Gosh, sorry about that. Maybe you should watch where you are going." I will then step back, out of the frame, and Olive will take the picture. I will then say "Maybe we should call it the Great Flour Fiasco of 2012." Having averted all attention from me to JayJ, she will then have to deal with all the pointing, the laughing and the whispering for a change. It was the perfect plan and the perfect opportunity to further hone my spy and acting skills.

By the time Olive and I got to Home Ec., I had gone over our plan about a million times in my head. I could have done it in my sleep. Everything was going according to plan. We would be making sugar cookies, so all the flour Tupperware containers had been pre-filled to the brim. That was one less step I had to worry about, making it one step closer to victory. I said a silent "yes" and did a mental fist pump, while walking to the cupboard to get all our ingredients. I walked back to our cooking station and said, in my best acting voice, "Oh my, I forgot the flour—silly me." I even embellished it a bit with a fake laugh. Sometimes, with plans like these, you just had to wing it.

I gracefully walked back to the cupboard. I sat there for a moment just looking at the Tupperware of flour. It was so much flour. It was perfect. I glanced over my shoulder at Mrs. Smith. Just as planned, her notebook was consuming her full attention. I grabbed the flour and began walking back towards the cooking station. Everything around me seemed to slow down to a crawl. It was like I had superhero powers. I stealthily removed the lid and let it fall to the floor. Nothing was going to stop me. I was now in perfect range to dump the flour on JayJ. Soon, JayJ would be covered head to toe in flour and humiliation. Everything was working just as planned.

Until out of nowhere, Mrs. Smith looked up from the notebook and blurted out, "Miss Picklepants, I believe you dropped the lid to your flour."

It was too late to abort, I had already committed to my "trip" and the flour was already on its path towards its intended victim, JayJ Rothefeller. However, JayJ, upon hearing Mrs. Smith say my name, looked up just in time to see that she was about to get 5 pounds of white flour dumped all over her. She moved just in time while grabbing the first person she could to cover her, which in this case was none other than Jiminy. Yes, that Jiminy.

Wait! What the heck was Jiminy doing in cooking class? He was supposed to be in Wood Shop.

And just as everything had started to move in slow motion, everything now sped up, and within seconds, I was on the floor, face down, while JayJ was gaping, and Jiminy was covered—head to toe mind you—with 5 pounds of flour.

"Oh my gosh, Penny!" JayJ shrilled. "Could you possibly be any more of a klutz, Klutzy-pants?" Her voice seemed to be echoed by everyone throughout the entire 6th grade home economics class with the exception of Olive. Olive was standing there pointing to JayJ, then to me, then to Jiminy with her mouth wide open.

"But you... her... then him..." was about all she could get out.

Mrs. Smith grabbed Jiminy and took him to the office so he could get cleaned up.

"Seriously Penny, I can't believe your parents let you out of the house. You are such nuisance to society. Isn't there like an island that you could go to so the rest of us can remain safe." JayJ said.

"I hate you," was about all I could say, said in a whisper while still lying on my stomach, not daring to get up.

I tried to find Jiminy after school to apologize, but he was no-where in sight. Olive pointed out that if 5 pounds of flour had just been dumped on her, she would probably go home.

I couldn't believe it. It seemed like whenever my bad luck caught up with me to settle its next score, Jiminy was always getting caught in the middle of it.

That night, I proceeded to tell Frannie everything that had happened while we were making pickle pizza, which was fabulous. I didn't really want to tell her about how I sought revenge especially since she made me promise not to, but I couldn't lie to her. "Frannie, I am starting to think that you were right—revenge doesn't feel so good in the end."

"Well, maybe it's just one of those things that you have to learn for yourself, but at least you have learned your lesson right? No more plans of attack. The only person who ends up getting hurt is you and I think you have been hurt enough. Now, Penny Pickle-pants, I want you to promise me that you will never do this again and this time I am going to hold your hands while you make that promise so you cannot cross your fingers."

"I, Penny Picklepants of the Pottsville, Pennsylvania Picklepants clan," I said, holding out both hands, "do solemnly swear that I will never, ever, ever, ever, ever take revenge upon the devil's spawn otherwise known as JayJ Rothefeller. If I do, may my hair turn green, my eyes fall out and my arms and legs turn into jelly—pickle jelly if I can help it—thus becoming a shunned member of society with my family disowning me, my friends dis-friending, and all memories of me being erased from all thought."

"A simple, I promise, would have sufficed, but a good promise nonetheless," Frannie said, with a chuckle.

CHAPTER FIFTEEN

Dear Secret Pickle Society,

Thought you might enjoy the following list of facts about the incredible, never regretable, totally gettable, 100% edible pickle:

FACT: Cleopatra claimed pickles made her beautiful. Duh!

FACT: In Mississippi, Kool-Aid pickles have become popular with kids. You cut a dill pickle in half and soak it in Kool-Aid for a week. I've been trying to get Kool-Aid to make a pickle flavor for years!

FACT: The average American eats 8.5 lbs. of pickles a year. Whatevs! Try more like 85 lbs. of pickles a year.

FACT: When the Philadelphia Eagles thrashed the Dallas Cowboys in September 2000, many players attributed the win to one thing: guzzling down immense quantities of pickle juice.

FACT: Christopher Columbus rationed pickles to his sailors to keep them from getting scurvy. Ahoy thar, eat ye some pickles!

FACT: Napoleon loved pickles and had a contest to figure out the best way to pickle food for his troops. The reward was $250,000. Perhaps he should have rigged the contest and then put the money in an offshore account to use when he was banished.

FACT: H.J. Heinz used pickle-shaped pins to lure customers to his out-of-the-way booth at the 1893 Chicago World's Fair. By the end of the fair, he'd given out over 1,000,000 pickle pins.

FACT: Berrien Springs, Michigan hosts a parade, led by the Grand Dillmeister, who tosses out fresh pickles to parade

watchers. The last time I threw a pickle at someone, well, let's just say that my lawyer has advised me to plead the 5th.

Sincerely,
Penny Picklepants ♡

JayJ never did get in trouble for the whole assembly debacle. Principal Q asked her if she had anything to do with it and she denied everything. Of course, he believed her. It's funny how wealth makes some people believe you no matter what you say. When the junior high Principal asked the 7th grade cheerleaders, who were in charge of the slideshow, if they had anything to do with it, they claimed they didn't know how the pictures ended up in the presentation. So the issue was dropped and by the next week the cheerleaders received brand-new uniforms from an anonymous donor. I have thus decided to not try out for cheerleading next year. My pep and energy will be better suited elsewhere. Most likely chess club, but still, chess club needs pep and energy too. I just need to learn how to play chess first, but I that can wait until next year.

After the Great Flour Fiasco of 2012 plot went horribly awry, and promising Frannie that I would no long plan plots of revenge, my life took on a certain *je ne sais quoi*—Frannie taught me that one. When I explained to Olive that it was Spanish for "JayJ says squat," she just rolled her eyes and laughed, but it was true. Over the next few months JayJ didn't say much to me and I stayed well away from her, especially in Home Ec. She would occasionally roll her eyes at me, but compared to having my life utterly ruined, I'd take eye rolls gladly.

I filled my days with the usual—school, Olive and Frannie. My days usually consisted of coming home from school, doing homework, then running over to Frannie's to cook something amazing. I called our cooking "pickle-licious." Frannie just called it "fabtabulous." Acutally, I taught her that one. Anyway, after Frannie and I would finish our latest pickle concoction, most days Olive would show up after finishing her own non-pickle concoction.

Today was no exception.

There we were talking about fashion and true love, when Frannie said, "That reminds me of my days in New York."

"New York? When were you in New York?" I asked.

"When I was younger, much younger," Frannie said, with a slight laugh. "It was brilliant. Better than I could have imagined."

"Did you grow up there?" Olive asked.

"No, I..." Frannie paused, with a far-off look in her eye, and a soft sigh. "I worked in the Garment District, when I was younger—in my early twenties, just out of college."

"What did you do?" I asked.

"I designed dresses."

She what?!

"You what?!" I said almost falling out of my chair. Can you believe it? Frannie designed dresses! In New York City!

"Who did you design for?" I asked.

"I mostly worked with a boutique called Jane Derby."

Okay. I had never heard of Jane Derby, but I'm sure it was unbelievable.

"You've got to tell us stories!" I demanded.

"Oh, it was so long ago, I don't want to bore you. Besides, it's getting late," Frannie replied.

"Bore me? Are you kidding?" I said. "There is nothing more in this world I want more than to hear about your days as a designer."

"Oh, I don't know," Frannie said.

"Please, please, please," Olive and I begged. Was Olive finally coming to her senses and developing an interest in fashion? Mmm, on second thought, she's probably just interested in the history. Well, that and the potential for a love story.

"Well, I suppose one story wouldn't hurt." Frannie said, probably knowing it was certainly not going to be the last if I had anything to do with it.

"That was how I met my Frank all those years ago," Frannie started.

"Frank was the late Mr. Frankincense," I said, turning to Olive, quite pleased with my depth of inside information and knowledge into Frankincense lore.

Olive nodded solemnly. Then I could tell the gears were starting to turn. She gave me a smiling look of "His name was Frank Frankincense? Are you serious?"

To which I responded with a look of "Yeah, and your name is Olive Oliverson. What's your point?"

To which she responded with a look of "Well, your name is Penny Picklepants."

To which I responded with a look of "Exactly!"

With all that settled in a matter of split seconds, we both returned our full attention to Frannie and her story.

"There I was, right out of college, in the biggest city I had ever seen. It was marvelous. And the people I worked with were so fabulous. There was Jeannette of course, and John, whom we called Johnny. And then there was Oscar. Oscar was so gifted, and still is. We would go to fancy parties and meet important people. It seemed great, and truth be told, it was."

Frannie let out a big sigh, then got a big smile on her face.

"And so one day Oscar invited me to a party, at a friend's of his. A lot of important people were there. It was to celebrate the christening of a new building, which was magnificent. Oscar's friend was the architect, and Oscar introduced me to him. His name, of course, was Frank. Frank and I hit it off in an instant. And, as they say, the rest is history."

Then her voice trailed off, and she had an even farther look in her eye. I wanted to ask why she and Frank had not had any children, but I figured that was a question for another time.

"Do you think I could wear one of your dresses to school?" I asked, causing quite a laugh from Frannie.

"I think it better if you leave the dramatics to me, Penny," Frannie said, which I take was a no—dang it!

I could tell Frannie was getting tired. She would get that way from time to time, which made Olive worry.

"What if something's wrong?" she would ask.

In case you haven't been paying attention, Olive is something of a worrywart. And so I would have to remind her.

"That is just what old people do, they get tired."

Olive would reluctantly agree. Sometimes I think it would worry me to death to be Olive.

CHAPTER SIXTEEN

The next day I went over to Frannie's as usual. But when I got there, there was a note on her door. It read as follows:

Dear Penny,
I'm afraid I won't be able to join you today, but please help yourself to the kitchen if you would like. You know where the key is. Sorry for the late notice. I had some last minute errands to run.

Love,

Frannie

I really wasn't in the mood for cooking without Frannie, so I came back the next day. After we cooked an amazing rendition of parmesan chicken with pickles—I called it parmickle chicken, or was it chickle parmesan?—I was curious where she had gone to at the last minute. "So, where were you yesterday?" I asked.

"Oh, I just had some errands to run, nothing important," she said.

"Hmm," I said, figuring there had to be more to the story. Maybe she was going Christmas shopping for me already. Or maybe even for my birthday gift. I mean, this would be my last year before embarking upon those legendary years of epic proportions and endless glory otherwise known as the teenage years. Certainly, such a once-in-a-lifetime event required some preparation.

"So, what kind of errands?" I asked, with keen interest.

"Now Penny, a lady is never nosey."

"But I'm not a lady," I reminded Frannie.

"Well, not yet anyway," Frannie said with a reassuring smile.

"Do you know what I think?" Frannie asked, slyly changing the subject—oh, but I'm not going to let it drop that easy, not when there are gifts of monumental significance at stake.

"Hmm," I said, as I thought for a moment. "I give up."

"I think you should take me on a tour of your family's pickle plant. That's what I think."

I of course jumped at the chance. "That is a fantastic idea," I said... what was it again that I said I wasn't going to let drop? Oh well, if it was important, I'll think of it. "Really? You'd want me to take you on a tour?"

"I would love for you to, Penny."

"When should we go?"

"You tell me."

So that night I asked my dad. Of course he was excited that I would want to take Frannie on a plant tour. He said we could come any time. I called Olive and asked her if she wanted to join us, to which she replied, "I like to eat pickles, therefore, I do not want to see how they are made." It's not like it was a hot dog factory for crying out loud. Oh well. She'd seen most of it anyway.

So everything was set... well, everything except how we were going to get there. I didn't know if Frannie had a car or not.

The next day I went over to tell her the good news, as well as to ask her how we were going to get there.

"I talked with my dad, and he was so excited when I asked him if I could take you on a tour," I said.

"Oh, that is wonderful Penny. When shall we go?"

"Anytime. My dad said as long as the plant's open, we just have to show up."

"Well, there's no time like the present. Are you free to go now?"

"Yeah, actually," I said. "But there's just one problem."

"What's that?"

"How should we get there?"

"Well, I had supposed my driver would take us."

What?! Frannie had a driver? Just when I thought she couldn't get any cooler.

"You have a driver?" I asked incredulously.

"Yes, I do," she said with a laugh.

"Well, where is he?"

"Well, he does other things for me, but he's usually available whenever I need him."

Wow! Just when you think you know a person. Fifteen minutes later, Frannie's driver showed up in the most amazing car I had ever seen. She said it had belonged to her dad and it was from the 1940's, or was a 1940, and called a Lincoln Continent or something. All I know is that it was convertible and it was for sure the most amazing car I had ever seen. And just like that we were off to the pickling plant in style.

I was really excited about showing the plant to Frannie. Ever since I was kid—like, when I was 10—I would practice what I would say if I was giving tours of the plant. I would put on my mom's green blazer—yes, my mom owns a blazer that is the exact color of a pickle and it is awesome—and I would recite all the important facts, but I would throw in some jokes here and there to keep things moving along, like, "What happens when you stick a pickle in your ear? You get Pickled Hearing, of course." Or, "Why did the pickle close his eyes?" Wait for it. "Because he didn't want to see the salad dressing." Never a dill moment at the Picklepant's Pickling Plant, I always say. Finally, I end with, "Here at the Picklepant's Pickling plant, our cucumbers just relish the idea of becoming one of our pickles." When it came to tours of the pickling plant, I always brought my A-game—or should I say, my P-game… you know, my Pickle-game.

Now that I was older, however, not to mention so much more mature, I figured I would leave the jokes aside and give Frannie just a good old-fashioned tour. So we started with the selection room.

"We hand pick every one of our cucumbers," I said. "This adds to the overall cost of our pickles, but the best cucumbers make the best pickles." From there we went to the preparation room. "One misconception about pickling plants is that a cucumber becomes a pickle the moment it is placed in a jar. But this is not the case. They are actually still considered cucumbers up until the cucumber is fully pickled, which usually take around two days."

Frannie nodded her head, clearly impressed.

From there, we went to the barrel room. "Every cucumber is pickling within 24 hours of being picked. From the time we hand-pick them, wash them, and let them sit in the barrels, they could be jarred and on their way to the stores within two days. However, we find that ageing them just the right amount of time significantly enhances their flavor. So we age every batch for an undisclosed amount of time before shipping them."

"Penny, this is fascinating," Frannie said. "How do you know so much about your family's pickle plant? It doesn't seem like you spend very much time here."

"Well, I have wanted to be a professional pickle taster for my entire life. I used to spend a lot more time here when I was a kid. My actual home was more like a second home compared to the plant."

"Well, to say I am impressed with your vast knowledge on how this plant works is an understatement. But I wonder if I could stump you with a hard question, let me think for a moment." She suddenly snapped her fingers and said, "I know. Why are pickle lids so hard to open?"

Ha! Like that was going to stump me. "No offense, but that's an easy one. While making a lid, our lid maker applies a sealing compound to the inside of the lid. When its placed, the lid is heated with steam to soften the compound, making it easier to form the hermetic seal required to keep bacteria from growing inside the jar. But most importantly, a vacuum is created when the jar is heated and the lid is placed, which is why the lid is sucked down into the jar before opening, keeping the pickles fresh. This also happens to make the lids really hard to twist off."

"Well, Penny, color me impressed. You really know this factory inside and out. Your love of your family's pickle plant really shows."

"Thanks Frannie. Actually, one day I hope that I can run the factory. It's been in our family for generations and I hope it will be that way for generations to come. Patrick is being groomed to take it over, but I secretly hope that he will turn it over to me. I have the passion for the pickles like no other in my family."

"Well, I like to imagine what this factory would be capable of in your well-abled hands."

I didn't know what to say. It was a novel feeling having someone place so much confidence in me.

"Thanks Frannie, that means a lot coming from you."

Of course I gave her a hug.

"Now. Are you ready for the best part?" I asked.

"What would that be?"

"The Sampling Room!"

The day ended with us eating way too many pickles, if that's even possible. I challenged Frannie to a pickle eating contest—my personal best was 10 baby pickles in 1 minute—but she declined the offer.

"You know Penny, with sampling all these delicious pickles and Halloween coming up, I couldn't help thinking you should dress up as a pickle," Frannie said, with a hint of sarcasm. At least I think it was sarcasm. Okay, that better have been sarcasm.

"No way!" I said. "Only kids dress up like that kind of stuff." Of course right when I said that, Patrick walked into the Sampling Room with Ginger. Why were they at the factory?

"Whatever little sis," Patrick said. "You dressed up like a pickle just last year."

"Oh Pay-at-rick, y'all so funny," Ginger said.

Do you think it would be okay if I said, "Oh Gee-in-jar, y'all so annoying"? Better not. Patrick is awfully close to the knives.

"Patrick, shut up!" I said. "Why are you even here?"

"Ginger wanted to see the plant so I brought her."

I highly doubt that his tour was as good as mine, but I figured we both knew it so why say it. Turning back my attention to Frannie, "Well, Frannie, to answer your question about Halloween, I was actually hoping that you would let me wear one of your dresses. I mean, I know they are amazing, so I would take really,

really, really good care of it and I wouldn't let anything happen to it. Please, please, please!"

"Well, how about I think about it."

"If you let me wear one of your dresses, I promise I won't ask for anything else ever again," I said, eliciting quite the laugh from Frannie.

"Well in that case," Frannie said, with a smile. "If you promise to take good care of it, I suppose it wouldn't hurt, seeing that they're just sitting in an old trunk gathering dust."

"Oh thank you so much Frannie," I said giving her a big hug, eliciting an "Oh!" and another laugh from Frannie.

"Do you think it would be okay if Olive wore one as well?"

"I thought you weren't going to ask Frannie for anything else if she said yes," Patrick said.

Big brothers are so annoying.

"Go away Patrick!" I said.

"I suppose it wouldn't be fair if Olive didn't get to wear one as well," Frannie said.

I of course turned around to look at Patrick and stick my tongue out at him. Two can play this immature game.

"Olive will be so excited," I said giving Frannie another hug. "I can't wait to tell her."

CHAPTER SEVENTEEN

Dear Secret Pickle Society,

In honor of Thanksgiving, I am sending you the recipe to my amazing pickle stuffing, called puffing, or stuffickle—still undecided—but whatever its name, I think it is going to catch on like wild fire and overtake the nation. I hope that your Thanksgiving tables will be graced with my... piffing—yes, piffing. And you're welcome!

* 2 loaves high quality sandwich bread (Italian or French)
* 8 Tablespoon butter
* 1-1/2 pounds sage sausage, removed from casing
* 1 large onion, finely chopped
* 4 large stalks celery, finely chopped
* 2 cloves garlic, minced
* 1/4 cup minced fresh sage (or 2 tsp dried sage)
* 1/2 cup diced dill pickles
* 32 ounce chicken or turkey broth, preferably homemade
* 3 whole eggs
* 1/2 cup minced parsley leaves
* Kosher salt and freshly ground black pepper

For the directions, I'm afraid you'll just have to contact me.

Sincerely,
Penny Picklepants ♡

Okay, so I know what you are thinking: "Wow! Penny and Olive must have an amazing Halloween night planned." And I would respond, "We most certainly do! If you consider a night of trick-or-treating as amazing a festivity as I do!" I may be on the cusp of adulthood, but I am not ready to give up Halloween. Hello? Free candy! It's going to be amazing.

Typically, we meet up at my house, down a big heaping bowl of chili—Oh! That gives me an idea for a recipe, chili with pickles, or should I say, chilickle!—and then we trick-or-treat until we can no longer carry our bags of candy. We have used pillowcases in the past, but it's always such a pain to carry that amount of candy in a bag without handles. So we got smart this year and got some reusable grocery bags the same ones that are meant to carry about 20 lbs. of frozen goods. But instead of 20 lbs. of boring good-for-you food, they are going to be filled with 20 lbs. of sugary sweet goodness.

I heard a rumor that Jiminy was going to have a big Halloween party this year. I kept hoping that Olive and I would get an invite, but knowing that Jiminy and JayJ were together. I doubted either of us would be on the list of invitees. And since the flour incident, the bleacher incident, not to mention the bike incident, Jiminy tended to scare easily around me as of late. I certainly can't blame him. Still, it makes me go red in the cheeks whenever I see him get a little jumpy when he sees me. Of course JayJ just laughs, says something stupid, and then everybody laughs. I just can't figure out if Jiminy is jumpy to be mean or to be safe. I am hoping it's to be safe.

With one week to go before Halloween, Olive and I, as well as Frannie, sat down and figured out our best route to maximize our candy opportunities.

"I say we hit up all the rich areas first and then our neighborhood last," I said. "That way we will have the first pick of the king-size candy bars and then can go for the little stuff after that."

Of course Olive didn't agree, "No, no, no. We've always hit our neighborhood first. Our neighborhood has shorter drive ways and we can hit more doors quicker and faster. The rich neighborhoods have huge driveways, thus they will cost us valuable time just getting to the front door."

Because we couldn't reach an agreement, we let Frannie decide for us.

"Well, going for the quick kill certainly does make sense," Frannie said, nodding to Olive. "But perhaps going after the king-sized candy bars while you still have the energy makes the most sense, so that you could run up and down the drive ways and be back in your neighborhood before you know it."

After Olive's begrudged "Fine!", Frannie looked at me and winked. I think she liked me the best, but I didn't want to hurt Olive's feelings. So I said, "See? Frannie agrees with me because she likes me the best." Of course Olive rolled her eyes and Frannie quickly changed the subject.

With our countdown to Halloween to just four days, I found myself daydreaming about king-sized candy bars and all the sugary goodness of trick-or-treating. So much so, that I almost missed Jiminy calling my name at school.

"Hey Penny," Jiminy called. "Penny, wait! I have something for you."

Unfortunately, what I didn't miss was the light pole directly in front of my path. WHAMO! And right down on my keister again. I had wanted to act as nonchalantly as possible while I was turning around to look at Jiminy. Unfortunately, I hadn't really practiced the "turn your head and look back while continuing to walk forward without running into any stationary objects directly in front of you" routine.

"Holy cow! Are you okay?" Jiminy asked, running up to me, or rather, running up to be by my side.

Dang it! Why do I keep making such a fool of myself in front of Jiminy? Just play it cool for once, Picklepants! Just play it cool.

"Oh, hey Jiminy," I said. "Yeah, um… so, hey… uh, what were we talking about?" Was that cool?

"Haha, haha," came the sound of a laugh of a most despicable creature. "That had to be the funniest thing I have ever seen," JayJ said.

I had decided, perhaps right then and there, that JayJ was just like the Teenage Mutant Ninja Turtles. Except she was only a pre-teenager, the only thing she was ninja at was destroying my happiness, and she just smelled like a turtle.

"JayJ," Jiminy said in a give-it-a-rest sort of way. My knight in shining armor!

"Whatever," JayJ said. "I'm just sorry I didn't get *that* on video. That had all the makings of a classic Picklepants moment." She then laughed again, causing an eruption of laughter among her wannabes. "Let's go girls."

Finally! Now, it was just me and Jiminy, like it was supposed to be.

"Oh man, you might want to get that checked," Jiminy said.

"Get what checked?" I asked.

That was when I felt the searing pain on the right side of my forehead.

"That goose egg on your forehead," Jiminy said. "It's huge, and growing."

Oh, great! Make a fool of yourself: check. Right in front of Jiminy: check and check. Morph yourself into a hideous creature right before Jiminy's eyes: check, check and check. Sigh!

"Are you gonna be okay?" Jiminy asked.

"Yeah, I'm fine," I said, as he helped me up on my feet again.

"Okay, well, anyway," Jiminy said, while blushing. Yes! He was blushing! "I just wanted to give you an invitation to my Halloween party this Saturday. You didn't have any plans did you? I mean I know they wouldn't be trick-or-treating plans, because we all know we are getting a little too old for that."

I guess right then wouldn't be the right time to tell him about the trick-or-treating map that Olive and I had revised 6.7 times.

"Oh yeah, right, totally. Trick-or-treating is so for kids, which we are so not." Oh, but truth be told, I still so loved the sugar, coated in sugar, deep-fried in more sugar. Sigh! I guess it was the one and only thing left holding me back, keeping me on the "cusp" of maturity instead of fully entering and standing squarely within the realm of all things grown-up and mature.

"What about JayJ, though?" I asked.

"What about her?"

"Isn't she going to be a little upset if you invite me?" Please say she isn't invited. Please say she isn't invited. Oh please, oh please, oh please!

"Why would she be upset?" Jiminy asked. "I mean, we're just friends. Besides, she actually really likes you."

Do you think he noticed my jaw dropping to floor? Okay first he and JayJ are just friends. Yes! Mental double-fist pump. Yes, yes, and yes! And a whole lot of "uh huh, that's right, uh huh, that's right." And what was that part about she likes me? So I guess this would be a bad time to tell him about my theory of JayJ being the devil's spawn? She just laughed at me for running into a pole for crying out loud. She hated me.

"Sure," I said nice and confused-like, "we are regular besties." I was about to point out that I said that with a hint of sarcasm rolled in a whole heck of a lot of "whatevs," but then he spoke before I could.

"I know you think she doesn't like you, and sometimes I can see why, but she was just telling me the other day how she wants to become friends and she thinks that the Halloween party would be the perfect time for you guys to make a new start."

Alrighty then.

"So, will I see you at the party then?"

"Yeah," I said. "Of course. But what about Olive?"

"Oh, I meant to say you both were invited," he said handing me another invite. "Could you give her her invite?"

It was hard concentrating on homework, let alone cooking that night. I kept going over all the scenarios with Olive and Frannie.

"But why didn't he give me the invitation himself?" Olive asked.

Picky, picky, picky. "I have no idea. All I know is that there is no way JayJ wants to be friends," I said.

"You know, Penny, maybe JayJ has finally seen the error of her ways," Frannie said.

Yeah right!

"Do you think it's possible?" Olive asked.

"Not even remotely," I said.

"So did Jiminy say anything else about me, like what I was going to dress up as or what our colors will be when we get married?"

"Olive, focus. And you aren't going to marry him. I am. Anyway I think that we just need to be cautious at the party. I have a feeling that girl is up to something."

"Penny stop being paranoid. Maybe she really does want to start over and be friends."

Whoa! Olive the fussbudget calling *me* paranoid? Well, okay, maybe I can get a little worked up from time to time. But seriously, Olive is the worrywart. Really, she is. Anyway, even though I was skeptical behind JayJ's motives, deep in the furthest recesses of my mind laid a dormant thought that perhaps there was some possibility JayJ really did want to be friends. Maybe, I thought, she's just been using her insults as a defense mechanism to protect herself because she is so intimidated by my own awesomeness. I mean, hello! Jiminy did come and personally hand me an invitation. Clearly, if my magnetic personality was too much of a draw for Jiminy to resist, then how could JayJ resist wanting to be friends with me? And Ginger had told me now and then that JayJ really did want to be friends and that JayJ felt that I didn't like her. I would typically answer her with, "That's because I don't." She would then laugh, slap my leg and tell me I was "hi-uss-terical." I think she was trying to say hysterical, but I was never quite sure.

An hour before the party, Olive and I met over at Frannie's to get ready. We had already picked out our dresses, the hats, and even the gloves, all thanks to Frannie's personal time-warped closet, aka the antique steamer trunk in her attic. She set our hair and she even let us wear some of her Mary Jane kitten heel pumps that matched the dresses, which had to be stuffed with tissue paper to help them fit. To say that we looked like we were straight from the 1950's is an understatement. We were 1950's HOT!

"First of all, you both look amazing," Frannie said. "And you both could be models. You are both so pretty. But please be careful with these dresses. I know I will never wear them again, but they still hold so many memories for me, so many good memories."

"Frannie, first of all, thank you so much for letting us wear your dresses," I said. "But trust us, we will not let anything happened to these amazing dresses, I promise."

After we arrived at the party—and after 10 minutes of "Ohhs" and "Ahhs" over our costumes (yes, Jiminy was so totally checking me out)—things settled down and we started to do what you always do at 6th grade Halloween parties: sit there looking at each other wondering what to do.

After the bowl of Doritos had all been eaten and after the 15th cycle of Monster Mash and Dead's Man Party had played on Jiminy's stereo, JayJ decided to take things into her own hands.

"Okay, I think it's time to play some games," she said. "How about ghost in the graveyard? But this time we will actually be playing in the graveyard."

The graveyard wasn't all that far from Jiminy's house. But still, it was the last place I wanted to be on any night, let alone Halloween night. I mean, I know the spirits don't come out and all that stuff—at least, I hope they don't—but still it's Halloween. There's a full moon. And well, cemeteries are freaking scary. Maybe I should say I will stay back and hand out the candy to the kids that are trick-or-treating.

"I know some of you may be scared," JayJ said, then looking squarely at me added, "Penny. But no one is staying behind to hand out candy to the trick-or-treaters. Jiminy's parents can do that."

"What are you even talking about?" I said. "I wasn't even thinking that. I was thinking... thinking... let's do this! Cemetery, here we come." I quickly turned from JayJ to Olive and said, "Did that sound convincing? Because I didn't feel convinced." Olive gave me a reassuring smile with a little head nod. Then we left.

We gathered at the house across from the cemetery gates. From there we entered in groups. We figured we couldn't all go in all at once because the police patrol the entrance to the cemetery to make sure kids don't go in and play games on Halloween night. Everyone had entered the cemetery except for Olive, me, JayJ and one of her friends.

"Okay," JayJ said, "meet us at the Pott Mausoleum,"—the Potts for whom Pottsville was named—"We'll be waiting for you there. Maybe we can conjure up Mr. Potts' spirit and ask him a few questions." Of course JayJ would recommend this. "Let's not," would be my recommendation. JayJ and her friend then disappeared into the fog. Did I mention there was fog?! Agh!

It figured that Olive and I were the last ones to enter, all alone. "Olive, let's just go home right now. We could still get a few hours of trick-or-treating in. We'll just tell everybody that we got lost. Nobody would even know that we left."

"I don't know Penny," Olive said. "Let's just go find them, stay for 5 minutes, and then go trick-or treating. We have to show them we're not scared."

We did?

We walked hand in hand towards the cemetery gates, which was oozing scariness and fog. I swear I could hear ghosts moaning, but Olive told me I was just imagining it. But, as you well know, I never imagine anything.

When we reached the gates, there were no police in sight, so we strolled right in. Okay, we didn't exactly stroll right on in, that would suggest that we were excited to be there. We actually were huddled shoulder to shoulder, legs shaking so hard we could hardly walk, while holding hands.

"Olive, do you even know where Mr. Potts' mausoleum is?"

"No. I thought you knew."

"Olive, I don't know anything about anything and now at a time like this you think I know something about something?"

"Could I get that in writing?" she said, with a little smirk. Oh, now Olive decides to become the witty one. "Let's just think for minute."

"Oh, now you want to think? It's a little past the time for thinking when you've already entered a cemetery."

"Penny! Calm down. We are both scared, but we can do this. There are no other mausoleums in the Pottsville cemetery so let's just look for the big building with Potts written on it."

"Sounds like a good plan, if we could see!" Even with a full moon the cemetery was creepily dark because the huge trees blocked out any hope of light from the moon. "Seriously, how are we supposed to read if we can't see? I think we should just turn around and go home while we still can."

"Penny, if we turn around now, JayJ will make fun of you for the rest of the school year. Or longer! Let's just find this stupid mausoleum, prove that we are not cowards, and then go straight home, okay?"

"Fine!"

I knew Olive was right and seeing how she is right 99.999% of the time, I doubted this would be the one-thousandth of a percent of the time that she was wrong.

We continued to walk huddled together, blindly calling out in hushed voices for the others. We didn't want to yell too loud in case the police were patrolling—or worse, the ghosts were listening.

I just had to chuckle, however, at the mental picture of two girls whispering people's names in a cemetery as if we were two ghosts straight from the 1950s. I was about to tell Olive how ironic this whole scenario was when she blurted out, "WE FOUND IT!"

"Shhhhhh!" I said.

"Sorry, we found it! Look," Olive said, pointing to a creepy looking building in the middle of the cemetery. There, standing in all its scary glory, was the Potts mausoleum.

"Wait!" I said. "Where is everybody? You don't think they went into the mausoleum, do you?"

"Pretty sure they keep the door locked, but it wouldn't hurt. Let's do it together. I don't want to wake up the spirit of Mr. Potts."

"Well if your yelling didn't already wake him up already." What the heck was I talking about? I sounded like I wasn't scared, oh, but how I was. We were two girls in front of a creepily huge metal door in the middle of a dark and dreary cemetery. I was wondering what the heck we were doing, when I blurted, "Okay on the count of three we will open the door together. Okay, one, two... th... th..."

"Will you just say three and get this over with."

"Olive! You might not be scared half to death, but my legs are shaking so hard it sounds like I am tap dancing, okay? So I will say three when I am good and ready."

"Well, you just said three. Does that count? Or do we have to start all over again?"

I would have given her a total crusty, but seeing that we could barely see at all combined with the fact that my eyes were closed because I was so scared, I decided to skip the crusty and just count to three. "Okay, here we go again and yes this time I will say three." After a brief pause, I said, "One." After another brief pause, I said,

"Two."

"Just say it!" Olive said.

"Fine! One, two, three!"

I'm not exactly sure what happened next, seeing how my eyes were closed. But the next thing I knew, I was wet, cold and I could hear laughing. Wait, did ghosts have a sense of humor?

"Did you seriously think you guys were cool enough to be invited to Jiminy's party?" a voice said, followed by further laughing.

Huh, that's weird. The ghost that just spoke sounds an awful like JayJ. Wait! JAYJ?

"Go home Picklepants. Nobody wants you here, especially Jiminy. And in case you were wondering this was his idea." And then I heard the sounds of laughter fading into the darkness.

Somehow Olive and I managed to find our way out. It's amazing how much clearer your mind thinks when you just want to get out of a place. By the time we made it out to the street lamp to toll the damage, we just stared at each other. Everything we had borrowed from Frannie was ruined.

"What just happened?" Olive asked. "All I remember is that we were about to open the mausoleum."

I was so dumbfounded that all I could do was just look at Olive. I couldn't find anything to say. I was literally speechless. It wasn't until somebody drove by and yelled, "Hey, Carrie! Love the costume," that I finally snapped out of it. Wait! Why did someone think I looked like their friend Carrie? I mean, how could someone even tell it was their friend Carrie if she had red paint dumped all over her?

"I just can't believe that Jiminy would do this to us," I said. "I guess I was wrong about him. You know what, Olive? You can have him and I hope you have the worst wedding ever! And I hope you make his life miserable! And I hope you guys have really ugly children!"

"Are you kidding me? He's all yours."

"Actually he is perfect for JayJ. And that is last I will ever talk about him. But what are we going to say to Frannie? She is going to kill us!"

"Let's go home and see if we can't wash this paint off. Let's just hope that they used a water-based paint," Olive said. "If they did then we should be fine. If they didn't, we are so in trouble."

After three days of hand scrubbing, four trips to different dry cleaners, each refusing to take the garments—"Oh honey, nothing's ever gonna take out that red paint. You just have to learn to live with it," being their common response—as well as an additional day or two of procrastination, I finally decided that I was going to have to tell Frannie what happened. I had been putting it off all week hoping beyond hope that something, anything would get the red paint out. The only luck on our side was that the paint didn't get in our hair. The gloves, dresses, and hats took the brunt of it, saving us from washing red paint out of our hair for the next three months. But to be honest, I would have rather had to wash out red paint from my hair for the next three months than have to tell Frannie her dresses were ruined. And it wasn't even us who had ruined them, but I doubt JayJ and Jiminy would be confessing anytime soon. They would probably deny we were even at the party or ever invited. I could just hear JayJ saying, "As if we would invite them!"

To add insult to injury, Jiminy came up to me on Monday and had the nerve to ask me what happened to us at the cemetery. I gave him my best crusty and told him to never talk to me again. I turned around and walked away. Take that, jerk!

And so the day finally arrived that we had to explain to Frannie what had happened to her beautiful dresses. I had been telling her all week that I hadn't been feeling good, which to be honest wasn't that far off. I had been having stomach cramps just thinking about what had happened. But I couldn't put it off forever.

As I walked slowly to Frannie's house, with the ruined clothes in one of the reusable grocery bags, I started to think of what I was going to say. I thought about pulling a "I only speak Spanish now" routine, however, I wasn't sure how to say "I only speak Spanish now" in Spanish. I thought about hanging the dresses on the door knob and then doorbell ditching, and later saying that a thief had stolen the dresses, must have ruined them, and by sheer intuition realized where to return them. But then I realized, even I wouldn't believe that story. By the time I arrived at Frannie's house I decided I would just say, "Wait! What? There's red paint on everything? Well, it must have been there when you gave them to us." Then again, I knew Frannie was a smart lady (dang it!) and little would get by her.

With my heart pounding practically out of my chest, my palms clammy for real this time, and my knees shaking just a smidge, I rang the doorbell. I kept my eyes closed, because I was secretly hoping that if I kept my eyes shut Frannie wouldn't see the red paint. I know it didn't make sense, but there was nothing else left. Well, I guess there was keeping the bag hidden behind my back as long as possible.

"Why, hello, Penny. What a nice surprise," Frannie said. "Are you feeling better now?"

I just stood there, not breathing, my eyes closed, my mouth pursed.

"Is everything alright dear?" Frannie asked. "What do you have behind your back?"

Oh boy! "Olive and I wore your dresses to Jiminy's party and everybody thought we looked amazing, and then JayJ, the spawn of the devil, suggested that we play ghost in the graveyard, but instead of just playing in Jiminy's backyard like a normal person would do, she had the brilliant idea of us going into the city cemetery and playing it in there, and we were supposed to meet everybody at the Potts Mausoleum, but we had to go into the cemetery in small groups because of the police that patrol the cemetery, so Olive and I went in together, and we couldn't see anything because it is pitch black in that cemetery, as if it isn't creepy enough alone, and then we got lost, but then we found it, and then I didn't want to count to three, but Olive wanted me to, and then I finally did, and then… and then… and then somebody poured red paint all over us and we ruined your dresses."

At that point, I burst out crying.

"Penny, darling, I didn't catch a single word of that. Won't you come in and I will fix us something to eat. Bad news is always easier to take while eating something delicious."

I took a big breath and walked in to tell her the story in slower, less hyper-ventilating detail. "Frannie, I am not even sure how it happened," I said. "I said three, a number I now despise, and I tried to open the mausoleum's door and then next thing I know we had red paint all over us. Apparently Jiminy had it planned for a while. Maybe it was his way of getting back at me for the Flour Fiasco of 2012, a little overkill I would say. I'm so sorry Frannie.

It's all my fault. If I had listened to you and not tried to get back at JayJ, then I wouldn't have dumped flour all over Jiminy, and then he wouldn't have dumped red paint all over me and ruin your dresses." I couldn't say any more without the threat of unleashing more tears. I couldn't even look at Frannie. I was so upset with myself. "And then, I come here, and… and…." Oh boy, here come the tears. "And you act like you're not even mad."

"Oh no my dear, you did nothing wrong. What upsets me is that there is a person who would do such a thing to you and Olive. Whoever did this did a horrible thing. But at the end of the day, the dresses are still ruined and the culprit has to live with the guilt of their actions. Sometimes living with guilt is the worst punishment of all."

"I am so sorry that we ruined your beautiful dresses," I said, choking back the tears.

"Penny, they're just things. Besides, you didn't think I would let you wear my nicest dresses did you?"

"But all the memories they hold," I said, trailing off.

"Now, we will have new memories. From now on we will always remember the Halloween that you got red paint dumped on you and we will laugh about it, at least one day we will. Now enough about the dresses, what are we going to cook today?"

And just like that, the Red Paint Fiasco of 2012 was put to rest. Maybe Frannie was right—in a few years Olive and I would take out the dresses and have a good laugh. But for now, I still felt like crying.

CHAPTER EIGHTEEN

Dear Secret Pickle Society,

The art of fresh-packed pickles is being lost. Not because people don't like pickles—I mean, that's just crazy talk. No, it's because of the process takes a lot of work and a lot of time. But at the Picklepants Pickling Plant, we know it's worth the time and effort.

When canning fresh-packed pickles, you, the pickler, must place the cucumbers into a jar with dill, garlic, and spices using a low-temperature process. Why a low-temperature process? Well, you want your pickles to be crispy, because nobody, and I mean NOBODY likes lifeless, limp pickles—that's just more crazy talk.

After placing the cucumbers into the jar with dill, garlic and spices, you pour in the pickling solution. You then place the jars in a canner, which instead of the small stovetop ones you may have used, we have giant industrial ones that are in the ground.

After the jars have been processed and sealed, the jars of pickles must sit on a shelf for weeks, not hours, not minutes. WEEKS! Sometimes the hardest part of life is waiting.

Sincerely,
Penny Picklepants ♡

P.S. The Picklepants Pickling Plant is in trouble. Please, if there is anything you can do to help our little plant, we would so much appreciate it.

Since Halloween, I decided to stop worrying so much about school and to focus more on helping my parents save the pickle plant—not that I ever worried too much about school in the first place. It's hard to help, though, when they never talk to me about it. Whenever they do talk about it and I happen to walk into the room, they stop, look at me, quickly turn their frowns upside down, and ask, "Do you need something dear?" which apparently is Parent for "Can you please leave the room. Mommy and Daddy are having a grown up discussion." Hey! I know another foreign language. I speak Parent. Well, okay—I don't speak it, but I definitely understand it. I would so much like to say, "I know what is going on and I can only help if you let me, but since you won't I am going to help anyway." But I don't say anything.

Since I have stopped worrying about school and altogether ignoring Jerk-face—aka Jiminy, which he will now and forevermore be known as, but since I never think about Jerk-face you will never hear me talk about Jerk-face... jerk!—the situation with JayJ has become somewhat bearable. When I say bearable, I mean I just ignore her and her crusty looks. I also try to ignore her crusty sayings like, "Penny what's that in your hair? It looks like red-paint," and "Look everybody, it's Penny Paintpants." Yes, I have gone from Penny Peed-her-pants to Penny Paintpants. Actually, it's quite an improvement, and with Thanksgiving coming up, I will have a JayJ-free five-day weekend.

The Friday before Thanksgiving Mrs. Smith dropped a bomb on us in Home Ec. She wants us to contribute something major to our Thanksgiving Feast. When I raised my hand and asked if buying pies from a local restaurant was considered a major contribution she responded with a snarky, "Absolutely not!" Turns out our contribution had to be something we cooked from scratch.

"What do you think you are going to cook for Thanksgiving dinner, Penny?" Olive asked.

"No idea," I said. "I'm still trying to figure out how to boil water."

"I thought you were past learning how to boil water with Frannie. In fact, didn't you just tell me last week how much you enjoy cooking?"

LAST WEEK'S CONVERASTION:

Me: "Wow, cooking is a lot of fun... who knew?"

Olive: "I did."

Ugh! I hate when Olive is right in her flashbacks. I need to find a friend who doesn't have such a good memory.

"Okay," I said in my best woe-is-me voice. "Fine! I do like cooking. I was just looking forward to a low-stress week and to leave all the cooking and stress of Thanksgiving to my mom."

"Wow, so sweet and considerate."

"I'm going over to Frannie's today—maybe we could figure something out together."

When I got home, I told my mom my most un-awesome news ever. She got really excited and showed me a new recipe she had found for something called a turkey roll. She then went into a ten minute explanation of how to do a turkey roll when she said it would only take one minute. Isn't that always the case with parents?

"So you take a turkey breast, pound it flat, you put the stuffing in the turkey, roll it, then wrap it with bacon. I was thinking of doing this instead of our traditional turkey. What do you think? Do you want to do it?"

"Sure, right after I finish with my courses at 'Le Cordon Bleu' in Paris." That's sarcasm for "I don't think so," but I don't think my mom needed an explanation.

"Listen, ever since Halloween you seem a little off, a little bit sad. Maybe this could help you get your groove back by focusing on something fun and exciting."

"Mom—first of all, who even talks like that? Groove back? Seriously? Secondly, I would hardly call cooking a turkey roll fun and exciting." Deep down I knew she was right. I hate when that happens. "But maybe you are right. I'll talk about it with Frannie."

"So you will do it?" she asked excitedly, the biggest grin covering her face. How could I turn her down?

"Let's just see how the test run goes." Dumbest thing I ever said. I should have known that the experiment would go perfect with Frannie's help. We cooked it on the grill to give it a little bit more flavor and it was so delicioso.

I decided that Frannie had to be a part of our Thanksgiving Feast. I mean, she had just spent the last three hours helping me with the main course. How could I not invite her? Plus, I didn't want her to be alone for Thanksgiving.

Naturally, my mom was ecstatic when I announced that I would cook the turkey roll. When I told her that I had invited Frannie, she grabbed me by the shoulders, smiled and got a tear in her eye, then hugged me.

As the Thanksgiving week quickly passed, I was starting to look more and more forward to Thanksgiving Day. I even got in the mood Wednesday morning, when I woke up, to start cooking. I figured if I prepared the turkey roll the day before, all I would have to think about the day of was cooking it. Best plan ever! Okay, I know what you are thinking: the last time I said that—aka the Flour Fiasco—it turned into just another fiasco—but holidays are completely different. Nothing bad ever happens on holidays.

With my metaphorical party balloon filled to the hilt with helium, I bounced down the stairs in my super chipper mood so happy to start preparing the turkey roll. Then I heard chit-chat and laughter—Ginger-like laughter. Ugh! My metaphorical happy balloon just popped. Better yet, it just flew around the room making that pffflllllgggghhh sound balloons make when you let them go right after filling them up. By the time I got to the kitchen I couldn't help blurting out, "What are you doing here, Ginger?" in a really snotty voice.

"Penny, don't be rude. Ginger is here because she wants to help get our Thanksgiving ready."

"Mom, I'm not being rude." Okay, I was, but I couldn't let my mom know that. "I'm just asking why Ginger is HERE, and not at her own house helping her mom get ready for their own dinner?"

"Oh, Mee-suzz Pick-ul-pay-ints, iss oh-kay-eee, I think Peh-nee is a riot." I started to tap my foot, with my arms crossed waiting for a really good answer when Ginger said, in her really annoying accent, "Pam, you didn't tell Peh-nee the good news? Peh-nee, we're all spending Thanksgiving with y'all."

"And by y'all, you mean your family, the Rothefellers, and only the Rothefellers, right? Not including my family, the Picklepants family, right? Please say right, right?"

"Oh Peh-nee. See what I meeen, y'all are such a riot. No silly, my whole fam-uh-leee is comin' on over here to your place and we are eatin' together."

All I could manage to think was "NOOOOOOOOOOO!" and then "NOOOOOOOOOO!" and then some more "NOOOOO-OOOOOO!" in my head.

"Penny, quit yelling," my mom warned.

Oh man, did I say that out loud? I totally didn't mean to. "Did I just say that out loud? Because I totally meant to!" I said.

Are you kidding me?! I have to spend Thanksgiving Day with

JayJ? Okay, settle down, I told myself. Take the advice of Frannie and be a lady. Smile and say things like, "Oh, that is just fantastic. I can't wait to get caught up with JayJ. She is such a delight." Okay, here goes: "Oh that sounds utterly morbid. I can't wait to glare at JayJ from across the table." Oh wait! That came out… exactly how I wanted it to. "I'm going to go upstairs," I said, while still thinking, "NOOOOOOO!" Wait, I think I'm still saying it out loud.

"Penny, stop yelling, and go take a shower," my mom said. "Then come down and help me and Ginger get ready for tomorrow. Trust me—you have nothing to worry about."

Yeah because I have nothing else to worry about than my stupid turkey roll. Oh yeah, I don't have to worry about the fact that I have to spend my favorite holiday (after Christmas), with the person I despise the very most. And I don't have to worry about the fact that the boy I have had a crush on since pre-school dumped red paint all over me on my other favorite holiday (after Christmas and Thanksgiving). I don't have to worry about the fact that my dad may be losing the pickle factory just in time for my most favorite holiday, Christmas. And I certainly don't need to worry about the fact that my life may be in absolute ruins by my very most favorite holiday of all, my birthday (after Christmas, Thanksgiving, Halloween and St. Patricks' Day… and yes, I left Valentine's Day out on purpose—and yes, we are part Irish… at least I think we are).

"Yeah you're right, Mom, nothing to worry about. I'll be down in two-shakes of a lamb's tail."

"Okay, sounds great!"

What? If she couldn't pick up that hint of sarcasm with a pinch of "whatevs," then so much for her superhuman mom powers.

When I finally came back down to the kitchen—three hours

later—Ginger had finally left. Actually, I just waited until I heard the "un-kay guyz's, see y'alls tuh-mar-uh," then I came down and Mom and I started on the turkey roll.

"Listen Penny, I know there have been a lot of things on your mind and I know you don't want to spend Thanksgiving with JayJ, but just smile. Who knows, you might just enjoy yourself, maybe even make a new friend."

Why are moms so pushy to make friends for you? "Mom, she is the devil's spawn. I will never be friends with her—and to be honest I can't figure out why Dad spends so much time with Mr. Rothefeller."

"What do you mean?" my mom said, looking up from cutting some celery. "How did you know that?"

"Mom, I may be younger than you, but I'm not stupid—I see things, I hear things. But why, OH WHY, do they have to come here tomorrow? You know that Thanksgiving is my favorite holiday."

"You mean after Christmas, your birthday, but before Halloween, and St. Patrick's Day?"

Okay, I'm impressed, but it doesn't mean she has superhuman mom powers. "Mom, seriously, they are going to ruin Thanksgiving."

"Penny, the Rothefellers are good people and Mr. Rothefeller has given your father some really good ideas for the plant."

"Well, I have good ideas for the plant too, but Dad never listens to me. And so what if Mr. Rothefeller has good business ideas, it doesn't mean they need to eat Thanksgiving Dinner with us. Don't they belong to a country club or something?"

Right then Parker walked into the kitchen, "Actually, they were going to go to the country club, until Mom insisted that they eat with us. Like Mom always says, 'Thanksgiving is best when you share it with your friends,' and you know what, Penny? I think she's right."

I decided to not call out Parker on his blatant buttering up, probably for the latest DS game he just had to have. "Great, then I will be spending Thanksgiving with Olive."

"No you won't. Besides, isn't Frannie coming tomorrow?" my mom pointed out.

Okay—at least I will have one friend with me.

Despite being upset, the afternoon went by fairly quickly. It was fun preparing the turkey roll with my mom. Who knew moms could be so fun? We started talking about my cooking blog and I told her how much I enjoyed writing on it about my cooking adventures with Frannie.

"The good thing is now my recipes don't include a generous heaping of burnt," I said. "I just really enjoy writing about everything, like why I include pickles in all my recipes and my life as a pickle heiress."

"Guess that makes me the Pickle Queen?" my mom said, making us both laugh.

"You'll always be a queen to me, Mom," I said, and I meant it, which totally got me a shopping trip. Score! Who knew being nice to your mom had so many advantages.

"So is your recipe ready to be the crown jewel of our Thanksgiving Day feast?" my mom asked.

"Mom, you know I am always ready to be the center of attention," I replied with a smile. And before we knew it, the turkey roll was ready.

It's amazing what a good night's sleep can do. I dreamt I was the queen of a feast and JayJ was the servant girl who dropped my pie, on herself of course, so I sent her to jail. It was fabulous. I woke up happy and ready for the day. So I had to spend Thanksgiving with JayJ and her family—things could be worse. I wasn't going to let it get in my way of having the best Thanksgiving ever. Yeah, you heard me—EVER!

After a quick breakfast, we headed to the movie theatres, per tradition, to watch the latest Hollywood blockbuster, an animated one this time around, while eating popcorn. I glanced down the row and looked at my family watching the movie. With a smile on my face, I thought how lucky I was. Turning my attention back on the movie, I thought, "What could possibly go wrong today?"

When we got home, the mad dash began to finish the last minute details before the Rothefellers arrived. My dad fired up the grill for me because he didn't trust me to do it. "The last time you started the grill you left it right next to the side of the house, and almost started the house on fire." I was about to retort when he pointed out the warped siding on the house.

With the grill heated to a crispy 450 degrees, I was ready to finish the crown jewel of Thanksgiving. Everything was going well when my mom yelled out to me that I had a phone call—and yes, I was standing guard—I did not want anything to happen to that turkey. Okay, I had to make this phone call fast.

"Hello?"

"Hello, Penny. It's Frannie."

"Hi, Frannie! When are you coming over? I just put the turkey roll on the grill and I can't wait for you to taste it. It's going to be amazing."

"Well, that is why I'm calling. I'm afraid I'm not feeling well and think it would best if I stayed home."

"No, you have to come."

"I wish I could, dear. Have fun for me. I know everything will be wonderful."

"I will bring you a plate over later. Then we can both marvel over my incredible cooking skills."

We had just said our goodbyes when my dad ran into the kitchen and announced, "Umm, Houston, I think we have a problem."

"Oh no! What is it?" I yelled, running outside. I instantly knew something was wrong when I saw flames billowing out from the grill. And in the center of the flames lay a black, crispy fried mass somewhat resembling a turkey roll.

"No, No, NO!" I screamed. "This is NOT happening." Our Thanksgiving Day feast was literally going up in bacon-grease flames. By the time my dad got the fire out—note to future turkey roll grillers: water and bacon grease fires do NOT mix—my turkey roll was a black log of burnt, wrapped in more burnt.

"Well," my mom said, "it is most likely cooked on the inside. I will just scrape off the burnt parts."

"Will there be anything left?" asked Parker.

Then the doorbell rang. There was a collective gasp throughout the house. Okay, mostly just from me. "Don't open the door! Let's just pretend we aren't home" I begged.

"Penny, it will be fine," my mom said. "We will just explain what happened and everything will be fine."

By the time the Rothefellers walked through the door and they were told the story of the burnt turkey roll—thanks Parker!—I wanted to go up to my room and curl up into a ball. But I didn't. I stood there, smiled and told myself to be strong.

Of course JayJ had plenty to say about it. "Well, luckily everybody knows that the best part of Thanksgiving dinner isn't the turkey, it's the pies. And seeing how I made the pies, they're perfect." She would be the only one with enough nerve to say such a thing out loud.

"Well in our family it's all about the turkey." Take that JayJ.

"It's a shame then they let you have anything to do with it, I suppose."

Finally, it was time to eat. "As you have heard," my mom said, "there was a little incident with our turkey, but I've tried it, and if you avoid any remaining burnt parts, it's really quite good."

Unfortunately, I had completely lost my appetite. Not because of the burnt turkey roll that nobody was eating or the fact that everybody was going on and on about how perfect the pies looked, but because of the smug look on JayJ's face. I didn't get it. Everything always worked out for her, and everything always ended up a fiasco for me. By the way, I am not about to call this the "Turkey Roll Fiasco of 2012." Nope, not gonna do it!

Later, before the Rothefellers left, they tried to compliment my uneaten, burnt-to-a-crisp turkey roll. "Well Penny dear, your turkey roll was just, um, delicious," Mrs. Rothefeller commented.

When I responded, "Well, how would you know? You didn't eat any," my mom quickly added, "Penny!" in that way that only mothers know how to say while making you feel like you're three years old again.

Of course, JayJ just had to jump in with, "Don't worry, Mrs. Picklepants, we've come to expect nothing less from Penny."

The nerve of that girl—well JayJ could be rude all she wanted because in three weeks, we would be out of school for Christmas break with nothing to do but watch movies, play in the snow—I mean my little brother to play in the snow, of course—and take comfort in knowing I would be enjoying JayJ-free peace and quiet for two whole weeks!

With the disaster otherwise known as Thanksgiving 2012 over, I went straight to my room to try to recoup and to regroup. On my way up to my room, I decided that JayJ really was the spawn of the devil and should hereafter be known as JayJ Devilfeller. Okay, that made me laugh, but it wasn't enough to pull me out of my really bad, no good mood. I even wasn't in the mood to sit down and watch "A Wonderful Life," another of our traditions. I just didn't think I could stand hearing Zuzu say, "Every time a bell rings, an angel gets his wings," without screaming at the TV, "Every time JayJ opens her mouth, a devil gets its horns!" I knew nobody would appreciate it as much as I would, and most likely my mom would then turn to me and say, "Now Penny, be nice—she isn't that bad," which I would respond with, "Now Mom, but you know she is." Then my mom would eventually send me to my room, so best to start the night where I would end up anyway.

After sitting in my bedroom awhile, I decided I would at least be productive and clean it. It didn't take long before I realized the futility of such drastic measures. I then figured it would now be safe for me to emerge from the confines of my bedroom. So I went downstairs to warm up a plate of leftovers because frankly, everybody knows the best part of Thanksgiving is leftovers, which reminded me that I was supposed to take a plate of leftovers to

Frannie. Great! One more thing I screwed up today. I was giving myself a stern talking to about screwing things up when I noticed my dad sitting in his office.

"Hey Dad, what's up?"

"Oh just some work. It seems to be nothing but work, work, work lately. I feel badly it hasn't left me much time for you and the family. How are things at school?"

I sat there for a minute wondering what I should reveal to my dad. He has always been a good listener, when he has the time, but lately with everything that was happening I didn't know where to start. Since I knew he was busy, I decided to not take up a lot of his time and I would just give him the Cliffs Notes version.

"Dad my life is in shambles!" I then continued to tell him everything that happened at the hands of JayJ and everything else that has plagued my mind in the last few months, "and Dad, all I want is to just be a professional pickle taster and work at the plant." I could tell by the look on his face that he was having a hard time keeping up with all my dilemmas, dramas, and fiascos. He was probably thinking twice about asking me how things were going.

"Wow, you really do have a lot going on. I had no idea. Have you talked with Mom?"

"No way," I said. "I've tried. She just doesn't get me."

"Well, you might want to give it another try. I think you'd be surprised just how well your mom gets you. And as far as working at the plant, I received an interesting call the other day. It was from Frannie, and she was calling me to tell me how much she enjoyed the tour you gave her of the plant. She was quite impressed with your extensive knowledge. Now, I figure if you are as passionate about it as you say you are, then maybe you should start coming down on Saturdays and giving tours. What do you think about that?"

YES! YES! YES!

"YES! YES! YES! I would love that Daddy," I said, giving him a giant hug. "When do I start? Do I need to give you my resume? Will I need to be interviewed? Let's just do it now. To answer your question about where I see myself in 5 years, I would say being even more fabulous than I am now! And to answer your question about my greatest strengths, I would say pickle tasting, shopping, and more shopping. How was that?"

After a hearty laugh, he hired me on the spot.

"Oh my gosh, Dad, that sounds so great, I can't wait! Thank you so much! You won't regret this, I promise!"

As I sat in the kitchen eating leftover sweet potatoes and stuffing, I allowed myself to wonder if maybe, just maybe my luck was finally turning around.

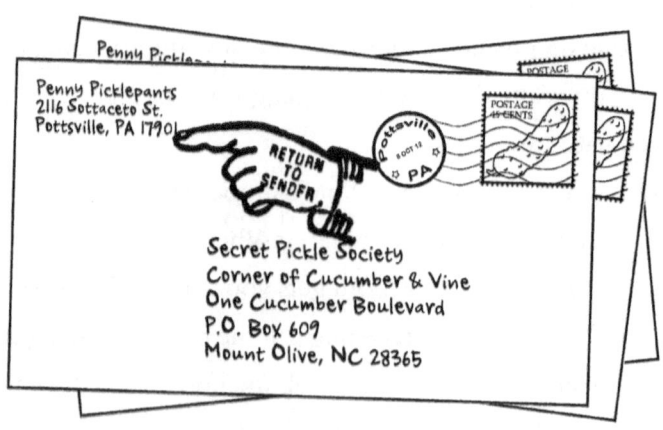

CHAPTER NINETEEN

Dear Secret Pickle Society,

The small German village of Essigdorf had a long tradition of decorating the Evergreen trees in the center of the village in honor of St. Nicolas. The tradition started... well, nobody was quite sure, but it was tradition, so they did it. They would decorate the trees with brilliant ornaments and St. Nicholas would leave presents. Exquisite glass spheres hung from the branches of each tree. But one year an awful thing happened. All the ornaments vanished. They looked high, they looked low. They looked to the east, they looked to the west, but they couldn't find them. There was no time to make new ones, nor could they afford to do so.

When Hans, a simple seller of essigs, saw what had happened to his beloved, small German village of Essigdorf, he knew he had to do something. So Hans walked to each tree and started to hang essigs from each branch because they were the only thing he had. He knew it would make him even poorer, for then he would have nothing left to sell, but he did it anyway, for he loved the people of Essigdorf.

On Christmas morning, the villagers woke up expecting nothing to be under the trees, but one by one, the villagers came out from their warm homes to find a huge amount of presents. The older villagers were shocked not only by the presents, but also by the trees lined with the most beautiful essigs they had ever seen. Of course, the children were ecstatic to see such big boxes wrapped in the fanciest shiny paper and filled with the best toys. You see, St. Nicholas was touched not only by the beauty of the decorations that year in the small German village of Essigdorf, but by the love of one man who gave everything he had to decorate the trees and make the others happy.

In the very center of the village was a box with the name "Hans" written on it. The only thing inside was a piece of paper, but on that paper was written the greatest essig recipe ever formulated. Armed with the new recipe, soon Hans found he could no longer keep up with demand, so he opened the now world-famous Hans Essig Plant, putting Essigdorf on the map. And in case you haven't already figured it out, an essig is of course none other than a pickle. And the tradition of hanging pickles from Christmas trees continues to this day. While decorating Christmas trees, parents hang a pickle as the last ornament. On the morning of Christmas, the child who finds the pickle ornament receives a special gift from St. Nicholas.

Sincerely,
Penny Picklepants ♡

P.S. If you would like a copy of the greatest essig recipe ever formulated, you're just going to have to contact me.

After I told Frannie the exciting news, she gave me some pointers on how to make the tours the best pickle tours ever. "Remember to just be yourself. Your sense of humor is a wonderful complement to the vast knowledge you possess of your family's pickle plant. Above all, remember to have fun! If you are having fun, then your tour group members will have fun. I know you will do a great job."

"Thanks Frannie. Actually, I was wondering if you would like to come to the pickle plant Christmas party. I am trying to get my dad to change it to the "Picklemas Party," but he didn't think that was such a good idea. Anyway, if you came then you could be there with me on my first official tour."

"Oh, Penny, that sounds delightful," Frannie said. "I would love to come. I can't even tell you the last time I went to a party."

Somehow I persuaded my mom to let me and Olive go to the mall to find a new dress for the Christmas party. She did try to use the excuse, "You have so much stuff in your closet already," but I used the ever useful rebuttal of, "But Mom, I need something new if you want me to look nice for Christmas," to which she replied with her infamous motherly rebuttal of, "You most certainly do not," to which I then responded with my everly persuasive rebuttal of, "But Mom!" Needless to say, she caved when she realized how futile it was to resist my awesomeness.

"Olive," I said, as we looked at a rack of party dresses, "do you think it should be black or red? Or black and red? Or should it be white? Or should it be white with a hint of black with a smidge of red? I just don't know which to choose!" Of course, after looking at about a hundred dresses—okay, more like 256.8 dresses—she told me to not stress about it.

"Trust me Penny, when you find the dress you will know."

Poor Olive. I hope she gets it one day... "Oh my gosh! This is it. This is my dress. You were right Olive. I knew it the second I saw it."

Having found the perfect dress, I knew the Christmas party was going to be a perfect night—now, just to get through the next week of school.

With only five days before the Christmas party, I had had a hard time concentrating on getting my last big assignment finished in Home Ec. Mrs. Smith had given us an assignment to write a talk on any type of food. I had wanted to do it on pickles, but when Mrs. Smith finished telling us about the assignment, she looked right at me and said, "And you can't do your talk on pickles Picklepants." Ugh! So not fair!

Instead, I decided to do it on condiments, which included pick-les (ha!) and my turn was next. I didn't feel nervous at all. I mean, I had written some pretty good jokes in this talk. I was going to have my classmates eating pickles out of my hands.

At first, things were going well. JayJ wasn't even paying attention, which I figured was a good thing. I had talked about tomatoes, pickles—Mrs. Smith shot me a death glare at the mention of pickles, so I only talked about them for a second and I didn't even pitch Picklepants Pickles, which I thought was quite generous of me. Next, I mentioned onions, but when I started on the lettuce, things went from smooth sailing to white squall in about 1.45 seconds.

"Now lettuce discuss Lettuce while you Romaine in your seats." Huh? No laughter? That was my best joke! Frannie laughed. Even my mom laughed at that one.

"More like, Asparagus the details," JayJ said, followed by laughter, lots and lots of laughter. Of course, JayJ didn't get in trouble. She never did. Mrs. Smith just said, "Quiet down class."

But the damage was done, I was too upset to finish. I was so flustered the rest of my speech unraveled into a total mess.

"So…, um…, see…, as you can…, see that is, um, your condolences are just as important as your boogers. I mean condiments… your condiments are just as important as your burgers. Um… just remember to not, um, use lemons…, yes, lemons, not good… so, yeah." What did I just say? I was completely off script! And did I just end my speech on lemons? What the heck was I thinking?

Of course JayJ had one more zinger left in her. "Orange you glad that's over with," she snipped, followed by lots and lots of laughter, AGAIN!

By the time I sat down, Olive had a concerned look on her face, "What happened, Penny? You were doing so well."

"What do you think? Jay and J happened to me. I swear she is out to destroy me." I wanted to yell out a big, fat "JERK!", but I knew I would get into trouble and of course JayJ would somehow turn it around and make me look like a complete idiot.

"Are you screaming 'big, fat JERK' in your head again?" Olive asked.

"Yes, and give me five more seconds."

Of course I am sure I looked like a complete idiot because I had my eyes closed tight with my cheeks puffed out. I'm sure I looked every bit the fool, but I didn't care. I had to get my frustration out somehow. "See what JayJ has reduced me to? A red puffer fish—she has reduced me to a red puffer fish!"

"There's no such thing as a red puffer fish," Olive said.

I guess the look I gave her made her quickly change tactics.

"I know Penny, I know," she said, perhaps the five most comforting words a friend could utter on such an occasion. "But don't worry—Christmas break is coming up and you get to have your Christmas party. You always love the Christmas party. Your dress is so cute—you look amazing in it. It's going to be a great night and one without JayJ."

Okay, now I know why I am friends with Olive—seriously, she is the best!

Like everything else that involved JayJ, I tried to put the Great Speech Fiasco of 2012 behind me and dwell on something less fiasco-ish. The Picklepants Christmas Party—my dad ended up going with the usual tradish name—was set for Saturday. In true Penny Picklepants fashion, I started getting ready the minute I woke up. I mean, I only had nine hours to get ready. I was definitely cutting it close.

I started the day off with a brisk walk. You always want to get ready for a big party with exercise, but nothing too hard because you don't want to be sore for your night of fun, frolic, and fashion. Olive then came over. We gave each other a mani and a pedi, as we discussed such important topics as whether red toenail polish will always be a staple of good fashion sense or become totally six minutes ago. I sided with a staple of good fashion sense, but Olive just rolled her eyes and laughed. I guess that was her way of siding with six minutes ago.

After Olive left, I spent the next hour taking a refreshing bath. I even added some Calgon to help strip away the stress of the last few months. I washed my hair twice—once for good measure and a second because I didn't want to get out of the bath just yet.

I then spent the next couple of hours eating lunch and getting caught up on my blog. After that, it was time to focus on my hair. I had let it air dry so the natural curl would add extra volume. Having hair that's sometimes really wavy—when the humidity is totally out of control—does not help in the fabulous hair department. I usually straighten it, but today I felt curls would be best. I borrowed my mom's hot curlers and proceeded to burn the heck out of my fingers trying to get them in my hair. After spending another hour of pulling and tugging and speaking a few under-my-breath choice words—don't tell my mom by the way—my hair was perfect. After all my primping, checking my primping, and double-checking my primping, I was ready to go.

Then I got a phone call.

"Penny," Parker yelled, "phone's for you."

"Hello?"

"Hello, Penny."

"Frannie! I'm so excited for tonight. I've just spent the past nine hours getting ready."

"Oh, I bet you look stunning. Please take a picture."

"Well, okay, but you're going to see me anyway, so…"

"I'm afraid that won't be possible. I'm calling to tell you that I won't be able to make it tonight."

"But you have to, Frannie. You said you were so excited, you just have to come."

"I'm sorry, Penny. I'm just not feeling well. But do have fun for me, won't you?"

We said our sad goodbyes. When I hung up the phone I hoped it would be the one and only disappointment for the night.

In years past we—i.e., the entire Picklepants family—would have to stand by the door and greet each person as they entered. I have to admit, by the end of the evening, my face would be sore from smiling. I would become so used to the same set of questions it wasn't long before someone would ask me something—anything—that I would just give the same long-winded answer: "I'm doing well. It's so good to see you too. Yes, I have gotten two inches taller. School is fine. Of course, I'm looking forward to junior high. Haha, yes. Coach Shoe is still coaching PE. Yep, I hope I'm not on the naughty list too." This would usually make the other person look a little confused, especially when all they had asked me was whether I could pass the salt.

This year, however, we did things a little bit differently. We had the employees' break room set up with tables of food, juices, and soda—which reminded me, I needed to talk to my dad about a possible Pickle Soda—kids would love it! Anyway, this party was a lot more relaxed, a come-and-go-as-you-please kind of party, sitting around casually while eating some good food.

To be honest, I was getting a little nervous about remembering all my lines for my first official tour. Then my dad grabbed me and said, "Penny, I want you to meet our new Marketing Director. His name is Mr. Jams." I wasn't really paying attention to what my dad was saying, as I was mentally practicing my jokes. "When can you put pickles in a door?" I said to myself. "When it's ajar." I know—funny right? Anyway, I was at the door part when my dad said, "And this is Mr. Jams' son, Jiminy. Jiminy this is my daughter, Penny. I believe you two are in the same grade, if I'm not mistaken."

To say my mouth dropped to the floor was like saying Karl Lagerfeld would be wearing a black coat, a white buttoned shirt with a really high collar, and sunglasses to Fashion Week, in addition to every other minute of his life. To the fashion illiterate, that's like saying, "Duh!" It wasn't until my dad nudged me that I finally snapped out of it.

"Um, Penny?" my dad said, patting my on the back, "Penny? Say hello to Jiminy and Mr. Jams."

"Guhhhhiii," was all I was able to get out.

"I'm going to show Mr. Jams his office, so why don't you show Jiminy around the factory. Probably a little late for a family tour."

"Hi… um… the red… and flour… and… you are right here now." Wow! That is one for the record books.

After a little chuckle—oh my, how his chuckle is like music to my… Wait! I don't like him anymore—focus Picklepants, focus!

Okay Penny, here is your chance to show Jiminy how graceful you can be. You need to show him that you are above his childish hijinks. Granted, you haven't talked to him since Halloween—still, show him the graceful woman you are, or becoming—or are… yeah, that you are—and that you can put more than two words together in a sentence for crying out loud!

"Way let's go this," came falling out of my mouth. Oh good gravy! After my nerves settled down and I stopped sweating buckets, I was able to show Jiminy some of the different areas, all while giving him a coherent tour of the plant. After the tour, we ended up sitting on the walkway overlooking the factory floor.

"I have been wondering what you've been up to," he said. "It's almost seemed like you have been avoiding me ever since Halloween."

"Avoiding you? Me? Heavens no. Why would I do that?" Oh confrontation, how I loathe thee.

"Did something happen at the Halloween party? We went to the cemetery, then I didn't see you after that."

"Halloween? Pshaw! Like I can even remember Halloween, it was like a bazillion years ago," I said, still dodging. Just breathe, take a deep breath—just say a little something about what happened—nice and steady.

"Okay Jiminy. I can't take it anymore. I just have to say that the whole red paint thing was so not cool. Those dresses that Olive and I wore belonged to my friend Frannie. They were her original designs. They were priceless originals. We tried for a week to get the red paint out, but nothing worked. I promised Frannie that I wouldn't let anything happen to those dresses. She didn't want me to take them, but I promised I would bring them back safe. I was crushed that I had to return them completely ruined." I think I overwhelmed him because the look on his face was one of total shock.

"Penny, what are you even talking about? What red paint?"

"Seriously, Jiminy? Is that how you are going to act? Like you had nothing to do with it? JayJ made it painfully clear it was all your idea. She made it even clearer that we were not welcomed at your party. But why red paint? Having a bucket of flour dumped on you is nothing compared to a bucket of red paint."

"Okay, I admit I wasn't thrilled about washing flour out of my hair for like a week, on top of you falling on me on the bleachers and crashing into my mail box and then landing on me."

I couldn't help it, I started to laugh, and so did he. "I'm so sorry for all that."

"I know you are," he said, "but I swear to you I had nothing to do with any red paint. I had no idea until you just told me."

"You swear you didn't have anything to do with it?"

Oh goodness he was looking at me with those big blue eyes. And his beautifully blond hair was, of course, perfection. I was hoping he couldn't hear my little heart's pittering and pattering every time he smiled. He also sounded like he was telling the truth.

"Penny, I swear I didn't. If I had, I…" he said, shaking his head. "After waiting a while, we eventually all met up in the cemetery. I asked where you were, and JayJ said she you and Olive had gone home. So we played a few games and then JayJ suggested that we should go back and watch a scary movie."

Of course it was all JayJ. Why would I think for ten seconds that she wasn't behind the whole thing? I had been played like a fool again! I ended up telling Jiminy the entire story from gory detail to gory detail. I wanted to ask why he even hung out with JayJ, but I didn't want to seem pushy.

"Why do you even hang out with JayJ?" I said. Ahh, to heck

with not being pushy. "She is so evil and just plain mean. You are too nice of a guy to be someone like her."

"First of all, you think I am a nice guy?" he asked, with that smile. Oh that smile! "And second of all, JayJ and I are just friends, we are not together. Besides, we are 12—how are we supposed to "date" when we can't even drive? I mean, meeting up at the mall and or going to a movie in a group is fun, but it isn't dating. And to be honest, it's pretty disappointing to hear what she did to you and Olive."

Oh Olive! I'm so sorry, but you can't have him anymore. He's all mine! "First of all, yes, I do think you are nice. Despite my wreaking havoc upon you, you have always been so nice to me. So I apologize that I thought you were capable of pulling a stunt like that. And second of all…"

And then he kissed me. OH! MY! GOSH! Did you hear me? Jiminy Jams just kissed me!!! I am never washing my lips ever, ever, and ever, ever again!

"I'm sorry," he said, blushing. "I couldn't help myself."

"Oh, please, in that case then, don't ever help yourself."

Best Christmas party ever!!! I kept reminding myself to not do anything stupid like drop my shoe or myself onto the conveyer belt. We ended up talking for close to 2 hours and would have stayed longer, but Jiminy's dad found him and said it was time to go. I have to admit, I felt a little sad, but seriously, best Christmas party ever. Ha! And you thought I was wasting my time with my 9 hours of prep time, didn't you? Admit it!

"Well, Penny," Jiminy said, flashing his gorgeous smile, "thanks for the tour. You are going to do a great job being the new tour guide. Also, don't worry about JayJ."

Easier said than done. "So you're never going to talk to her again because she is the devil's offspring?" Did I just say that out loud?

He just laughed and said, "Anyway, Merry Christmas Penny."

"Merry Christmas, Jiminy." Well at least it was worth a shot right?

While lying in bed that night, I couldn't believe how the night had turned out. In true girl fashion, I kept going over and over my conversation with Jiminy. The way he smiled, the way he laughed, the way he said good-bye and of course THE WAY HE KISSED ME! I couldn't wait to tell Frannie and Olive about the party! But not the kiss of course. I don't kiss and tell... well, maybe just one or two people wouldn't hurt. I didn't even care what I got for Christmas. My present had arrived early!

CHAPTER NINETEEN-AND-A-HALF

Dear Reader,

Yes I know it is weird to see a half chapter. Why not just call it **CHAPTER TWENTY** like normal people? Well, in case you haven't picked it up in the previous nineteen chapters, the Picklepants are anything but normal, and I'm furthest thing from an exception to that rule. So in true Penny Picklepants fashion (tee hee, I have a fashion. Yes!) I am calling the other half of my Christmas vacay chapter 19-1/2. It is filled with romance (in case you didn't realize, I am shifting my eyebrows up and down to emphasize the romance part), intrigue, and espionage set in a far, exotic land.

Ha! Who am I kidding? It is filled with more situations of me making a fool out of myself, but then again, have you come to expect anything less from the one and only Penny Picklepants?

Love,
Penn ♡

Christmas Eve was filled with all things traditional. We ate tacos on the floor by the Christmas tree, because everybody spreads a blanket on the living-room floor and eats tacos on Christmas Eve, right? And yes, I totally put pickles in my tacos. Always have. Always will.

Later on we went caroling and took our traditional drive around the town of Pottsville to look at the hard work and dedication the townspeople put into expressing the holiday spirit in lights. Ever since I was little I called this drive "Twinkling." I even made up a song when I was a little girl: "Here we go a twinkling, here we go a twinkling," and started to sing it. But every time I did, Parker would ask me to stop because it made him want to go to the bathroom.

Of course we ended the night by reading the Christmas story, and then opening one present from our parents—"Wow, pajamas, again, like the last 11 years of my life"—tradition are traditions. Lastly, we set out a plate of cookies and milk, as well as a dill pickle, of course, for good measure.

Traditionally, I have a hard time falling asleep on Christmas Eve. But this year was different. Ever since the party—okay, it was like two days ago, but still—I felt like my Christmas came early. So I wasn't a ball of nerves like I usually was. Actually, I like to think of myself as having grown up. I mean, I am going to be 12 soon, practically on the verge of adulthood, so it was time to act like it. I figured with my new found maturity, I would sleep in and just chill in the morning until we all felt like it was time to open our presents.

"Mom! DAD!! It's 5'oclock in the morning. Wake up! PLEASE, PLEASE, PLEASE!"

Okay, so much for maturity, but good gravy, it's Christmas Morning!

"Penny, you are the only one awake," my mom said, yawning. "Go back to bed and sleep for another hour."

"At least!" my dad added.

"Well, then I will go wake up Parker and Patrick and get this show on the road. Come on already!"

"Penny unless you want every one of your presents returned to the store, go back to bed for one more hour!"

"Sheesh, Mom. It's not like you need to be so snippy."

I tried going back to bed, but I couldn't sleep. I figured I hadn't thought about Jiminy for the last 10 minutes, so I thought I better do some more reflecting on our conversation. It never gets old.

Finally at 6 o'clock—isn't that like a form of abuse or something?—all of us kids went into my parents room and started jumping on their bed yelling, "Wake up, wake up." Not that we were excited or anything!

I have to admit, running down the stairs towards our stockings—we always opened them first, then tear into the really good stuff—there was always a feeling of elation wondering what you were going to get—were you going to be excited or a little bit disappointed?

When I opened my stocking, I was a little confused. I had gotten a passport, sunblock, sunglasses—they weren't Prada, but I guess I can overlook that—and a book of travel games. When I turned around to ask my mom what was going on, I saw that Patrick and Parker had received the similar gifts in their stockings. I think we were all confused at receiving such strange gifts. We all looked at each other and at the same time said, "Huh?"

"Well, this year, your Dad and I decided to do something different. Instead of filling up your stockings with stuff you don't want, we got you thing you would need." Of course she had the goofiest grin ever emblazoned on her face.

"Um, the last time I checked Mom, it is like 15 degrees outside and even though Pennsylvania is a strange state sometimes, you don't need a passport to live here. Although that would answer a few questions…"

"Sweet," Parker said, "Now, when I start traveling in space I will have my passport all ready."

"When's the next flight, Parker?" I asked.

Okay, that wiped the grin of off Mom's face.

"I'm kidding," I said, looking at my mom.

"Well," my mom said, "who's ready to start opening their presents?"

Patrick went first. A set of luggage.

"Are you trying tell us something?" Patrick asked.

"Yes, we want you to move out, Patrick," I said, but my mom still didn't appreciate my honesty, I mean humor.

More luggage, new swimming suits, and summer clothes—we were more confused than ever.

"It will all come together with the scavenger hunt," my mom said.

So, we have a tradition in our family where the last gift, usually the big family gift, is found by us, the kids, searching for clues Santa has left behind—typed instead of handwritten in case one of us recognized Santa's handwriting. As in all previous Christmases, the first scavenger hunt clue is placed by the base of the Christmas tree. Parker found it first.

CLUE 1

Although these gifts may seem a little crazy,
And your parent's thoughts a bit hazy,
You will find there is a point to all this madness.
If you find Clue 2 in Patrick's room of badness.

"You know it! My room is so full of badness," Patrick said, after reading the clue.

Upon entering Patrick's room, I doubted we would be able to find any clue in the heaps of "badness" littering his room without requiring a tetanus shot. Beyond the typical dirty clothes and boy stuff lying on the floor, there were dirty dishes and other things that were so dirty they were no longer recognizable. As we started to toss his "badness" about, I luckily found Clue 2 under a pile of dirty clothes next to his closet door without too much effort.

"I feel like I need to wash my hands and eyes in bleach or something," I said. "Am I going to get a funky foot fungus from walking on your floor? This room is disgusting!"

"Oh, like yours is any better," Patrick said. "Let's just work together and figure out clue number two."

CLUE 2
You did it, you did it, you found Clue 2.
Now you must go to where we bid our guests adieu.
But is it in the back, the front, or another way?
You are almost done - so shout hooray!

Since the front door was closest, we ran down the stairs to see if we had run right by a clue taped to the door. Of course, getting three kids down the stairs safely amidst the pushing, pulling, shoving, and dodging—Christmas Spirit right out the door, and yes, after all these years, we still fought to get to the clues first—usually took a Christmas miracle. But even with my ninja-like reflexes I was still last to get to the front door.

"I found it—I found it!" Parker yelled loud enough to cause permanent hearing.

CLUE 3

You found Clue 3, now where does Clue 4 hide?
Can only say that in the kitchen it may reside, but
You have to figure out whether it is in or it is out.
Or could it be just lying about?

There was a mad dash to the kitchen. When we got there, we all stopped not sure what to do. It's not that our kitchen is huge, but when you factor in all the cabinets, the refrigerator, the freezer, as well as the pantry—well, to say the least, our task was a daunting one.

"Penny, you take all the cabinets below the counter-tops," Patrick said, barking out orders like a Fashion Week runway director. "I will take all the cabinets above the counter-tops. Parker, you take the pantry and then the fridge and freezer."

After 10 minutes of looking and turning the kitchen inside out, I was starting to think my parents, I mean Santa, had sent us on a wild goose chase. They, of course, were standing in the doorway laughing their heads off, videotaping the entire ordeal.

"Seriously guys, did you really hide it or are you just videotaping us for further humiliation?"

My thought exactly, Patrick. I was about to yell a very loud and frustrated "Ugh!" when Parker yelled, "I FOUND IT! I FOUND IT!" causing me to drop my mom's biggest pot on my toe, but I would deal with the pain later. I was dying to find out what clue 4 held.

"Read it, READ IT!" Patrick and I yelled at the same time.

CLUE 4

Your gifts may make you think your parents are square,

Um… no, definitely thought that with or without gifts.

But with these gifts, you are now fully prepared,

For the one and only big magnifico,
Because you guys are headed to ol' MEXICO!

...BTW, we leave in six hours,
So be sure to use your packing powers!

Well that's funny—I think clue four just told us we are going to Mexico. "Um," I said, swallowing, not wanting to believe it in case it turned out to be some place I had never heard of like Mexico, Pennsylvania. "This wouldn't happen to be that same Mexico I have read about in my fashion magazines where they have amazing beaches and guys bring you amazing exotic drinks on the beach, and..."

"Yes, Penny, we are talking about that Mexico. And no, you cannot drink the exotic drinks," my mom said. "Kids, we are spending the rest of our Christmas vacation in Cancun, Mexico. So enough chit-chat—let's get packing and Patrick..." my mom paused, "you may need to do some laundry."

I think she was just as excited as the rest of us. But I have to admit I was still in shock. "Are you serious?" I said in a high-pitched squeal. "You are only giving me six hours to pack! AHHHHHH!" I screamed, running up the stairs. I mean usually it takes me a week just to plan out all my outfits and now I only had six hours. It was so unfair! I do have to admit, though, that having a bunch of new summer clothes to wear and a new swim suit certainly does help the situation. We were all in such a mad dash to pack and get out of the house that we didn't have time to consider our traditional Christmas breakfast.

I did however, call Frannie to ask her if I could come over and give her my gift. I had already given Olive her gift—a pedicure kit, she gave me a scarf—but I had to admit, just to myself of course, I was the most excited about Frannie's gift. I mean, I loved giving Olive her pedicure kit, and believe me when I say she needed it, but there was something about Frannie's gift that felt more from the heart.

Frannie quickly ushered me out from the cold into her warm house. My entire body felt like it was a frozen popsicle, making me even more excited about going to Mexico.

"You'll never guess where we're going Frannie," I said, my frozen tongue doing its best to keep up. "My parents surprised us with a trip to Mexico. Can you believe it? Mexico! The REAL Mexico!" I then proceeded to tell her all about the strange gifts we had received and about the crazy scavenger hunt that my parents had sent us on and how excited we were to find out we were going to be spending the next week in Mexico. I also told her how, if there ever was a Christmas trip, it had always been a trip either to Grandma and Grandpa Porterhouse, who live in the frozen wasteland otherwise known as WisCANsin, aka Wisconsin—no thank you, not in the middle of winter—or to my Grandma Picklepants (Grandpa Picklepants passed away when I was a baby) in sunny Florida, which was always fine by me.

"Oh Penny. That sounds fabulous. Did I ever tell you the time I went to Mexico?" Frannie spent the next 15 minutes telling me all about her adventures in Mexico—exploring the jungle, swimming in the ocean, and sitting on the beach watching the sunset with Frank. She painted the most beautiful images with her stories.

"Oh, I hope my trip will be as fun as yours Frannie," I said.

"You will have a wonderful time. Now let's get to why you came over, I have a gift for you."

She handed me her gift and after I unwrapped it, I sat there stunned for a few minutes not knowing what to say to Frannie as I held one of her beloved brooches in my hand.

"Frannie, I can't accept this, this one is your favorite," I said, choking back the tears. It was about 2 inches long of brilliant princess cut emeralds in the shape of a pickle. I figured the emeralds were fake, but I didn't dare ask Frannie. I didn't want to seem shallow. It seemed so unladylike.

"Are these emeralds real?" Okay, not quite a lady yet.

"Of course they are real, Penny. A lady does not deal in fakery."

"Frannie, really. I couldn't accept this present. It's too valuable." I continued to stare at the pickle brooch, certainly not wanting to give it up, but I couldn't take it. I really didn't know a lot about jewels other than what I had read about them in Vogue: "Always go for big, shiny, and real" is what they said. This definitely fell into every one of those categories. "Frannie, really, I can't. I once lost a necklace and..."

"Penny, I know you won't lose it. That pin will come to mean a lot to you when you are older and I really don't need it anymore. Take it and enjoy it."

I wasn't sure what Frannie meant by that, but I knew for one thing, I would enjoy it. I would wear it every time I gave a tour at the factory. And I would not lose it.

"Well, I feel like I should have gotten you more for Christmas," I said, feeling a bit dejected when I thought of the plainness of my gift compared to Frannie's.

"Nonsense! Whatever you have for me, I know I will love it, because it is coming from you. You seem to me to be the kind of girl who gives presents from the heart."

"You too, Frannie," I said, looking again at the brooch. Of course, Frannie just laughed and told me to hand over the gift. After she un-wrapped it, she looked at me, a tear in her eye.

"Oh, Penny. I absolutely love it… oh absolutely!" It was a picture of Olive and I in our Halloween costumes. Technically they were Frannie's dresses, but still, it was a picture of us. It was in a frame that Frannie had received when she found out she was pregnant with her and Frank's first child. Fargo Frankincense was stillborn. Then Frannie was told by her doctor that she could never have a child live through full-term pregnancy. Frannie kept the empty frame on a table in her living room. I instantly fell in love with the beautiful frame, and she told me I could have it. It wasn't until after she gave it to me that she told me the story.

"I figured you had everything except a picture of me and Olive. Also, this way you can see how the dresses used to look before JayJ so kindly redecorated them." I wasn't sure what else to say because Frannie's eyes were locked on the picture and the frame.

After what felt like a million years, she looked at me with tears in her eyes and said, "Oh, Penny, I love it. It is perfect, just like you my dear. It's the best Christmas gift you could ever have given me. I will cherish it forever." We then hugged, and cried, and talked, and laughed, like we always do.

Eventually, I told her I needed to get home. It was time to head to the airport—I felt so sophisticated saying that. She told me to have fun, don't get lost, and don't drink the water. Then she gave me a big hug and thanked me, again, for the picture.

By the time we landed in Mexico, it was a perfect 80 degrees out. Walking off the plane I turned to my dad and said, "If you want you can just leave me here forever. It's perfect." He laughed and said, "Tempting." I wasn't sure if he was kidding or being serious—then again, I wasn't sure if I cared either way.

We quickly got our luggage, and then found our driver—yes! We had our own driver! He was dressed in black and held a sign that read, "Picklepants." It was so cool. Then we were off on our Mexican adventure. I rolled down the window to breathe in the salty air and feel the warmth of the sun on my face. I closed my eyes and for the first time, in a long time, I felt like life was perfect. I slowly opened my eyes when my dad yelled, "We're here and it looks like our welcome party is here as well." A smile spread across my face until I turned my head. That smile quickly turned into a frown. "Yeah, I'm good," I said. "Mexico has been great. Driver can you please take me back to the airport?"

"Penny, get out of the car," my dad said, clearly upset, but with a smile on his face. "They arrived yesterday to make sure our Mexico trip would be perfect. Get out and greet our generous hosts."

"Umm, no, really I'm good. Mexico was amazing. I loved it, but I am done. Really, I've seen all I need to see. I can go home now," I said, turning to the driver. "Driver, how do you say 'Take me to the airport now before I scream in total frustration that I have to spend my Mexican vacation with them,' in Spanish?"

"Como?" the taxi driver said.

Wow! Spanish is so efficient. That entire phrase in a single word.

"Penny, you are not going back to the airport," my dad said. "You are going to get out of this car, and you are going to have a good time. The Rothefellers paid for our trip so you will be..."

"Wait! The Rothefellers paid for our trip?! You mean we didn't take this trip because the fact…" I stopped myself. I had figured that the trip to Mexico was a sign that the factory was doing better, so what I was about to say was, "because the factory is doing a lot better," but my parents still didn't know that I knew the factory was in trouble. Conversations are so hard when you know something that you aren't supposed to know, but what you know keeps coming up, you know?

"Because the what?" my dad said.

"Um," I gulped. "Because of the fact… the fact…, um, the fact that you love your family so much?"

"Penny, this trip is really important to me. So you are going to get out of the car. You are going to look happy, and you are going to tell the Rothefellers how excited you are to see them or you will be grounded for the rest of your life and if you think I am kidding just try me."

I never knew my dad could talk with such a happy face all while clinching his teeth so hard they could have turned coal into diamonds. I figured it would best if I got out of the car, looked happy and told the Rothefellers how excited I was to see them.

And that is exactly what I did. I got out of the car, put on my Frada's—my fake Prada sunglasses—smiled at the Rothefellers, and walked to the pool. I know—a bit dramatic—but I was really upset I was on a vacation paid for by the Rothefellers. I just didn't know if I was ever going to be able to relax, even in Mexico, knowing that our vacation was being paid by the Devilfellers. I decided I was going to spend my entire Mexican vacation pouting. I was just going to sit at the pool the entire time—I mean, really there was no reason I couldn't get a tan while pouting—and be mad at my parents. And there was no way, NO WAY, I was going to think about anything else except... wait, huh? That boy is really cute. And he is looking at me, and he is smiling at me.

Okay, new plan—be really mad at my parents and at the same time think about the cute boy who is looking at me from across the pool. Play it cool Picklepants, play it cool.

"Hey Penny, see that sign right there—it reads, **No Hacer Pipi**—which means don't pee in the pool. Maybe you should just avoid the pool altogether so the rest of us can enjoy it," JayJ said, smirking.

How am I supposed to relax and enjoy myself with her around?

"Just remember Penny, the dye doesn't lie." she said.

Wow! To think, even the middle of paradise could be ruined by the presence of JayJ! I turned to look at hot Mexico boy. He had a look of total horror on his face. Well, I guess now I don't have to think about him anymore.

"Are you just going to ignore me the entire trip?" JayJ asked.

"That's the plan," I said. Unfortunately, that wasn't the plan according to my parents. They called me to come to dinner while each simultaneously gave me the "you best behave" look.

Dinner was as expected. Patrick and Ginger couldn't keep their eyes off each other, while my dad and Mr. Devilfeller, I mean, Rothefeller—my mom said I couldn't call them that during our trip, but she did only said "during"—talked business, my mom and Mrs. Devil, I mean Rothefeller, talked about, well, whatever moms talk about, and Parker and Junior talked about whatever boys talk about. And who do you suppose that left? You guessed it—just JayJ and I. My view of talking to JayJ only included no talky-talky. JayJ's idea of talking to Penny only included making fun of Penny. See? Just one more thing we do NOT have in common.

"So, Jiminy and I were hanging out before this trip," JayJ said. "Well, I better not tell you the rest of the story. Everybody knows you have a thing for him. I wouldn't want to make you jealous."

I was about to tell her that I had undeniable proof that she and Jiminy were just friends—because as you know, Jiminy made it clear, ever so beautifully, crystal clear, that they were only friends, but then, that would require my talking to her.

The next day, the girls—oh yay, another day with JayJ—were sent shopping, while the boys got to go do whatever boys do on vacation. Okay, I know what you are thinking—"but it's shopping"—and while I would agree, I would remind you that there is "shopping" and then there is "shopping with JayJ," and the former is incomparable to the latter. So much so, I was actually trying to convince my dad to take me with him, but he said that Mr. Rothefeller—oh, how I wanted to say Mr. Devilfeller—had a special day planned for the girls and that I wouldn't want to miss it.

He was right. After breakfast, we hopped on a boat and headed to Isla de Mujeres—Island of the Women, our tour guide translated before I could, because I so know Spanish—for a day of shopping.

I was trying to stick to the "plan," you know, to ignore JayJ and to pout the entire trip, but the amazing boat ride was beginning to make me excited to spend the day shopping and chilling on the beach. As much as I hate to admit it—trust me, it's killing me to admit it—I was having fun shopping. The shops were filled with all sorts of things from bright colored clothing, amazing paintings, and intricate souvenirs—all of them made by hand. I was having a blast finding things for me, Olive, and Frannie. I was even able to avoid JayJ most of the time, which only added to the shopping experience. After shopping, we headed to the beach for a little rest and relaxation.

We had just finished setting up our beach chairs, when JayJ turned to us.

"Who is that guy? And why does he keep saluting us?"

"Oh dear," my mom said, "that is one skimpy bathing suit. Just look away girls."

"Oh my," Mrs. Rothefeller said, with a little laugh. "It certainly is—hmm, very skimpy indeed," she said, seemingly unable to keep her eyes off of the guy.

Gross!

Well, I guess I had to at least see what they were talking about. Actually, I spun around as fast as I could secretly hoping that it was my hot Mexico boy—when my jaw fell to the ground, so that I was barely able to utter, "Oh my gosh! Is that Coach Shoe?! In a Speedo?!"

How in the world did the crazy PE teacher from Pottsville Elementary School end up on the same island, on the same beach, at the same time as us?

I was about to launch into my Speedo speech—if you are not a swimmer, then you should never, ever, ever wear a speedo ever, and when I say never, I mean NEVER, EVER, EVER!—when JayJ and I said simultaneously, "AHHHHH! IT BURNS MY EYES!!"—causing us both to blurt out, "Jinks!" Then we looked at each other and started to laugh our heads off. I guess it was one of those "you had to be there" moments.

We continued to laugh about seeing Coach Shoe in a Speedo at dinner as we relayed the story to everyone at the dinner table that evening. For the first time ever, JayJ was talking and laughing not at me, but with me.

For the next few days our vacation was packed with adventure. From riding the historic Copper Canyon Railway, to looking at Aztec Ruins, to swimming with dolphins—I couldn't help myself, I was having fun. But as they say, all good things must come to an end.

By the time we flew home, I couldn't wait to sleep in my own bed. Vacays are amazing, but I always end up missing my own bed by the end. I wanted to call Olive and Frannie and tell them everything, but it was pretty late when we got home, and I was so tired. That night when I got in bed, I think I was asleep before my head hit the pillow.

CHAPTER TWENTY

Dear Secret Pickle Society,

If one is looking for good luck in the New Year, one only need look to our friends to the south in Mexico for inspirations. On the eve of the New Year, families put up piñatas filled with yummy candy, little toys and trinkets, and money. While the blindfolded hitter is frantically trying to break the piñata, those who are watching (and trying not to laugh), they sing the piñata song, "Hit it, hit it, hit it. Don't lose your aim. Because if you lose your aim, you lose the way. You hit it once. You hit it twice. You hit it three times. And then your time is up." Every swing that finds its mark brings the family luck for the New Year. But you will never guess what they say will bring the family not only good luck, but good fortune as well. The secret I learned was to put a pickle in the piñata. And if you want not only good luck and good fortune, but are seeking good looks as well—because everybody knows it's never too late to have good looks—you must form the piñata to make it look like a pickle. I just so happened to learn how to make a perfect-looking, luck-and-good-looks-bringing pickle piñata when I was in Mexico. If you would like to learn how, you know how to contact me.

Sincerely,
Penny Picklepants ♡

When I woke up the next morning, I was glad to be home. I wasn't glad to see the snow, the wind and the general cold that had swept Pottsville since we had left, but still home is home.

After Olive came over and oohed and ahhed over my tan— yeah, it was the perfect tan—we went over to Frannie's. I was excited to see her and to see how she handled a week without me.

When we got to her home, no one answered. I couldn't imagine where she would be on this frigid day in January. But Olive said to keep knocking so I did. Finally, Frannie answered the door, by which time my hands were so frozen I thought they were going to fall off. Then I noticed how tired Frannie looked.

"Oh hello girls," she said. "Sorry, I was just taking a nap."

Well, that explains it.

"Please come in, it's quite chilly outside, and Penny you must be really cold after being in that nice Mexico heat."

As we walked in, I couldn't help noticing that the glow that usually shone from Frannie's face whenever she saw Olive and I had diminished.

"Frannie are you okay? You look, um, kind of tired."

Of course Frannie started to laugh and said, "Just recovering from a cold. Unlike some," she said, smiling at me, "I have not been lying on a beach all week long soaking up the sun—speaking of which, tell me everything about your trip."

And just like that I dived into the details of my Mexico adventure, telling them all about hot Mexico boy, the amazing beaches, and Isla de Mujeres; how JayJ and I saw Coach Shoe, what he was wearning, and how JayJ and I were actually getting along.

After chatting for a while, and of course after some good old fashioned pickle-based cooking—pickle burritos, trust me they were delicious!—Olive and I said our good-byes and left. Frannie had barely shut the door when Olive turned and looked at me.

"I really liked cooking at Frannie's house. Do you think I could..."

I knew it! "Yes, you can cook with us."

"No," Olive said. "What I was going to say was do you think

she would mind cooking separately with me?"

I think by the look I gave Olive she realized her mistake.

"It was... just a thought." Olive said. "But don't you think Frannie looked a little pale?"

Of course being one that is totally in-tune with my friends, I quickly answered, "Relax, Olive. She's recovering from a cold and just needs some sun. Speaking of which, have you ever thought about going to a tanning booth?"

Olive answered by throwing a snowball at me. I took that as a no.

Making our way home, Olive and I parted and I told her I would call her later to find out what she would be wearing on Monday. She laughed and said, "Whatever."

I hadn't taken but a few steps into the house before I heard muffled voices coming from behind the closed door on my dad's office. I had noticed that my dad's office door had been closed a lot lately. Of course, it made me curious and made me want to put my ear up to the door to see if I could hear anything important. But I was a lady now, I was growing up and grownups don't snoop. So I did what any mature, graceful, adultish person would do—I tip-toed over to the office and put my ear to the door.

"Just as long as you keep it running essentially the same way," I heard my dad say.

"Of course, of course," I heard another man say.

"There are a lot of good people there and I just..."

"I understand, Peter. Trust me."

Then my dad's noisy printer started printing.

I was straining to hear what was being said when the door opened and I fell into the office. So much for being mature and graceful.

"Oh, hello there, Penny," my dad said, holding out his hand to help me up, "did you need something?"

As I took my dad's hand, I saw not only my dad smiling down at me, but Mr. Rothefeller as well. "Umm, no I was just… and then I… um, fell." That made sense, right?

"Well, in that case, why don't you see Mr. Rothefeller to the door?"

I guess I deserved that.

After I saw Mr. Rothefeller out and we said our pleasant-ries—"How is school Penny?"—"Fine."—I found my dad in his study looking over some papers.

"Hey, Dad," I said, entering his office. "So, what was Mr. Rothefeller doing here?"

"It was business, Penny—none of it concerns you."

"Were you guys talking about the plant?"

"Penny, like I said, it doesn't concern you."

"If it's about the plant it does concern me. It concerns me a whole lot, in fact."

"Penny, everything is fine with the plant. You needn't worry yourself. You are too young to worry so much."

Gaining no ground, I decided to change tactics.

"Why did the Rothefellers pay for our trip to Mexico?" I would not be deterred this time.

"Again, Penny…"

"It's business," I said mockingly.

"Penny. Mr. Rothefeller is a very knowledgeable man. He has a lot of advice to offer regarding the plant. Beyond that, all I can say for now is you will know everything in due time, okay? All in due time."

I guess I was just deterred. I was about to ask why adults always talk in riddles when my dad looked down at his papers that cluttered his desk and said, "Don't you need to figure out what you are going to wear to school? Doesn't that usually take you a few hours?" Of course, he looked up for a moment and smiled, but I knew it was his round-about way of politely asking me to leave.

I was bugged that he was keeping me in the dark. "It's my future too, you know," I said, walking out. I figured it would be more dramatic that way, but I wasn't sure if he heard me over the stomps and the huffing.

CHAPTER TWENTY-ONE

Dear Secret Pickle Society,

MY FIRST TOUR, by Penny Picklepants

In case you didn't already know, I am now the official tour guide of the Picklepants Pickle Factory. There I was on a Saturday morning, when out of nowhere come two very lost Japanese tourists. "Wow!" I thought to myself, "People are coming from all over the world just to see my tour of the plant."

"Hello," I said standing there in my pickle suit, which I only wore to get people to take the tour mind you. "Would you like to take a free tour of my family's pickle factory?"

They then proceeded to point at me with one hand and laugh while covering their mouth with their other hand.

Oh-kay, I thought to myself. Let's try that again, shall we?

"Would you like to take a free tour of my family's pickle factory?

They then said, still pointing at me, "Pic-cha?"

"Did they just call me Pikachu?" I thought to myself.

"No, not Pikachu," I said, pointing to my costume, "Pickle, like you eat, yummy pickle. My family has a pickle plant. Do you want a tour?"

They again said, still pointing at me, "Pic-cha?"

"Sorry, no Pikachu, just pickles. Do you like pickles?" I said, mimicking eating a pickle.

"No, no, no," they said, still pointing at me, "pic-cha?"

I had no idea what to do so I took them on the tour, which they loved by the way. Turns out, however, they just wanted to take a picture. After the tour, they told my dad, "This girl really needs to learn English."

There are a lot more stories where this came from, but to hear them you'll just have to contact me.

Sincerely,
Penny Picklepants ♡

Between school—where every teacher had decided that we were way behind and that we needed to double our efforts, aka double our homework—and giving tours at the plant on Saturdays, I had hardly had time to make plans for my birthday. Spring was almost here, as well as my birthday. But I found my thoughts more and more focused on the factory and less and less on my social life, or lack thereof. I guess that's what happens when you are a career woman—your social life suffers.

The tours were going great, lost Japanese tourists aside, and being at the factory was an eye opening experience. Mr. Rothefeller had been to the plant more times than I cared to count, but whenever I pressed my dad for details, he just smiled and would say something philosophical and parentish like, "Don't worry about it. Isn't your birthday coming up? Don't you usually take about six weeks to plan it?" Man he was good at redirecting my thoughts.

I would then usually tell him something like, "Yeah, so for my birthday I want a full day at the mall with Olive. We are going to..." and then I listed all the things Olive and I were going to do at the mall when I turned the ol' 1-2!

Finally, the big day had arrived.

"Happy birthday to me," I sang in my head. "Happy birthday to me. Happy birthday dear..."

"Penny?!" my name reverberated, but not in my own voice.

"Penny?! Wake up—the phone's for you," my mom called from downstairs.

Ah, my birthday. Already the phone calls are starting to pour in to wish me a wonderful, fabtabulous birthday.

"Coming, Mom!" I yelled.

I quickly glanced at my bedroom mirror to see if I looked older and more mature—to my shock, I did!—I couldn't believe that turning twelve made me look so much like a teenager. I mean, starting today when people asked how old I was I could officially tell them, "Almost 13." How awesome was that? But for today, I would enjoy being 12 and I would enjoy it with my besty Olive.

"Hello?"

"Hey Penn, it's Olive…" Olive said, like she had just woken up.

"Oh my gosh, Olive—guess what!—I am twelve today. Can you believe it? I am TWELVE! I can't wait for the day to get started…"

"Penn…"

"I mean, I could hardly sleep last night. I kept going over and over in my mind how this day is going to be like the BEST DAY EVER!"

"Penn…"

"Oh and the mall—I can't believe we are going to spend the entire day at the mall. I can't wait to try on shoes, and jeans, and sweaters, and of course, dresses. Don't you think we should try on prom dresses for fun? I want to find the one with the…"

"PENNY!" Olive said, sounding very stuffed up. "I'm sick."

"What?" I said. "Olive, you are not thick, you're just a little bigger around the waist. I mean it's just baby fat, but once you turn twelve it will disappear. I mean, I looked at myself in the mirror this morning, and I couldn't believe how much older I looked."

"What?" Olive said. "I'm not thick! What do you mean I am bigger around the waist? I want you to know that the doctor says I am the perfect weight for my age, and…"

"Exactly. That's what I meant." Phew, dodged that bullet.

"Ugh! Penny, I said I am SICK—I've been throwing up all

night."

"Well, then you're done throwing up, right? So you mean you *were* sick. That's fine."

"No, Penny. I was sick, and I still am sick. I'm not going to be able to go to the mall."

I was stunned, my brain was trying to decode what Olive had just said and all that I could come up with was my computer voice saying, "Does not compute, does not compute."

"No!" I said. "You can't be sick! Not on my birthday of all days!"

"Like I had a choice. I feel really awful."

"Well you should," I said. "You are ruining my birthday!"

"No, I mean I feel like I am about to throw up any minute."

Silence. I didn't know what to say.

"Penny? Are you there?"

"Yes."

"Well, I also feel bad about missing your birthday, but we can go to the mall when I am feeling better."

"Yeah, that sounds… sounds great. Call me when you feel better, okay?"

I couldn't believe that my birthday was already ruined because my best friend decided to get sick. I mean I would never let myself get sick on Olive's birthday. I would just push through the pain. I would sacrifice my health for my friend because, yeah, I am just a good friend like that.

"Penny?" my mom asked. "Are you through with the phone? I need to make a call."

I hadn't moved since Olive had hung up. I had no idea how long the operator had been saying, "If you would like to make a call, please hang up and try again. If you would like to make a call, please hang up and try again."

I knew that if I turned around and looked at my mom I would start crying, but almost-teenagers don't cry. I also knew I wouldn't be able to stand with the phone in my hand and my back towards the world all day. I was going to have to turn around eventually. And plus, I really needed to pee.

Okay, I will just concentrate on heading to the bathroom, having a good cry, and then walking out like the lady I was. I had seen it in the movies a hundred times and if it happens in the movies, then it must happen in real life. I turned around, looked at my mom, then ran into her arms and started to cry.

"Olive's sick and she can't spend the day with me and now my birthday is ruined, Mom, it's ruined!" Okay, so much for acting the part of an almost-teenager.

"Oh, Penny," my mom said, "I am so sorry." We sat there hugging each other while my mom brushed my hair with her hand like she always used to do.

"Tell you what," my mom said, "you and I will spend the day shopping at the mall and going out to lunch. I know I am not Olive, but we could still have fun together. What do you say?"

Oh great! The first day of being an almost-teenager and I have to spend it with my mom, but I couldn't say that to her—mature almost-teenagers don't say those kind of things.

"Great! The first day of being an almost-teenager and I have to spend it with my mom."

Oops! I guess I better start filtering my thoughts before saying them out loud.

"I am just going to ignore that because I know you are upset.

Listen, I will make your birthday breakfast feast and after that we will figure it out. I just have a feeling that your day isn't going to be as bad as you think."

"Mom, you are only saying that because you are my mom and mom's by law are supposed to say stuff like that."

She just laughed, gave me another hug and started to prepare my birthday breakfast, featuring chocolate waffles, fresh fruit, and whipped cream. Before my dad had left in the morning for the pickle factory, he had left me the most important birthday gift a girl could ever get: money! But even that wasn't making me feel better.

As Patrick and Parker came into the kitchen, my mom filled them in on my birthday's demise. Parker, being Parker, then said, "Maybe she just got sick of you?" I gave him my best crusty, which apparently did not faze him, as he nonchalantly returned his attention to the DS that never seemed to leave his hands.

At least Patrick made an effort, "Penny, I was going to spend the day with Ginger. You are more than welcome to spend the day with us."

"Yeah, like I want to spend the day with the older sister of my mortal enemy. All I know is that my birthday is going to be completely, 100% Rothefeller-free!"

"Suit yourself," Patrick said, shrugging his shoulders. Like I said, at least he tried.

But then Parker decided he wasn't finished. "Penny, I'm sorry that Olive is sick and I am sure she isn't sick of you. I was just joking. But if you want, you could always spend the day with me," Parker said, with those puppy brown eyes of his. He was such a cute little brother, well, when he wanted to be.

"Oh Parker. You are so cute—when you want to be," I said,

with a smile. "Thanks for the offer, buddy, but I'll be fine, though."
I figured the more I said it, the more I would believe it.

During breakfast I got a call from my Grandma Picklepants and
then a little later from my Grandma and Grandpa Porterhouse.
They each wished me a happy birthday and told me their birthday
cards were in the mail—hopefully more shopping money, which
hopefully would arrive today.

After Parker left the kitchen, I figured I should act the mature
twelve-almost-thirteen-year-old woman that I was becoming and
help my mom do the dishes. My mom always wanted to teach me
how to do the dishes. I don't know why though. Didn't she know
that when I was old enough to actually have my own dishes, I
would just hire somebody to wash them for me? When I told her
that, she just started to laugh and said, "I thought the same thing
when I was your age, Penny." I just couldn't believe that my mom
had once been my age!

We had the kitchen almost cleaned up when I heard the doorbell
ring. I secretly hoped it was Olive and she would yell, "PSYCH"
when I opened the door. But it wasn't Olive at all. It was Frannie.

When I saw Frannie standing in the door way, holding a beautiful gift bag, I told myself to remain calm, and do everything that
Frannie had taught me about being a lady. I then said, with utter
despair, "My birthday is ruined, my twelfth birthday is ruined."

"What do you mean your birthday is ruined, what happened?"

"Unfortunately for our birthday girl here," my mom said coming up to the door, "Olive is sick with the flu and will be unable
to spend the day with Penny at the mall. Won't you come in for a
moment, Frannie?"

"Oh, just a moment, yes. Thank you."

Hearing my mom say it again made it seem even worse. I just couldn't believe that with everything I had to deal with, that my birthday was ruined. Fate must have really had it out for me.

"Oh Penny, I am so sorry to hear that. I know how much you were looking forward to spending the day with Olive."

I had talked to Frannie so much about my birthday I bet she could have likely repeated what we were going to do word for word:

"First, I'm going to wear my pink oxford with my favorite white skirt. I'm going to have my mom drop us off at the west entrance. Then we are going to hit the first floor of stores, and yes we are going to go to every store."

"Every store, Penny?" Frannie would ask with a wide grin.

"Every store, Frannie!" I would say. Then I would proceed to tell her where we were going to eat lunch, I mean you have to keep up your shopping strength. "After lunch we are going to hit the second floor shops and end the day at the Prom Dress store. I cannot wait for that one."

But alas, it wasn't meant to be, even though it so totally was. Now Olive and I would never spend my birthday together. We would never go into every store together. We wouldn't have lunch together. And we wouldn't even be able try on dresses together. My birthday was ruined!

"Penny, what about spending the day with me?" Frannie asked.

Huh? Well that got my attention. "Frannie, you would want to spend the day at the mall and trying on prom dresses?"

"Heavens no," she said with a laugh. "I wouldn't want to do that, but I would like to spend the day with my favorite birthday girl. You just have to agree to spend it the way a lady would spend her day."

"What do you mean?"

"Well, for starters, you would need to put on your favorite dress. Then you would have to do your hair. A lady always does her hair. We would then have my driver pick us up at my house and take us to real shops, where they serve you tea and sandwiches while you try on beautiful clothes, the store employees fussing over you the entire time. We would then eat lunch at the country club, and finally wind down the day at the spa. A lady always ends a day out at the spa."

Should I pinch myself now or later? "Frannie, are you kidding me?" I did not want to get my hopes up only to have them dashed once again.

Frannie took my face into her gloved hands and said, "I never kid about a lady's day out. You be at my house in one hour. That should be plenty of time for you to get ready for the best twelfth birthday ever."

I was racing up the stairs before she could even finish, but quickly turned around because with all the commotion I had forgotten to ask Frannie about the birthday gift she had brought me. "Frannie, wait—your gift. Do you want to give it to me now?" I asked, but honestly what could be better than a day of shopping?

"Oh this? No, it is nothing important. I will give it to you later. Now, go get ready and I will see you in one hour."

I was so excited that I couldn't stop smiling, which is really a pain when shampoo is running into your mouth as well as all the other products to help your hair reach its maximum fabulosity. Even with a mouth tasting like mango shampoo with a hint of lemongrass, I just couldn't stop smiling, as well as wondering what other tricks Frannie has up her sleeve. She never ceased to amaze.

Finally, it was time to go. I gave my mom a quick hug good-bye, grabbed my birthday money, and headed out the door. I think I skipped the entire way to Frannie's. I knew 12-year-old girls that are on the cusp of womanhood do not skip, but I just couldn't help myself, and I didn't care. I was just so happy. When I got to Frannie's front door, I started to knock when a strange man opened the door.

"Oh hello," the man said, "you must be Penny."

Whaa...? How did this guy even know who I am and what was he doing at Frannie's?

"Um, yes," I said, forgetting the first rule of strangers. "And who are you?"

"Penny," Frannie said, appearing behind the man, "this is Mr. Lawson. He is my attorney. We were just finishing up some last minute business. He is on his way out and it looks like our car is here, so I will go grab my things and then we will be ready to go."

"I'll take care of the rest Frannie," the man said, turning towards me. "Nice to finally meet you, Penny. Oh, and happy birthday." He then stuck his hand out like I knew what I to do with it. So I did what any lady would do. I gave him a high-five on the side.

"Yeah, nice to meet you too, Mr...." Yeah, I already forgot his name.

"Penny, are you ready for the best birthday ever?" Frannie asked.

"Like you even need to ask. Let's go!"

When we got to the first store, the ladies made such a fuss over me. "Oh look at this beauty. How did you get to be so beautiful?" was all they could say and of course the compliments didn't stop the entire time I was trying on the clothes. "You look like Miss America. What a beauty queen." I must admit, I was lapping it up.

Lunch at the country club was, well, just as equally amazing. When we walked into the door, which was opened for us, everybody kept saying, "Well hello, Mrs. Frankincense. It is so nice to see you again. And who is this charming young woman with you today?" They kept calling me, "Miss Picklepants!" They would say things like, "Would you like more Sprite Miss PicklePants?" and, "Would you like more fries with your hamburger Miss Picklepants?" A girl could get used to this kind of lifestyle. They even brought out a big piece of chocolate birthday cake, with twelve candles. The entire staff then sang me Happy Birthday. When we were getting ready to leave, I noticed that they hadn't brought the check yet. "Frannie, we can't leave, they haven't brought the check."

Frannie smiled and said, "Penny, they never bring me the check." She just raised her eyebrows and then laughed. I was worried we were about to pull a "dine and dash" when Frannie explained, "It just goes on my bill." How cool is that?!

The spa was amazing. The minute we got there, we were ushered to a beautiful room and told to change into a plush, white robe. We got facials, which was just this side of heaven. I was tempted to taste the green goop they put on our faces, but I didn't want to embarrass Frannie, so I did it when nobody was watching. It tasted like avocados! When I suggested to the facial lady they should use pickles instead of avocados she just laughed.

Then we got massages—they were so heavenly! Andre, my masseuse, kept telling me that I was tense in my shoulders and neck and that I needed to relax more. I told him that if he had to go to school with JayJ Rothefeller he would be tense too. He laughed, and said, "It can't be that bad," to which I replied, "Oh, but it can.' Again he just laughed.

As we drove home from the "best birthday ever" day, I couldn't help but put my head on Frannie's shoulder and go over and over in my mind how amazing my birthday turned out to be. I was tired, but I didn't dare go to sleep in case I woke up and found that this had all been a dream.

"Frannie, thank you so much."

"You are so welcome."

As the driver pulled up to my house, I felt like I needed to say more to Frannie—to thank her for the wonderful day.

"Frannie, I just want you to know that this has been the best birthday I have ever had. Thank you for spending not only my birthday with me, but seriously, for spending all that money on me. I felt like a princess. I hope one day I have as much money as you do so I can do this every Saturday!"

Frannie smiled and looked at me very seriously and said, "When one is your age, one thinks money can buy happiness. But when you reach my age, you realize that it is not having money but what you do for others with your money that makes you happy."

Hmm, I thought. Then I said, "I don't really see the difference. I mean, I could do a lot of great things if I had money, like go shopping, or travel. I could even spend a week on a Mediterranean Island. How amazing would that be?"

"A vacation to a Mediterranean island is amazing, trust me, but the highlight is usually looking forward to being home with friends and family. If you do good things with your money, like helping others, well, it beats a vacation anywhere, any time."

"Oh, I get it." I said with sly smile, "It makes you happy when you spend money on ME. Well if that's the case, I've got a whole lot of happiness planned for you."

Frannie just laughed.

"Oh Penny, what a thrill it has been for me to get to know you. You make feel young again."

I opened the door to get out of the car, then I said, "Frannie, you make me feel old, I mean, not old, like old…, I mean, um, well, you just make me feel like I am already thirteen!" Mouth: insert foot here.

Frannie laughed again. "Oh Penny. What a rare, precious gem you are. You have been so important to me, and I am so happy you let me spend your twelfth birthday with you. And when I was your age, I thought old people smelled weird too."

I wanted to melt right there on the car floor. It felt like the entire ground beneath me had given way and I was half way to China. "You read it?" I could hardly breathe. "You read the blog entry?" Hyperventilation was setting in. "Oh, Frannie! I am so sorry. I can't believe in a million years I ever wrote that. Please forgive me!"

"Penny! There is no need to ask for forgiveness. I forgave you a long time ago."

"You did?"

"Well, of course I did."

"But why? I never even apologized."

"Growing up, my father would always ask us, with a big smile on his face, 'Is life sweet or is life sour?' After waiting a moment for us to think about it, he would always tell us, 'Only you can decide the correct answer to that question. No circumstance, person, or thing can make it for you.'"

I had no idea what she was talking about.

"What he meant, was that it's up to you which it is. Life is what you make it."

Luckily Frannie explained it to me.

"Life is much too short Penny to live offended and bitter. In the future, just make sure you truly get to know someone before passing judgment. I think it will help you see things in a whole new light."

Oh my gosh! Frannie was so wise. If only I could ever be half as wise one day. Though I hated having to leave Frannie, it was late and it was time to leave. I pushed the car door open slowly and got out of the car.

"Well, bye," I said. I was almost to the front door when I remembered that Frannie had never given me the present she had brought to my house that morning. I ran back to the car and motioned for her to roll down the window.

"Sorry," I said, "I just remembered you never gave me my birthday gift, I mean, the one you brought over this morning."

With a sweet smile Frannie said, "I left it at your house so you could open it when you got in."

"Oh, of course," I said. "Okay, well, since you didn't get to see me open it, I will come over and personally give you the biggest hug ever since I know I will love it."

"I will count the minutes," she said with a big smile. She then slightly hesitated, looked at me and said, "I do love you Penny."

I always felt awkward saying "I love you" to people other than my parents, but when I really thought about it, I did love Frannie. She was an amazing person who had become one of my best friends, in spite of our age difference.

"I love you too, Frannie," I said, with Frannie's face beaming. And with that, she left, as a tear rolled down my face.

After I watched the car drive off, I ran into the house and tore open her gift—as if spending the day with Frannie wasn't already enough. I started to laugh when I saw it. I kept turning it over and over not believing my eyes. My whole family came to see why I was laughing. When they saw what I had in my hands they started laughing too.

"Only Frannie" I kept thinking to myself.

"A cookbook? Frannie got you a cookbook?" Parker said. "Well, that was weird."

"Parker, this is my cookbook."

"Yeah, I know it's *your* cookbook. Frannie gave it to you."

"No, I mean, it's *my* cookbook. Look," I said, holding it up.

Upon closer inspection, Parker's eyes got really big and suddenly he understood. My present from Frannie was my cookbook: "Penny Picklepants and the Twenty-Pickle Pie," by Penny Picklepants. She had taken all the recipes and my commentary from the blog and put them into one compilation, my very own cookbook. I thumbed through the pages—there was the recipe for Dilly Beef Sandwiches and Dilly Pickle Dip—and Frannie's favorite that she taught to me, Pickle Poached Salmon. "Where did all these pictures come from?" I thought to myself. Nearly every page included a picture. Inside the cover it read:

Dearest Penny,

Variety is the very spice of life, that which gives it all its flavor... that and well, pickles.

With Love,

Frannie

P.S. I hope you enjoy the photos that some friends of mine generously contributed to the effort.

That night, I couldn't take my eyes off of my cookbook. I kept saying to myself over and over while laughing, "My cookbook. I, Penny Picklepants, have a cookbook!"

Now this had been a good day, perhaps the best day. And it was all because of Frannie.

CHAPTER TWENTY-TWO

Dear Secret Pickle Society,

I just wanted to write you a quick note to tell you the exciting news. I, Penny Picklepants, your #1 faithful fan and follower am happy to announce that I am now an officially published author. My best friend in the whole wide world, Mrs. Frannie Frankincense, fellow pickle aficionado, compiled all of my pickle recipes (created with her help) as well as all of my beyond-her-years insights, into "Penny Picklepants and the Twenty-Pickle Pie," by Penny Picklepants. Can you believe that? Isn't that great? Plus, Frannie had some friends take some amazing photos for it. Just thought you would like to know. Drop me a line and I'll send you a signed copy, although I think I own the only copy that exists for the time being.

Sincerely,

Penny Picklepants ♡

Monday started out like any other Monday. I got up and looked in the mirror—right side of the face no zits, left side of the face no zits—it's going to be a good skin day. Then I showered—mmm, the smell of mango, pomegranate, and lemongrass in the morning… it's no wonder I always get so hungry taking a shower. Next, I got dressed—favy jeans: check. New shirt from birthday shopping that I so love: check. The perfect belt and shoes to bring it all together: check and check. Lastly, I grabbed a bite to eat and then headed out the door. A new year, a new shirt and a new age—it was going to be a good day.

School was, well… school—boring with a dash of homework with a hint of ogling and goggling at Jiminy. And get this, JayJ even smiled at me without a hint of sarcasm.

Olive asked, "What was that all about?"

"I don't know."

And Jiminy couldn't stop smiling at me either.

Olive asked, "What was that all about?"

"I don't know."

Maybe he figured it was too improbable that I was going to throw myself or any other thing at him… scratch that—the probability of my throwing myself at him was very high.

At the end of the school day Olive asked if I wanted to come over to her house, but I told her that I was going to Frannie's for a cooking session. I told her to come over later and try out our latest creation, pickle chimi-chungas.

"Let me guess, pickmi-chungas?"

I responded with a, "Not even close! They are called pimi-pi-chungas."

I couldn't tell if her eye roll this time signaled a "whatever!" or something else, so I just ignored it. As I started to work on my homework, my dad walked in the front door and announced: "FAMILY MEETING! Everybody in my office, now!"

I started to laugh. The last time we had a family meeting was, like, well, never. What does one do at a family meeting? I have already met my family. Why would I want to meet them again?

"Dad, I really don't have time for this 'family meeting,'" I said, saying "family meeting" with air quotes. "I have homework then I need to get over to Frannie's so I can do my cooking assignment. We are going to make…"

"Penny, in my office, right now," my dad said, wearing a very stern look on his face.

Now I will admit, I don't take my parent's looks all that seriously. But there are times in one's life that the look on a parent's face makes one pause and ponder the wisdom of doing what they say—this seemed like one of those times.

As we all sat down in the office, there was a strange silence wrapped up and deep-fried in tension that filled the room. From the looks of it, Patrick and Parker, in addition to my mom, all understood the seriousness of the situation. I figured it was the perfect time to try out some of my new pickle jokes, because everyone knows there is no better way to break the tension in a room than with pickle jokes.

"So a Rabbi, a pickle and a truck driver walk into a bar..."

"Penny," my dad said, "neither the time nor the place. This is serious and I need you all to understand what is going on."

Then it dawned on me—he was about to tell me everything I wanted to know about the factory, revealing all the secrets of those hushed conversations between my mom and my dad. I could finally stop acting like I didn't know that I knew something was going on, but trying to act like I didn't know to not let them know that I knew, you know? Sheesh, keeping secrets is really hard, but I had done it. I had proven I was the Fort Knox of keeping secrets!

"Well, your mother and I have been talking a lot about the future of the factory..."

Huh? Future of the factory? There is a future? Maybe all the secrets shared between him and my mom weren't about the factory's demise after all. Maybe they are going to announce that I am going to be the newest and youngest—best ever—professional pickle taster. They must have taken notice of all the hard work I had been putting in at the factory and come to the same conclusion I had—

that I, Penny Picklepants, am the future of Picklepants Pickles.

"We are selling it to the Rothefellers."

Say what?

"They have given us an offer that simply we cannot refuse."

What? Did my father just say what I think he just said? Everything started going in slow-mo again. "Okay," I told myself, "just breathe—focus and breathe."

"What? Did you, the son and heir of grandpa Picklepants, just say what I think you just said?"

"Penny, listen. Your mom and I have decided to sell the pickle factory to the Rothefellers. They have made an incredible offer that, in light of everything else, we cannot refuse. We really don't have any other choice—"

When I looked around the room, everybody seemed fine with it. Patrick looked relieved. And Parker, well, I don't think he ever cared. When I looked at my mom, she looked happy. Yes, HAPPY! And my dad? He just looked relieved as well.

"Besides," my dad continued, "with this offer, we can finally do all those things your mom and I have dreamed of doing, but never could because the money just wasn't there, like seeing the Taj Mahal, and…"

"So in order for you to live your dream you have to kill mine?" I said.

"Penny, this isn't just for your mom and I—it's what's best for all of us." I guess that was that. "Now, there is one thing that I need you guys to do," my dad said.

As if I was in any mood to help my dad, the dream killer. He had just dashed… completely decimated… obliviated… pulverized… banished to death and ruin my childhood dreams. My dream of becoming a professional pickle taster, the youngest ever professional pickle taster, was dead. Did anyone in this family even care an ounce about the plant as much as I did?

"You need to keep a tight lid on this."

"Like Picklepants pickle jar lid tight?" I couldn't resist.

"Yes," my dad said, clearly not amused. "You can in no way talk to or tell anybody about this. And yes, I am looking at you, Penny, when I am saying this." What was that supposed to mean? "The truth is that if we kept the factory we would just end up losing it anyway. I thought the factory had been paid off, but turns out the bank made a mistake, and, well, not to get into specifics—if we don't sell the factory, the bank is going to take it and auction it anyway. And then, I don't know what would happen, and there are a lot of jobs at stake here. Now, before anything can happen, there are papers and forms that need signing as well as a bunch of legal technicalities that needs to take place before this goes public. If any of this gets leaked to anybody—and I mean anybody—it could mean the end of the deal. The truth is, we've barely been able to keep the factory afloat. But by selling the factory to the Rothefellers, I think a lot of people will be able to keep their jobs."

"Why don't you just hire Mr. Rothefeller to run the factory? You don't need to sell it, do you? I mean, I've been dreaming about working at the factory ever since I can remember. There's no way I can work there if the Rothefellers own it. I wouldn't even want to." Great! Now the tears are threatening to spill. I was bouncing between feeling angry, sad, disgusted, depressed, hopeless, and confused, as well as every other emotion that goes along with your dreams being killed. There was nothing I could do.

"Penny, I know you had dreams…" my dad said.

"Exactly! Had! I HAD dreams, but now they're dead, because my own father is a dream killer." I was so mad that I ran out of the office, out the front door and I ran to the first place that popped into my head—Frannie's house.

I started running as fast as I could to Frannie's—which by the way, if you ever want to make a dramatic exit from a room, make sure you have a coat on when it is unseasonably cold and blustery outside.

An ambulance whizzed by, nearly making me trip—flashbacks of somersaulting over mailboxes raced through my head. At first I thought my parents had called 911 on me because they were concerned that I had, oh so dramatically, left the "family meeting." But as I watched the ambulance turn down Frannie's street, my stomach dropped while my heart started to beat even faster.

When I turned down Frannie's street, I saw the ambulance stop at her house. There was also a fire truck and two police cars parked on her street. The lights from all the vehicles were twirling, whirling, and blinding. I beelined it to Frannie's house, but before I even reached her lawn, a policeman grabbed me. I started to freak out and yell, "Let me go! Why are you here? Where's Frannie?! WHERE'S FRANNIE?!" I screamed, struggling to free myself from the policeman's arms. My reaction must have alarmed him because he suddenly got down on one knee, grabbed me by the arms, and looked me in the eyes. He then asked, "Did you know Mrs. Frankincense?"

"Yes I know her!" I exclaimed. "Now, let me go!"

"Miss, I can't do that. You've got to settle down."

"Let go of me and I will," I said, struggling to free myself.

"Miss, how are you related to Mrs. Frankincense? Are you her next of kin?"

"What?" I said.

"Are you family?"

"Well, practically," I said. "I'm all the family she has left." I just wanted to see Frannie. I wanted her to tell me everything was going to be okay.

"Miss? I need you to tell me what your name is."

"Penny," I said, sobbing.

"And what's your last name?"

"Picklepants," I said. "Frannie is my best friend, and I just need to talk to her. Please, just let me go. I have had the worst day ever and I just need to talk with Frannie. Please let me go see her."

For as long as I live, I will never forget the look on the officer's face or the words he spoke at that moment.

"Miss Picklepants," he said, bowing his head down so that he could look me in the eyes. He then looked down at the sidewalk and shook his head, letting out a deep breath. He took another breath, swallowed, then look back up at me.

"I am so sorry, Miss Picklepants, but Mrs. Frankincense has passed away."

All time came to a stop. I couldn't hear a thing. All senses muted, it was like I was floating in the middle of space with nothing around me but a vast and empty sea of silent and utter blackness.

"What?" I said, finally coming to. "What do you mean passed away?" I said.

"I mean," the officer said, "Mrs. Frankincense is…"

Just then there appeared at Frannie's door a paramedic carrying a gurney, another paramedic carrying it from the other end. On the gurney lay a body, with a white sheet over it. They brought the gurney to the stairs, lifted it down the stairs, and placed it in the ambulance. The ambulance left slowly, without its sirens blaring.

"NO!" I screamed, covering my mouth. "No!" I said, collapsing on the officer and bawling.

"Miss," the officer said, placing a blanket over me, "I am so sorry for your loss. I have to go and take care of some business. But if there is anything we can do, please just ask."

I sat there crying for so long, wondering how in one day I had lost everything—my dream, my best friend, my entire life—that I had no idea how long I had been sitting there before I realized that Olive had her arm around me. How could a day that started out so well end up so horribly?

After everybody had driven off, and all the neighbors had gone back into their homes, Olive and I were the only ones left.

"Do you want to talk?" she asked, with tears welling in her eyes.

I looked at her, shook my head no, and started to cry again. "I think I just need some time." She gave me a big hug and I started to walk back to my house alone.

As I walked in a daze, I kept wondering how this day could have happened, why everything that had happened had to happen. Why did the Rothefellers ever have to move to Pottsville? Why did the factory have to be sold? And if it had to be sold, then why to the Rothefellers, of all people? But most of all, I wondered why Frannie… oh Frannie! Why did you have to die?! I knew she had been sick, but she seemed fine—even happy—on my birthday.

It was all too much, too much for a twelve-year-old girl. My mind couldn't fathom never seeing her again, her beautiful, smiling face. I couldn't believe that we would never get to stand in her kitchen creating our crazy concoctions ever again—that I wouldn't get to see the gleam in her eye whenever she told me her amazing stories—that I would never again get to roam through her house admiring all the amazing things it held.

As each "would never" hit me, a fresh wave of tears poured from my eyes as a fresh wave of sadness overcame my heart. "Oh, Frannie! Why did you have to leave me?"

As I walked into my house, my mom quickly gave me a hug and asked if I was alright. Why do people ask you if you are okay when they clearly know you are not? It wasn't that I didn't appreciate the hug—I was just still too numb to talk about it. There was a part of me that refused to believe it could be true.

I ran up the stairs mumbling that I just needed some time alone. I just needed to sort out all the thoughts swirling through my head. I realized I had to write a tribute to Frannie. Then I fell asleep before dinner and slept the whole night through.

CHAPTER TWENTY-THREE

That night I dreamt that I was sitting in Frannie's kitchen eating fried pickles and eggs—yes they are so delicious and even more so when you fall asleep on an empty stomach—Frannie walked into the kitchen wearing her favorite black dress that she had designed, her pickle brooch that she had given to me, and a smile, her signature smile. She didn't sit, but just stood there smiling at me. She then walked over to me, grabbed my hand and while looking straight into my eyes said, "Do not worry Penny, everything works out in the end."

I just sat there holding her hand, looking into her eyes, not wanting to let go when she said, "Penny, it's time for me to go. Frank has been patiently waiting for me—we are going to Paris. We always loved Paris."

"But Frannie, I need you more... more than ever—please don't leave! What am I going to do without you?"

"Penny, like I said, everything works out in the end—trust me." I wanted her to stay with me and explain how everything was going to work out. At that particular moment in time, I just didn't see how it could. I was still holding her hands when she turned her head towards somebody and said, "I'm coming...." She turned to me, smiled and said, "It's going to be okay Penny." With that, she let go of my hands and I watched her walk away. I yelled for her to come back, but she acted like she couldn't hear me. "Frannie! You can't leave me," I cried, tears pouring down my face. "I need you! Frannie! Frannie? Please... please don't leave me!"

I woke up hoping it was all a bad dream. But I knew it wasn't. I then hoped what Frannie had told me would be true, that everything would somehow work out in the end. But when I sat up in my bed, I had never felt so alone and for the first time since I had met Frannie, I doubted her.

I woke up before the sunrise. Everyone else was still asleep, even my dad. I crept down the stairs, avoiding the noisy parts of the stairs. I walked into the dark kitchen, leaving the lights off. I flipped on the computer and sat down at the keyboard. After the modem connected me to the internet, I went to the blog and started writing the following tribute to Frannie:

A few years ago, I lost my favorite necklace—a silver chain with a round aquamarine stone. I had worn it to the pool because I had decided that it looked perfect with my new swimsuit. My mom had distinctly told me to take it off when we got to the pool, because she was afraid I would lose it. I convinced her that it would be fine. But after a day of swimming and lying in the sun, I finally realized the necklace was gone. I looked everywhere—in the pool, in the girls' locker room, in the kiddie pool, in the deep end, by the diving boards—everywhere. It was gone. I was so upset, and my mom's telling me, "I told you so," even with just a look, didn't help matters much. By the time we got home, I was determined to earn enough money to buy another one.

I did extra chores, helped at the pickle factory—I did whatever it took to earn the money for a necklace to replace the one I had lost. The day arrived when my mom took me to the store to buy the replacement. I put it on right after I paid the worker and vowed to never lose it again.

Unlike the necklace that replaced the one that I lost—a

necklace that currently sits in my jewelry box—there are things in this life that we will never be able to replace. Frannie Frankincense, my best friend in the entire world, the greatest woman I have ever known, is a person that I will never be able to replace. She was older than me, wiser than me, funnier than me, more talented than me, but she always made me feel like I was the special one. She laughed at my jokes, she encouraged my ideas, and told me that I was smart. She believed in me. She was in every sense of the word, a friend who can never be replaced.

And not only did I lose my best friend, I lost my future. My father has made the decision to sell the family pickle factory—the same pickle factory that has been in my family for generations—having been passed down from father to son, generation after generation. My oldest brother, Patrick stood in line to inherit the factory, a proposition he was none too excited about. I, on the other hand, had dreamed ever since I was a little girl that one day I would run the factory. Perhaps certain Picklepants in the past had run the plant from a sense of obligation. I only saw it from a sense of adventure.

I had dreams of becoming the world's youngest professional pickle taster, of even traveling the world in pursuit of the most perfect tasting pickles. Granted, I also had dreams of marrying Jiminy Jams (if Zac Efron does not work out), becoming a fashion designer, and becoming rich and famous. But the dream that I thought was the one sure thing in my life, the safest dream I thought I had, was that of becoming the youngest professional pickle taster of all time. That dream was dashed to pieces because my dad thought it would be best to sell the family pickle plant to the most evil of family's, the Rothefellers, aka the Devilfellers, just for a little financial security. My dad said there are problems, we would lose the factory to the bank anyway, but I never thought he was one to give up so easily—especially, not to the Rothefellers. They may have paid our way to Mexico, their oldest daughter may be dating my oldest brother, but their middle child has made this middle child's life a living hell, and I know that selling the factory to them would kill the Picklepant's spirit of the factory. But as they say, business is business.

Oh, what am I doing? This is a tribute to you, Frannie, so enough about the factory. Good riddance.

Frannie, I love you and I miss you so much! I just hope the words you once told me—"everything works out in the end"— could actually be true, because right now, it feels like the end, and nothing is working out.

With all my love,
Penny Picklepants

Wow, that felt really good. By the time I finished my post, my mom was up and making breakfast. Now to delete the post.

There was a knock at the door.

"Penny, Olive is here for you," Patrick yelled from the front door.

"Okay, thanks, I just need to..."

"Penny, your friend is waiting for you at the door. Just go get her and bring her in here," my mom said.

Ugh! Why did this blog site have to make things so confusing? I just wanted to delete the stupid thing.

"Fine!" I said. "But don't let anyone touch the computer."

Of course when I saw Olive standing there with flowers, I

started to cry once again. We stood there crying for a few minutes before I remembered the post.

"Wait! Olive, I have to go delete something on the computer. Go wait for me in my bedroom and I will be up there in a second."

When I walked into the kitchen and saw Patrick sitting at the computer, my heart stopped. It was a good thing I was so young because with all this stopping and pounding, and flipping and flopping of my heart, I didn't think it could take much more.

"Patrick? Can I get on real quick? I just need to delete something."

Not paying much attention to me and paying more attention to his game or whatever boring stuff teenage boys do on the computer, he mumbled, "I already did it."

"What are you talking about? You already did what? You deleted it?"

"No, I posted it."

"You what?"

"I. Already. Posted. It."

"Patrick, please, please, please tell me that you DID NOT just post my blog entry. Seriously, Patrick, did you even read it?"

"I read some of the beginning… looked nice."

"PATRICK! GET OFF THE COMPUTER RIGHT NOW!" I screamed, as I tried to physically push him off the chair.

"Sheesh, what is wrong with you?" Patrick said. My effort to get Patrick off the chair was rather futile, but seeing how determined I was, he got off on his own.

"Fine!" he said, "but you have 30 seconds."

"Fine!" I said. After I calmed myself down, I figured out how to delete the post in just a couple seconds. And then it was gone.

"There! Now you can get back to your precious little video game." I got up and walked out of the kitchen with a big sigh of relief, thinking to myself, "That could have been bad."

After Olive and I talked for over an hour and went through a box of tissues, I finally realized I only had thirty minutes to get ready for school.

"Holy crap!" I yelled, "I haven't even picked out what I'm going to wear!" I thanked Olive again for the flowers and told her how happy I was that she was my best friend. As I watched Olive leave my room I felt comforted that I would always have Olive as a best friend and nothing would change that.

I then proceeded to take the fastest shower in the history of Penny Picklepants showers, and picked out some jeans with a cute top. With my hair still wet and my stomach growling like a wild animal, I ran downstairs to grab a bite to eat.

As I walked downstairs to the kitchen, I heard the telephone ring. Now, I am no expert in telephone ringing, but I have heard that when the phone rings before 9:00 in the morning, it is never to deliver good news. I heard my dad answer the phone in his office—guess he was working from home today—while I made my way to the fridge to get some juice. I really wanted fried pickles and eggs, but that made me think about Frannie, which made me cry, so I settled on orange juice. As I was pouring the juice, I about dropped the pitcher, when I heard my dad yell, "What?!" loud enough to wake the neighbors.

Luckily, I caught the pitcher before a juice-induced disaster struck. I crept into my dad's office. He looked livid, but he wouldn't look at me. He tried to flag me out with his free hand, but I wouldn't leave, not entirely. Like always, I just wanted to know what was going on. He said his final, "Yes sir. No sir. I understand, sir," then hung up the phone. He then gave me look of death.

"Penny! What did you do?"

"Well, I didn't have a lot of time to pick out an outfit or take a shower, so I know I don't look my best. And for breakfast, I just wanted juice, which I almost dropped when I heard you yell, but my cat-like reflexes kicked in and I caught the pitcher before it fell, so everything's fine." By then, my mom had walked in.

"Penny, it's time to go," my mom said.

"Penny, what have you done?" my dad demanded.

"Honey, can this wait? If we don't leave right now the kids are going to be late."

"Then let them be late!" my dad boomed. Wow! You knew my dad was angry if he didn't care whether we were late for school. But I still had no idea why he was so upset.

"What's wrong, Peter?" my mom said, in her remember-cool-heads-always-prevail voice.

"I just got a call from J&R Enterprises," my dad said.

"Okay, and what did they want?" my mom asked, checking her watch.

"Apparently your daughter"—another clue my dad was angry was whenever he referred to me as "your daughter,"—"got on her blog and decided it would be a good idea to write about how we stood to lose the factory if we didn't sell it to the Rothefellers, apparently even referring to them as the Devilfellers." Then my dad turned to me. "I told you that in the strictest confidence! I specifically told you not tell anyone about that. What in the world were you thinking, Penny?!"

I couldn't wrap my mind around what he was saying. He looked so angry, angrier then I had ever seen him—even madder than when my parents went on a vacation and Patrick, at 14-years-old, safely drove my mom's station wagon around town, only to wreck it into the back of my dad's parked truck when he was trying to park it where my mom had left it. Leave it to Patrick to wreck two cars at once. "Focus Penny!" I told myself, "take a deep breath, and ask him what the heck is going on."

"What you are talking about Dad? I am so confused?"

"Penny, do you realize what you have done?"

"No, Dad, I don't," I said, doing my best to hold back the tears.

"Did you really get on your blog and tell the entire world what was happening with the factory—that we were going to lose it?"

Oh no!

"The company that Mr. Rothefeller works for has now pulled out of the deal. Now we are going to lose the factory unless we can come up with a quarter of a million dollars, Penny! Do you have $250,000 sitting around? Because I sure as hell don't! So now, we have just lost everything. It's all gone."

My mom's jaw was on the floor next to mine. Yup, things just got worse.

"Dad, I don't know how that's even possible. It wasn't sup- posed to be published, but Patrick published it by accident. But I instantly deleted it. It's not my fault."

"Penny," my dad said, clearly disappointed, "that's your prob- lem. You never think anything is your fault. But guess what, it is this time. And now, thanks to you, we could be homeless in less than 30 days!"

"Peter!" my mom remonstrated, widening her eyes and cocking her head to send my father a double message to cool it. "There is no need to be so dramatic."

Wow! My mom actually coming to my defense—that's a new one. But the damage had been done, and at the same time my mom was speaking, so was I.

"Well, how many times have you seen your best friend being hauled out of her house on a gurney because she died before you could get there because of a stupid family meeting?!" I yelled, crying and running out of the office, and doing my best not to trip while going up the stairs. I slammed my door and yelled, "I am never leaving my room again!" Of course my dad answered with a, "Well you're gonna have to when the bank repos our house!" Just like life, parents, and particularly dads in this case, can be so cruel sometimes.

How could it be possible that in 24 hours I had lost my sure-thing of a dream, my best friend, my family, and now maybe my home? So much for things working out in the end!

For the next few days, to say things were tense in my house would be an understatement. My dad wasn't coming home from the factory, except to shower and to change his clothes. When I asked my mom what was going on, she forced a smile on her face and said that he was trying to find another buyer for the factory. But with the secret out, buyers were scarce.

To make matters worse, Patrick was mad at me as well. Ginger had broken up with him because of the "fall out" over the factory. She told him that it wouldn't look good if they were still together, so of course he blamed me. I, however, could see through that one clearly! When I pointed out to him the reason she had been dating him, he yelled that he hated me and that I had ruined any chances for happiness in his life—and they say I'm dramatic—hello! When I told him to "join the club," he went into his room and slammed the door. I hoped that made him feel better because it sure did when I did it. Of course, when I did it, my mom yelled at me to stop slamming doors—when Patrick did it, not a single word.

At school, things were even worse. Olive was doing an amazing job acting the part of supportive friend, but I think it was a bit too big of a role for her to carry all by herself—not that it was due to any fault of her own. Olive was amazing and always would be. It's just that I had grown accustomed to leaning on Frannie so much, even more than Olive. Olive just hadn't put in the years of experience Frannie's words of wisdom required. This then made me miss Frannie all the more, and I started to cry again.

Everything was back to normal with JayJ now, receiving her signature glares on a regular basis. Jiminy was another story. Let's just say things got a bit awkward. I hope, I hope, I so hope that Jiminy did not read my post, but at this point anything would be possible, and it would explain the sudden awkwardness, well, that and the fact that he kissed me. Oh my gosh! At least I still got to feel that same feeling whenever I thought about that perfect night. A happy memory floating on the surface of an otherwise endless sea of misery—okay, yes, I could be overly dramatic as well, but seriously, seriously?

I wasn't sure why JayJ was back to giving me glares of death and destruction though. It wasn't like her family wasn't looking at the possibility of adding an additional "aka" to their family car, aka the red-grocery-go-getter, and soon to be, aka the family home. I finally got up the nerve to ask her what the deal was before Home Ec.

"I just can't get over the fact," she said, "that I was forced to ruin what would have been the perfect Christmas vacay to Mexico by having to spend it with you and the other Pathetic-pants because your family was too POOR to take yourselves."

Well, that cleared things up!

"Oh, and I heard your old friend died," JayJ said. Don't even go there JayJ! "It must be rough when your best friend is an old lady."

How dare she! Okay, you are not going to believe this—oh, who am I kidding? Of course you are going to believe this—I totally took a swing at JayJ. Yes, I missed, but still, I've never wanted to hit someone so bad. Actually, I've never wanted to hit someone, but the look on her face—oh, you should've seen it—it more than made up for missing it with my fist.

I had really wanted to talk with Jiminy at lunch time, but I just couldn't handle another rejection. I felt like my life had turned into The World vs. Penny Picklepants. I didn't want to take the chance of finding out, yet one more person hated me.

World: 7,000,000,005. Picklepants: 1.

I found myself having to stay late at school to get caught up on my work—personal drama really wreaks havoc on your education. As I started to walk home after one of those days, I saw Jiminy walking in front of me. I debated with myself whether I should go talk to him or just walk really, really, slow so he wouldn't notice me. We reached the point where we had to go separate ways when he stopped, turned around, and looked at me.

"Did you even take into consideration other people's livelihoods were at stake?"

"Jiminy, that blog post was never supposed to be published… did you read it?"

"No, but…"

Phew!

"Jiminy, it was an accident. There was so much going on, I only wrote it to try to sort everything out. Then my brother published it on accident. All my hopes and dreams were pinned on the factory. And then my best friend died… and… and, do you really think I wanted any of this to happen?" I said, not being able to help start crying. At least it was only a little bit, not to the level of mascara running down my cheeks in front of Jiminy.

"Penny," Jiminy said, "my dad's probably going to lose his job, as well as a lot of other good people."

"What are you talking about?"

"My dad heard that Mr. Rothefeller's company is just going to buy the factory to shut it down now."

"What? So, they are going to buy it anyway? Isn't that good?"

"No! It's not good. My dad said the company will pay a lot less, and I guess since they'll get it so cheap, the company is going to close it immediately instead of keeping it going. They may have planned on shutting it down anyway, but it would have been years later after they had made some of their money back."

Wow! Jiminy really knows how to talk business, which makes him even hotter… focus Picklepants! Focus!

"Jiminy, if you don't think that my heart is broken into little pieces because everything I have done, then you don't know me at all. And now, on top of everything else, knowing that everybody from the factory will lose their jobs because of me! These people watched me grow up, some even babysat me. You don't think all of this is on my mind of every minute of every day? At least you still have your family and your friends."

We just sat there, Jiminy with a concerned look on his face, staring at the ground. It certainly felt good getting some of it off my chest, but I felt bad for dumping it all on Jiminy.

"Jiminy, I'm sorry for dumping all this on you," I said, wiping away the tears. "And I am so sorry about your dad losing his job. I feel… horrible." Oh great, more tears.

Not really sure what to do next, and with an awkward silence growing between us, I started to leave, but he quickly grabbed my arm—best day ever! Okay not even close, but hey he was grabbing my arm—and he said, "I'm sorry about Frannie." Then he paused as if he was going to say something else… but didn't.

"The one thing Frannie always told me," I said, turning back to face him, "was that everything works out in the end and to tell you the truth it is the only thing I have left to hold on to."

Jiminy looked at me and said, with a smile on his face, "What I was going to say, before you interrupted me, is that I will always be your friend." Then he opened his arms and said, "And another thing to hold on to."

OH! MY! GOSH! A hug from Jiminy! This may even top the kiss. Okay, it totally didn't, but definitely right up there.

I could've stood there with him forevermore. Eventually we said goodbye and I walked home, regularly turning back to watch him walk the other way. Oh, and yes, the mascara totally ran. Did I forget to mention I had started dabbling in F.M.S.? That's right, Facial Makeup Secrecy. My mom would've killed me if she found out, but I had to find something to occupy my mind with something constructive, if only for a few minutes a day.

World: 7,000,000,004. Picklepants: 2.

Knowing Jiminy and I were friends again lessened my load. But the dread of the next 24 hours hit me hard as I started again on my way home. Frannie's funeral was tomorrow. I was having really mixed emotions about it. I felt like it would bring me some much needed closure, but I knew it would also make it all the more real. Knowing that Frannie really had died and that she wasn't coming back—it was too much to comprehend.

I tried to get to bed early that night so I wouldn't feel like my head was in the clouds at the funeral, but I was having a hard time getting to sleep. I tried reading my newest Vogue, but it didn't help. I tried yoga—remembering to breathe in for 4 and exhale for 7— and I started to get lightheaded. I tried sleeping feetside up on my bed—or is it headside feet?—surprisingly it didn't work either so I decided a warm cup of milk just may do the trick. Figuring everybody else was asleep—I crept out of my room, and saw all the lights had been turned off. The coast was clear. When the kitchen came into view from the stairs, however, I noticed a light was on and I could hear my parents talking. I sat down on the stairs.

"Peter, she didn't mean for any of this to happen."

"No one ever does—but it was pure carelessness."

"Whatever it was, you know she loves that factory as much if not more than anyone. She would never do anything on purpose to hurt its future. She was upset, Peter!"

Wow! My mom, my great defender—who would've thought?

"I know she didn't mean it but... Agh! It just makes me so mad that she wrote about it on her blog."

"She probably felt like she had nowhere else to turn, or no one else to turn to, we've been so busy. A lot had been dumped into her lap. And then to lose Frannie on top of it all."

"I know," my dad said, with a big sigh.

"She never intended to publish it..."

"But why even put it on the blog at all?"

"I don't know Peter. I think she just wanted to write about Frannie. Then all the factory stuff came out, and then—"

There was a moment where neither spoke.

"Peter, you have to stop blaming her. It is so much for her to carry. Please, just forgive her. She's 12-years-old. But more importantly, she is your daughter, your one and only. And if you could forgive Patrick for wrecking two cars at once, then..."

"Yes, but that didn't cost us the factory and our home."

"But you did forgive him. I guess you just need to ask yourself what is more important—a factory and a home, or a daughter."

I had no idea how long I had been sitting on the steps. I knew it was wrong to eavesdrop—wait, they hadn't noticed me... because of my amazing spy skills, yes!—but for some reason, I couldn't get up and leave. Then my mom came walking out and saw me sitting on the steps. I was caught—great here comes more trouble, just what I needed—she then walked up the steps, gave me a kiss on the head and gave me the biggest hug she had ever given me.

"I love you, Penny," she said. I guess parents aren't as predictable as I thought. Of course, my tears were, though.

My entire family agreed to come with me to Frannie's funeral. It was at the city cemetery. In fact, I could see the Potts Mausoleum from where I sat. I think I could even see speckles of red.

I figured there probably wouldn't be a lot of people there and

I just couldn't stand the fact that the other seats would be empty. I was also hoping it would help ease the tension between me and my dad and Patrick. Neither had said much to me in the last few days, and it seemed my mom was the only person on my side. Actually, Parker didn't exactly hate me—he told me, "Penny, I don't hate you, but don't ever think of messing with my DS—I will disown you."

Note to self: never, ever, touch or even think about touching Parker's DS.

World: 7,000,000,002. Picklepants: 4.

Wow, only 7 billion and two to go!

With the exception of Olive, my family and I were pretty much it for the funeral party. Then, right before the service was to begin, a few others joined us and sat in the back. I looked back to see if I recognized them—a woman I had never seen, a young man wearing a suit, another young man wearing a suit, a hat, and gloves, and an older, slightly balding gentleman, wearing the nicest suit I had ever seen—although a couple of them looked vaguely familiar, I couldn't place them all. Then I remembered one—he was Frannie's driver.

One of them, a woman, stood up and walked towards the casket. Before reaching the front, she stopped right by my side. She bent down, and admiring my brooch, she told me, "I just love your pin." She stood up and continued walking to the front, turned, and faced the rest of us. I inhaled a breath of surprise. "Oh my gosh," I said to myself, "she's wearing a pickle pin just like mine." But it was a little different.

"Frannie Frankincense was an amazing woman fighting an up-hill battle against cancer," she said.

I started to think back to all the time we spent together—from that first awkward meeting on her doorstep all the way to her telling me that she loved me. I started to cry thinking about how much I missed Frannie and before I knew it, my mom and dad had their arms around me. When I looked at my dad, he gave a smile. Maybe Frannie was right, maybe at least some things would work out, if not everything—for that brief, passing moment, it certainly seemed like it was possible.

"And may we always remember Frannie," she said, pausing, then looking straight at me, "as the wise, if not spunky, woman that we who knew her best knew she was. She touched many lives in ways that only Frannie could have. She was much loved in life and will be sorely missed in her passing."

Before I knew it, the service was over. The woman who spoke came up to me, shook my hand, and then left with the older gentleman. I never did find out who either of them were, or how they knew Frannie, but I figured from the way she spoke about her, they had known one another for quite a while. When we got up to leave, the man in the suit waved at me—at least, I think he was waving at me, because when I looked behind me to see if he was waving at somebody else, nobody was there—then he left with Frannie's driver.

As the rest of us began to leave, my dad grabbed my hand and said, "We need to talk." Ugh! I hate when conversation with your parents begin that way. The last time my mom said this she gave me a speech about how birds chase bees—remember Chapter 13? Yeah, trust me, you're not missing much—and how when they do this it somehow triggers me becoming a woman. I wanted to ask her why would birds would chase bees, and why would such a thing trigger me becoming a woman. But to be honest, the minute she said, "We need to talk," I knew she was going to be doing all the talking. I just sat there, gave a few "uh-huhs," and tuned out the rest. But maybe this time, maybe I could try tuning in a little more.

My dad walked with me over to stand under one of the cemetery's huge trees. "Penny, first of all, I just want to apologize the way I've been acting—the way I've been treating you."

Wow! My tuning in is really paying off this time around.

"Your mom told me that your posting the blog was somehow an accident, and that you never meant for it to be posted—I just can't figure out why you wrote what you wrote."

"I don't know, it started out as a tribute to Frannie and the next thing I know, the phone is ringing, and you are yelling about losing the factory and the house. To be honest, I just wish you had told us what was going on. Why did you keep it secret?"

Oh, that's good—answer the question with a question of your own—the lawyer plan is so back on.

"After all of this, do you really have to wonder?" my dad said.

Ouch! At least he was smiling when he said it.

"You're right, though, Penny," he continued. "Your mother and I should have leveled with you guys. I just figured that I could fix it before it ever became a problem. In the future, we'll tackle these kinds of problems as a family. I promise. Now how about a hug?"

I took it from the hug and the "I love you" that he whispered in my ear that he had forgiven me. But there was one more thing to say before we moved on.

"All I know," my dad said on the way out, "is that we have 25 days to save the plant, and I'm going to need all the help I can get if we are going to save it, including yours."

World: 7,000,000,000. Picklepants: 6.

Well, I guess six will have to do.

CHAPTER TWENTY-FOUR

I likened the next 25 days in my house to trying to find the perfect bathing suit in 15 minutes with a 20 dollar budget. My mom, on the other hand, said it was like trying to throw a barrel of pickles over an oak tree—whichever metaphor you prefer—I know you prefer mine—things around the house were really, really tense. We were all hoping for a miracle, but the days quickly dwindled, as did our hope. With only one day left, and no prospects of finding a new buyer, we sat down for another family meeting—I was beginning to hate family meetings.

"You know Dad, when I start going to therapy—and trust me, I will need therapy after all of this—the first thing my therapist and I are going to tackle are the words "family meeting" and how they now cause my pulse to quicken and my palms to go sweaty."

"Well it doesn't look like you will be going to therapy..."

"Did you find a buyer?"

"No, I meant we won't have money to pay for it. I couldn't find another buyer. As of this time tomorrow, the Picklepants Pickling Plant will be no more."

"And when you say everything," I said, "do you mean just the factory everything? Or like everything, everything?" As usual, I needed some clarity.

"Penny," my mom said, "what your dad is trying to say, is that we will be losing the factory and maybe our house."

Maybe clarity isn't that good of a thing after all.

"Well, why the house if it's the factory that needs money?" Parker said. "I have been paying attention you know. Just because I am on my DS doesn't mean I'm not paying attention."

"Well you sure have a funny way of "listening" when I ask you to do chores," my mom said. She had a point.

"Well, I always listen to the important stuff," Parker said, to which my mom was about reply when my dad continued.

"Let's focus on what's going to happen next. And Parker when your mom asks you to do chores, do them okay?"

Parker smiled and nodded, his eyes not leaving his DS.

"Tomorrow, we are going to go to the factory. The Sheriff is going to put the factory up for auction and the highest bidder will then receive the factory."

"Are they going to auction our house?" Patrick asked.

"No, but the second mortgage…" my dad said, as we looked on with very confused faces. "Listen kids, there is a lot of business stuff I could bore you with, but essentially it comes down to this. We have to move and the bank is taking the house and the factory unless we come up with a quarter-of-a-millions dollars. End of story."

After hearing the seriousness of my dad's voice, I again started to doubt if Frannie really was right. How could everything work out in the end? How could it this time?

"Dad, where are we going to go?" Parker asked. I think I was hoping that we would be able to move to another house. Maybe it would end up being a good thing. Expect the worst, hope for the best, right?

"Well, financially we can't afford much, and with our credit ruined, we'll most likely need to find a cheap apartment."

Expectations are so overrated.

"And because we can't afford much, you kids may be sharing a room."

Hmm, why am I surprised that it just got worse.

"Are you kidding me? There is no way I am sharing a room with my brothers!" I folded my arms to send a message that I was serious.

"Well, we are in the mess because of you so I think you can at least be a little bit more flexible."

Ouch!

"Penny, I apologize—I didn't mean that—just under a lot of stress. We just need to work together here."

"Let's just get to bed," my mom said. "Tomorrow is going to be a very long day."

When I was really young, like 10-years-old, I hated when people would say, "That was the longest *insert-number-here* minutes of my life." I mean, five minutes is five minutes whether you're freaking out or totally chill. But after today's drive to the factory, I was beginning to understand what they meant. The drive to the factory always took exactly 11.7 minutes from the house—I would have said our factory and our home, but after today, I guess neither would be ours anymore. However, today's drive felt like it took 11.7 years to get there. Not because I was anxious to get there— just the opposite. Everything was weighing down on me so much that it seemed as if time had ceased to exist. I bet we were all thinking the same thing: "This is the last time we will ever drive to *our* factory." Then I glanced over at Parker on his DS, and thought to myself, "Well, most of us, at least."

When we pulled up to the factory, the Rothefellers were already there. We all piled out of the van.

"Well, Peter," Mr. Rothefeller said, "I guess it's time to show you how the big boys play."

"And, what do you mean by that?" my dad asked.

"After entering today's winning bid, we are going to tear down this eye sore. You are looking at the future home of Pottsville's newest landfill."

"A landfill?" my dad asked flabbergasted. "You are going to put hundreds of people out of work for a land fill?"

"Oh, Peter. Landfills are big business, and they create jobs too. But, ya know, I would just like to thank Penny for blabbing on her blog," Mr. Rothefeller said, chuckling. "She saved J&R a lot of money. So thank you," he said, turning to me.

My dad made a fist with his right hand, took a deep breath, then relaxed his fist. "I thought we were friends, Jax," my dad said.

"Peter, it's nothing personal—it's just business."

In the course of my dad's and Mr. Rothefeller's exchange, Patrick couldn't take his eyes off of Ginger. He even tried to talk to her as we walked up to the factory doors, but Ginger quickly said in her annoying southern accent, "Pay-atrick, if ya'll can't fig-ure it out why I was dating you, then you are really are as sad and pathetic as Penny always said you were. I told y'all it was over."

Ouch! I was beginning to see evil did run in the family after all.

There was a lot more people at the auction than I thought there would be. Of course the Rothefellers, aka the Devilfellers, were there—and yes we are back to calling Devilfellers because that is what they were: smug and evil. The Devilfeller's lawyer was there: also smug and evil. The Sheriff: old and scary, with a gun. The Bank Representative: stuffy and bored. A bunch of guys I'd never seen: fat and chatty. And then of course, us, the Picklepants: stressed and overstressed.

I wasn't really sure why any of these people were here at the thing. I say "thing" because it still wasn't clear what was happening. My dad had tried to explain it, "The factory is under a Sheriff's auction which means..." and that is when he lost me. I really did try to keep up, but I was sick to my stomach knowing that we were losing the factory. Even though I had said I was sorry a million times, and my dad said I had been forgiven, I still felt responsible. I had played the "if only" game several times on the drive to the factory, but it only made me feel worse.

"Then the highest bidder will win the building and that is a Sheriff's auction. Do you understand now?" my dad finished. There are times in life where shaking your head and saying "No, I have no idea what you are talking about," makes a lot of sense. I shook my head and said, "Yes, absolutely!"

The Sheriff and my dad shook hands and the Sheriff said, "Sorry to have to do this to you Peter. I hate to see the factory go just as much as the next person." My dad just nodded and replied with a somber, "I know Herb. I know." Then things got started.

It started off with the Sheriff saying a bunch of legal mumbo jumbo that I couldn't understand. I leaned over and asked Patrick if the Sheriff was speaking English. Patrick shrugged his shoulders and mumbled, "I dunno." He then went into all the logistics of the auction: blah, blah, blah... must be certified prior to the auction, yada, yada, yada... you had to pay 5 percent of the bid price upfront, blah, blah, blah... you must pay the remaining balance due no later than 4:00 P.M. that day—and then a bunch more blah, blah, blah. I didn't understand, nor did I want to understand. The only thing I really and truly understood was that the Rothefellers were going to get our pickle plant and in the process destroy my dreams. JERKS!

"And now, the bidding will begin according to my clock, at ten o'clock this 6th day of April. Do I have any bids?" asked the Sheriff. "I bid $100,000," said Mr. Rothefeller's attorney. Another person said, "$125,000." Soon the bids were over $300,000. And just like that, I watched my dreams get sold to the highest bidder.

We just sat there waiting for some miracle to happen before the auction ended. But nothing happened. I thought of all the great memories I had of the factory growing up. There was the time that I bolted myself in the pickle pantry, a fancy name for where pickles are stored waiting for delivery, and started eating as many pickles as I could. I had eaten about two and a half jars before my mom found me. "Penny," my mom yelled, "how many pickles have you eaten?" I remember I told her, "I'm not sure, but it certainly wasn't enough!" Then for the next three days all I wanted to do was drink water. Who knew eating two and a half jars of pickles could make you so thirsty?

There was the time I walked into the break room and found some of the workers having a contest to see how many pickles they could stuff into their mouths. I discovered, much to my chagrin, the break room had all the pickles you could eat. Anyway, they asked if I wanted to join. How could I refuse? I only got three in my mouth, which I thought was pretty good. But the winner got seven, yes seven pickles in his mouth. The real fun was when he couldn't get them back out. I don't think they had pickle-stuffing contests after that.

Then there was the time I answered a phone call from Germany. My dad's secretary stepped out of the office for a quick bathroom break and left me "in charge." Well, little did she know that the phone would ring just then and it would be a call from Germany. Unfortunately, my German was a bit rusty.

"Guten Tag, Mr. Picklepants bitte," said the man from Germany.

"There's a good dog? But it bit you?" I said.

Laughter, "No, Mr. Picklepants bitte" said the man.

"Mr. Picklepants doesn't bite, I know that for a fact—he is my dad you know," I said.

Dead silence. "Ich rufe sie spatter," said the man.

"You see a spider on the roof?" I asked, in amazement.

Dead silence—then dial tone.

There were more memories that raced about in my mind. It was like time had stopped and I was watching a movie—a movie about my life at the factory. It felt like I had spent half of my life there. Then I realized, I had spent half of my life there. I just couldn't believe that in a matter of minutes, the pickle factory would be closed forever. When I finally realized that it would be gone forever, I took a deep breath, reached out, grabbed my dad's hand, and started to cry.

Somehow, between the uncontrollable crying and the uncontrollable sniffling, my dad figured out I was quite upset. He bent down and whispered in my ear, "Everything works out in the end, Penny." I caught my breath and looked up at my dad in surprise. "That's what Frannie always used to say, Dad!" He just smiled back at me and said, "Then it must be true." Only a few minutes remained.

I guess I had been so busy walking down memory lane while wiping my eyes of the tears that I hadn't even noticed that somebody else had arrived at the auction.

"WAIT! Wait, Sheriff Tate!" this somebody yelled.

Everybody turned around and looked at a man running from

his car with a briefcase in his hand. I immediately recognized him as the man from Frannie's funeral, but what was he doing here? The Sheriff raised his head and furrowed his brow at the stranger. "Auction ends in about two minutes. Are you here to make a bid? Are you certified?" inquired the Sheriff.

"My name is Mr. Lawson. I am the lawyer of the Frankincense estate."

"Yeah, so get to the point." said Mr. Rothefeller. I was really, really starting to dislike that guy, but it made me feel better that all of us—the Picklepants clan—gave him the death glare.

"I would get to the point if you would stop interrupting me," Mr. Lawson said. I was really, really starting to like this guy. I could see why Frannie would choose him as her lawyer. "I have the will of Mrs. Frankincense, which will forever change the outcome of this proceeding." Again, I am not one to understand the legalese of the legal profession, but I am pretty sure this is a good thing. "This is the last Will and Testament of Francisca Maria Frankincense. It reads, 'It is my will that the proceeds from the sale of my house and contents within, excepting those items specified, be used first and foremost to resolve the remaining debt of the Picklepants Pickle factory...'"

"Sheriff, if I may say something," Mr. Rothefeller asked. The Sheriff nodded. "I'm no lawyer, and I certainly don't mean to rain on anyone's parade here, but wouldn't the sale of the Frankincense home need to occur sometime in the next, um..." Mr. Rothefeller said, obnoxiously checking the time on his Rolex (I really hoped that it was a Fauxlex... yeah, let's just say it was). "Let's see here— by my reckoning, the next 60 seconds? Wouldn't this mean the gentleman would need to tender a check for the entire sum of the debt, as he is clearly not certified, sometime in the next 60 seconds?" Then with that smug Rothefeller smile, he said, turning to the crowd, "I highly doubt a house, even one as nice as the Frankincense home, could be sold in the span of a few seconds."

The Rothefellers and their lawyer all laughed.

As much as I hated to admit, he sounded awfully right—and trust me, I absolutely hated when the Rothefellers were right.

The Sheriff, with one of those "I've done everything I can do, and I'm really sorry, but it looks like evil has won the day today" kind of looks said, "Mr. Lawson, unless you can tender me a check in my hand in the next 30 seconds, I'm afraid that..."

But then Mr. Lawson interrupted the Sheriff again. "Sheriff, if I may." The Sheriff just nodded, waving his hands as if he wouldn't get in the way anymore. "The Frankincense residence and all its remaining content have already been sold. The money is deposited in the bank."

Like a very surprised choir, the Sheriff, Mr. Rothefeller, the Rothefeller attorney, and everybody in my family all in unison shouted a surprised, "What?!" If the situation hadn't been so serious, I probably would have said, "Jinx!" out loud, but I figured I would let it slide this time.

"Well," said the Sheriff, "That is certainly a step in the right direction Mr.—what did you say your name was again?"

"Lawson, sir—Mr. Lawson."

"Well, Mr. Lawson, that is certainly a step in the right direction, but unless you have a check backed by those proceeds in my hand in the next 20 seconds, I'm afraid the factory will be sold to the highest bidder," the Sheriff said, nodding towards the smug-faced Rothefellers, "with no period of redemption remaining. I suggest you give me the check if you have it."

The air was so thick with suspense I don't think a single soul there breathed a breath or twitched a muscle for the next 15 seconds while Mr. Lawson rummaged through his brief case.

He started to pull out pieces of paper, looking at them and saying "No, not what I am looking for." He even managed to say, "Oh, I have been looking for that—huh, that's where it's been!" I finally got his attention when I yelled, "Mr. Lawson, the check?!" "Oh, yes! The check," he said, smiling and winking at me while he pulled a piece of paper from his shirt pocket and handed it to the Sheriff. "I believe what you need is right here."

EXHALE

Was that exhale as loud as I thought it was?

"Well I'll be darned!" said the Sheriff, slapping the check with the back of his hand. "A check made out to the Pottsville Community Bank for two-hundred fifty-two thousand two-hundred twenty-three dollars and seven cents."

The Sheriff then handed the check over to the guy from the bank, who then walked up to my dad, with a great big grin on his face, and said, "Well, Mr. Picklepants, it appears that the mortgage to the Picklepants Pickling Plant…" The banker paused a moment with a smirk on his face. "Ha!" he said, "say that 10 times fast, I dare you!" Parker then proceeded to do just that without missing a beat.

"Parker!" we all yelled.

"I apologize," said the banker with a sheepish look on his face. "As I was saying, it would appear that the mortgage has been redeemed, and this time for sure. You are now the owners free and clear of the Picklepants Pickle Plant." They shook hands. We then went crazy.

* LAUGHING * CHEERING * CRYING *

Now, I know that was as loud as I thought it was! We all proceeded to jump, dance, cry, and laugh all at the same time. I didn't even care to see the look on JayJ's face. It didn't matter. Just as Frannie had said, everything had actually worked out in the end. I couldn't believe it. She was right! I felt so ashamed for ever having doubted her, though I knew she wouldn't have wanted me to feel that way.

After things settled down, I walked over to Mr. Lawson with my dad, his arm around me—my dad looked so happy, like Christmas-morning happy. We both exclaimed, in unison, "How?" We gave each other a quick glance, smiled and said, "Jinx!" at the same time, which caused another round of laughing and hugging.

"Well, Frannie had known the factory was in trouble for a while now. In fact Penny," nodding to me, "told Frannie about the factory some time ago."

"Penny! You knew and you didn't say anything?" my dad asked.

"I accidentally heard you and Mom talking about it a long time ago and I didn't want you to have to sell it. I told Frannie hoping she could help me figure out a way to save the plant."

"And as you can see, Mr. Picklepants, I think it is safe to say that in the end it was Penny and Frannie who did save the family pickle plant."

"Penny," my dad said, kissing me on the forehead. "I never should have doubted you."

My dad and mom, as well as the entire auction entourage were looking at me in amazement, that I actually had something to do with saving the factory.

After hugging me one more time, my dad turned again to Mr. Lawson and said, "But how did Frannie sell everything?"

"Frannie had quite an antique furniture collection, worth a small fortune in itself. When she found out about the factory, she had me begin selling the most valuable items. As far as the home, even though Frannie had received multiple offers, she arranged to have it sold to the Pottsville Cancer Institute. Now, cancer patients who are unable to pay to stay anywhere else will have a place to stay at the Frannie Frankincense House for free. Frannie's estate has received the majority of the money with the house and the things that have already been purchased. In addition to other trusts, Frannie requested that a considerable amount be put into a trust in Penny's name."

Huh? I had no idea what he was talking about, but it sounded good.

"The one condition Frannie stipulated was that Penny would not find out the amount nor be able to touch it until her twenty-first birthday. However, as trustee, the will gives me the right to withdraw money from the trust at any time for necessities."

"Mom! I am so getting a Hermès Birkin bag—I mean that's totally a necessity—practically an emergency," I said.

My mom didn't say no—unfortunately her not-in-a-million-years expression was definitely not a yes.

"What about the specified items that were not to be sold?" my dad asked.

"Oh, right—yes, the specified items: Frannie owned two antique steamer trunks filled with her most meaningful possessions, among them her dress designs, hats, gloves, as well as many other items. The will stipulates that these are to go to Penny. Also, her jewelry is to be divided between Penny and one Miss Oliverson—Olive I believe is her first name."

I couldn't believe it—to be able to keep something so meaningful to Frannie to always remember her by—I guess from the smile on my face and the obscene giggling, you could safely say I was overcome with joy.

So much was happening all at once that I had forgotten about the Rothefellers. I guess they had finally realized that they didn't get the factory because they were all leaving with their heads hung low. I think for the first time—ever, dare I say—the Rothefellers had lost. Let me state that again: THE ROTHEFELLERS LOST! Of course, as they walked back to their car, Ginger grabbed Patrick's arm and said, "You know what, Patrick?" Wait! What happened to the southern accent? "I was thinking we should give it another try," she continued. "What do you think?"

For a moment, I thought Patrick was going to give in—I was about to start yelling, "NO!" when Patrick removed her hand from his arm and in his best southern accent said, "I told y'all it's over."

As Patrick watched Ginger leave, I grabbed his hand and asked him if he was okay. "Yeah, I'm fine. I just can't believe she was using me this whole time."

"Sorry!" I said. "You'll find somebody else Patrick, but you've got to promise me you won't date anyone with a fake Southern accent ever again. Seriously, what was that all about?"

"Not sure exactly, but it was seriously annoying."

I couldn't have agreed with him more and knowing we would never see them again—well, hoping we would never see them again—I realized that I was finally ready to confront JayJ and say all the things that I wanted to say to her, but never could.

"JayJ, wait," I said, running over to her. "I need to talk to you. I've wanted to say this to you forever, so here goes." I took a deep breath, and within the span of a split second, all the wisdom Frannie had imparted to me seemed to course through my brain and even my entire body. "I forgive you." Wait! What did I just say? "I forgive you for everything you did to me. All your ridicule and your attempts to put me down—they only made me realize how blessed I am to have amazing friends and family who like me just the way I am. And though you may not believe it, I wish the same thing for you, because it is a wonderful blessing to have true friends. Okay, well, have a good day."

I couldn't believe what I had just said. I guess from the look on her face, she was just as flabbergasted as I was.

"JayJ," barked Mr. Rothefeller, "Get in the car, NOW!" And just like that, JayJ was gone. I couldn't help but smile—Frannie was right about another thing: The best revenge was forgiveness.

As we were leaving the factory after a round of hugs, more hugs, and even more hugs—Patrick put a stop to the even more and more hugs—Mr. Lawson walked up to me. "Penny, one more thing."

"There's more?" I said an octave higher than usual.

"Yes, there is more," he said, handing me a white envelope. To the untrained eye, it would've looked like any other envelope, but to the trained pickle-professional eye, I knew exactly what it was— the small green pickle in the upper corner, somewhat resembling Frannie's brooch, may have given it away.

Dear Miss. Picklepants:

Perhaps it shouldn't come as a surprise that Frannie had been a long-time member of our ranks. Her wisdom of life as well as pickles will be sorely missed. What does come as a surprise, at least to us, however, is that Frannie made it painfully clear that you were to be her replacement. Although we rarely (as in never) offer membership into the Secret Pickle Society to one of such a tender age as yourself, Frannie assured us that you have what it takes to join our ranks. Consequently, you can expect your first assignment in due time.

But for now, some rules:

First, wear the emerald encrusted pickle brooch, the official symbol of the Secret Pickle Society, proudly. Like I told you at Frannie's funeral, I really do love that pin. Each one is unique, but similar enough to be the perfect way for fellow members to recognize one another.

Second, never, ever, ever, tell anybody about us or that you are a member. Many have tried to get in (yes, we got all of your letters) and most are rejected. It is a lifetime membership and the many questions you may have will be unlocked as you go about your life as a member.

One last thing, Miss Pickelpants—with the Secret Pickle Society's seal of approval on your family's pickle factory, should it ever find itself in a "pickle" again, so to speak, we are here to help.

Sincerely,
Tabitha, President ❀

P.S. I look forward to your sending me the directions to the Pickle Stuffing, or Piffing, how to make the perfect pickle piñata, and all your other great ideas.

P.P.S. Frannie already sent us a copy of your cookbook. We lent a hand with some of the pictures. We were wondering what your thoughts were on publishing. We can certainly help.

After I read the letter, I thought about Frannie—everything she had done for me, my family, Olive, the plant, and all the workers. Then I started crying. And I wondered if I was ever going to stop.

CHAPTER TWENTY-FOUR-AND-A-HALF

...or Epilogue if you prefer, but I prefer 24-½.

Dear Secret Pickle Society,

I knew it! I knew it! I knew it! Not to sound boastful, but I SOO knew it... Holy cow! I know it! What do I do now that I know it? I have so many questions. Where do I even start? I mean, for starters: Who started the Secret Pickle Society? What is its purpose? Can I call it SPS for short? Do you call it SPS for short? Where do I go for the answers you say will come? More than anything: Thank you SO MUCH for making me a member. Whatever I do, I want to do it in memory of Frannie. I know I'll never be able to fill her shoes, but I promise I'll do everything I can to never let you down.

Sincerely,
Penny Picklepants

A smile came to my face as I walked home from school that Wednesday afternoon. The sun was out—summer was on its way, and more importantly, school was on its way out—life was good. I was in such a good place in my life that I even gladly got the mail on the way in. As I flipped through it, hoping that I had received another letter from the Pickle Society, I noticed a letter to my dad.

"Dad," I yelled, walking in the door, "you got a letter. I think it's from India... ana?"